MOU
NANCY CO

"Beautiful Mackinac Island provides the setting for a puzzling series of crimes. Now that Allie McMurphy has taken over her grandparents' hotel and fudge shop, life on Mackinac is good, although her little dog, Mal, does tend to nose out trouble. . . . Allie's third offers plenty of plausible suspects and mouthwatering fudge recipes."—*Kirkus Reviews*

"WOW. This is a great book. I loved the series from the beginning and this book just makes me love it even more. No one can make me feel like I am in Mackinac Island better than Nancy Coco. She draws the reader in and makes you feel like you are part of the story. I cannot wait to read more. FANTASTIC is the only thing I can say further about this book."—**Bookschellves.com**

To Fudge or Not to Fudge

"*To Fudge or Not to Fudge* is a superbly crafted, classic, culinary cozy mystery. If you enjoy them as much as I do, you are in for a real treat. The setting of Mackinac Island immediately drew me to the book as it is an amazing location. The only problem I had with the book was reading about all the mouthwatering fudge made me hungry."—**Examiner.com (5 stars)**

"We LOVED it! This   he pages of a book. If yo   d, you will long to vis   ill help you to recall   s." —**Melissa's Mocha**

"A five-star delicious mystery that has great characters, a good plot, and a surprise ending. If you like a good mystery with more than one suspect and a surprise ending, then rush out to get this book and read it, but be sure you have the time since once you start you won't want to put it down. I give this 5 Stars and a Wow Factor of 5+. The fudge recipes included in the book all sound wonderful. I am thinking that a gift basket filled with the fudge from the recipes in this book, along with a copy of the book, some hot chocolate mix and/or coffee, and a nice mug would be a great Christmas gift."
—Mystery Reading Nook

"A charming and funny culinary mystery that parodies reality show competitions and is led by a sweet heroine, eccentric but likable characters, and a skillfully crafted plot that speeds toward an unpredictable conclusion. Allie stands out as a likable and engaging character. Delectable fudge recipes are interspersed throughout the novel."**—Kings River Life**

All Fudged Up

"A sweet treat with memorable characters, a charming locale, and satisfying mystery."**—Barbara Allan**, author of the Trash 'n' Treasures mysteries

"A fun book with a lively plot, and it's set in one of America's most interesting resorts. All this plus fudge!"
—JoAnna Carl, author of the Chocoholic mysteries
(NAL)

"A sweet confection of a book. Charming setting, clever protagonist, and creamy fudge—a yummy recipe for a great read."**—Joanna Campbell Slan**, author of *The Scrap-N-Craft* and *The Jane Eyre Chronicles*

"Nancy Coco's *All Fudged Up* is a delightful mystery delivering suspense and surprise in equal measure. Her heroine, Alice McMurphy, owner of the Historic McMurphy Hotel and Fudge Shop (as much of a mouthful as her delicious fudge), has a wry narrative voice that never falters. Add that to the charm of the setting, Michigan's famed Mackinac Island, and you have a recipe for enjoyment. As an added bonus, mouthwatering fudge recipes are included. A must-read for all lovers of amateur sleuth classic mysteries."
—**Carole Bugge**, author of *Who Killed Blanche Dubois?* and other Claire Rawlings mysteries

"You won't have to 'fudge' your enthusiasm for Nancy Coco's first Mackinac Island Fudge Shop Mystery. Indulge your sweet tooth as you settle in and meet Allie McMurphy, Mal the bichon/poodle mix, and the rest of the motley crew in this entertaining series debut."—**Miranda James**

"The characters are fun and well-developed, the setting is quaint and beautiful, and there are several mouth-watering fudge recipes."—*RT Book Reviews* (3 stars)

"Enjoyable . . . ALL FUDGED UP is littered with delicious fudge recipes, including alcohol-infused ones. I really enjoyed this cozy mystery and look forward to reading more in this series."—**Fresh Fiction**

"Cozy mystery lovers who enjoy quirky characters, a great setting and fantastic recipes will love this debut."
—*The Lima News*

"The first Candy-Coated mystery is a fun cozy due to the wonderful location filled with eccentric characters."
—*Midwest Book Review*

Forever Fudge

Nancy Coco

KENSINGTON PUBLISHING CORP.

http://www.kensingtonbooks.com

KENSINGTON BOOKS are published by

Kensington Publishing Corp.
119 West 40th Street
New York, NY 10018

All Kensington titles, imprints, and distributed lines are available at special quantity discounts for bulk purchases for sales promotions, premiums, fund-raising, and educational or institutional use. Special book excerpts or customized printings can also be created to fit specific needs. For details, write or phone the office of the Kensington Special Sales Manager. Kensington Publishing Corp., 119 West 40th Street, New York, NY 10018. Attn: Special Sales Department. Phone: 1-800-221-2647.

Kensington and the K logo Reg. U.S. Pat & TM Off.

ISBN-13: 978-1-4967-1606-4
ISBN-10: 1-4967-1606-X
First Kensington Mass Market Edition: October 2018

eISBN-13: 978-1-4967-1607-1
eISBN-10: 1-4967-1607-8
First Kensington Electronic Edition: October 2018

10 9 8 7 6 5 4 3 2 1

Printed in the United States of America

This book is for the readers.
Thank you for being part of my life.

Chapter 1

"Allie, have you heard the news?" Jenn, my best friend and this season's assistant manager of the McMurphy Hotel and Fudge Shop came bouncing into the office.

"There's a town hall meeting tonight," I said, and didn't look up from my work on the finances. Labor Day weekend was the official end of the season on Mackinac Island. It was the Tuesday after and I was working up the numbers to see how successful the season had been and if I could stay in business.

"Yes," Jenn said as she sat on the edge of my desk. "But do you know why?"

I set down my pencil. "Tell me."

"They're announcing that a television pilot for a mystery series set on the island will be shot starting next week."

"A mystery series set on Mackinac?" I sat back. "That's cool."

"It is so cool. Marsha Goodwin told me that a Hollywood producer visited us on vacation a year or so back and wanted to do a series set here. They finally got up the funds to shoot the pilot. They will be doing outside shots here and then inside shots back in their LA studios." She wiggled into place on my desk. "Now, here's the fun part, for a mere two thousand dollars, they will include shots of the exterior of the McMurphy. We could be part of the opening credits for the run of the show!"

"I'm familiar with television shows," I said, thinking back to this summer's cooking show I got roped into. "While a pilot is cool, that doesn't mean a show will get made."

"But it's a shot you can't pass up," she said, and crossed her arms. "What if the series takes off? You could be on the opening for years and on reruns forever."

"Two grand is—"

"Not that much money for that kind of exposure. Think about how business has picked up since that cooking show."

I looked at my computer screen. Our online fudge sales had doubled. We only had a limited amount of rooms to rent so we were turning people away. "It has been good for business," I mused.

"And you want to keep up the exposure," she advised.

"But we are already running to capacity. Any more orders and I'll have to stop making batches by hand and start farming it off to a factory."

"Why would that be bad?" Jenn frowned at me, confused.

"Because we are known for our handmade fudge," I said. "Anyone can make fudge in a factory. We make fudge in the kitchen by hand."

"So hire in another candy maker and start another shift," she said. Then she hopped down and planted her hands on my desk. "The Old Tyme Photo Shop and all the others on this side of Main Street are pitching in for the exterior shots. You don't want to lose to the other side."

"What other side?"

"The other side of Main," Jenn said, and waved her hand and straightened. "People will be counting on your support tonight."

"No pressure," I muttered sarcastically, and rubbed my hands over my face. "If I do this, I'll have to take the money out of the roof remodel fund. That means we would not have the patio roof for events next year."

"They are both long-term investments," Jenn pointed out. "But I think this television show has a chance to really take off."

"Why?"

"It's starring Dirk Benjamin," she said with an exaggerated sigh.

"Dirk Benjamin?"

She jumped up and pulled out her phone. "Yes, you know—he did that made-for-TV movie about broken hearts where the older guy has Alzheimer's and the older woman falls for the younger handyman. . . ."

"I don't watch much TV," I said.

"Oh, you know him," she said. "I'll pull up his IMDb page." She flipped through some screens on her phone and then turned it toward me. "See?"

On the screen was a head shot of a very handsome man. I swore there was a twinkle spot of light coming off his teeth. "He is nice-looking."

"He's more than nice-looking," she said, and turned the phone back toward her. "He is the latest 'it' guy for the small screen. He's been slotted to play the local police detective. There is no way this pilot won't take off."

"So wait, that guy is playing Rex Manning?" I chuckled at the idea that a young Hollywood actor with so much hair and a toothy smile would be playing Rex. Rex Manning was rougher around the edges, with a bald head and more action-movie-guy looks than romantic hero looks.

"Well, not exactly," Jenn said. "The series is about a Mackinac Island writer. You know, an updated version of Jessica Fletcher. She finds clues to murders and he steps in to arrest people."

"Oh boy, I bet Rex loves that idea," I said. Rex wasn't very happy with my meddling with his investigations. I highly doubted he would be happy about a television show depicting the Mackinac Island police as needing an old woman's help to solve crimes.

Jenn smirked. "Rex hates it. I heard that Dirk is shadowing Rex for the next week to get a feel for how he does his job."

That thought made me laugh. "Okay, now I have to call Rex and see how he's taking it." I picked up my phone.

"Before you call," Jenn interrupted. "Are you in for the two thousand?"

"I don't think so," I said with a shake of my head. "The pilot could get made and not picked up or even shown to anyone for years. I think I'll keep my roof improvements."

Jenn stuck out her bottom lip in a pout. "Sad. I think your neighbors aren't going to be too happy."

"We just can't do everything," I said with a shrug. "They are business owners. They'll understand."

* * *

Later that afternoon I took my bichon poo puppy, Mal, out for her afternoon walk. We went out the back of the McMurphy and across the alley to Mal's favorite patch of grass.

"Allie," Mr. Beecher called my name. Mr. Beecher was an elderly gentleman who wore three-piece suits and walked twice daily around the island. He reminded me of the snowman narrator from the Rudolph stop-motion television show. Or more specifically, he reminded me of Burl Ives.

"Hello, Mr. Beecher. How are you today?"

"I'm well, thanks," he said. "I hear that you aren't going to put in for the pool to get the television show to shoot your side of the street."

I sent him a weak smile. "Word travels fast around here."

"You've got some folks up in arms over it," he said, then reached into his pocket and took out a small treat. Mal raced over and did her tricks for him. "I told them that you were entitled to spend your money as you saw fit."

"Thank you," I said. "I'm saving up to remodel the rooftop. It will make a great space for weddings and bridal showers and other kinds of parties. The view of the straits is awesome."

His eyes twinkled. "Like I said you are entitled to spend your money as you see fit. I think your grandfather would be proud of what you've done with the place."

"Thanks," I said. "I wish Papa were here for my first season, too."

"What's our little friend up to?" he asked, and

pointed out that Mal was sniffing around the side of the Dumpster two buildings down.

"Mal," I called. "What are you doing? Get over here." I clapped my hands. Mal refused to come. "I'm sorry," I said. "Sometimes she can get really stubborn."

"Do take care. They like to put poison out by the Dumpsters to keep the rats away."

"Oh no." My heart rate sped up. I don't know what I would do if Mal got poisoned. I hurried down the alley to the Dumpster calling her name. "Mal. Mal, come here, girl." It wasn't rat poison she was sniffing around, but a pair of men's tennis shoes . . . with the person still wearing them. "I'm sorry," I said, and pulled her off the man. "She has never met a stranger."

The guy was half sitting, half lying down against the side of the building. His head rested against the Dumpster, a hat covering his face as if he needed a nap and wanted to keep the sun out. He didn't make a sound. I froze.

"Is he sleeping?" Mr. Beecher asked as he rounded the Dumpster.

"Oh, boy," I said, noting the dirty jeans and torn sweatshirt he wore. "Hello? Sir?" I reached down and jiggled his shoulder. The hat popped up and revealed brown eyes wide open, but opaque, staring at nothing. "Sir?" I put my hand on his neck to feel for a pulse, but one touch let me know he was dead. The body was cold.

I straightened, my nerves on edge. Mal wiggled in my arms. Mr. Beecher stuck his hands in his pockets and whistled.

"So you've found another dead man," he stated.

"I think so," I said, and fumbled for my phone. "Do you recognize him?"

"He sort of looks like Jack Sharpe," Mr. Beecher mused, tilting his round head to get a better look at the body. "Of course, Jack is a better dresser."

"9-1-1, what is your emergency?" Charlene the dispatcher's voice was clear on the other end of the phone.

"Hi, Charlene, it's Allie."

"Oh, dear me, who's dead now?" She sounded pained.

"I don't know," I said. "I'm in the alley behind Main Street . . ." I stepped back to look at the store names stenciled on their back doors. "Behind Doud's Market and Mackinac Gifts."

"I'll send Rex out," she said. "But he isn't going to be happy."

"I'm not responsible for making Rex happy," I replied.

"That's not what I hear," Charlene chuckled. "I've sent a text out to Shane as well to get CSU over there. There is a dead body, right?"

"Yes," I said solemnly. "But just because I call you doesn't automatically mean someone died."

"Honey, the only time you ask for help is if someone dies," she pointed out. "Are you alone?"

"No, Mr. Beecher is here, too."

"Well, good. Who found the body?"

"Mal did," I answered.

"That pup has a nose for the dead," Charlene said.

In the distance I heard sirens. The alley wasn't very far from the administration building where the ambulance and police were housed. The ambulance was one of the only motor vehicles allowed on the island.

"I hear them coming," I said into the phone. "Thanks, Charlene."

"Take care, Allie."

"Well, this certainly is an interesting turn of events." Mr. Beecher kept his hands in his pockets and bent over to peer at the body. "I wonder what killed him?"

"Let's hope it wasn't foul play," I said, and gathered Mal up in my arms. Movement caught the corner of my eye and I turned to see Rex come striding down the alleyway with a tall, impossibly handsome man behind him.

"Allie, Mal, Mr. Beecher." Rex acknowledged us all but didn't introduce the man with him. He turned to the body. "You reported him dead?"

"Yes," I said. "Mal pointed him out and we thought he was sleeping. So I knelt and shook him to wake him up, but he was stiff and cold."

"Wow, a real dead guy. Just like that . . . in the alley," the handsome man said, and ran his hand through his mass of blond hair, which was thick and glossy.

"Hello," Mr. Beecher said, and stuck out his hand. "I don't think we've met."

"Right, Dirk Benjamin," the man said, and shook Mr. Beecher's hand. "You're Beecher?"

"Mr. Beecher," he replied.

"The man is definitely dead," Rex said, interrupting. He knelt beside the body and used his pen to pull the hat off the dead man's head. There was blood and gunk on the inside of the hat.

Dirk Benjamin turned very pale. "Is that like brains?"

"Yes," Rex answered with his mouth in a grim line. Dirk turned and got sick on the other side of the Dumpster. "Amateurs . . ."

I looked from the hat to the dead man's head and saw that he had a bullet hole right above the eyes.

"I'm thinking it was foul play," Mr. Beecher said out loud.

"Do you think?" Rex muttered sarcastically.

The ambulance—one of only two motorized vehicles allowed on the island—cut its sirens as it crept along the alley toward us. George Marron and Walt Henderson got out of the vehicle. George had long, black hair that was pulled back in a single braid, copper skin, and high cheekbones of his Iroquois ancestry. Walt was a tall, thin man with gray hair and a hawklike nose. He had sharp features and dark brown eyes. His skin had the weathered look of a fisherman or at the least someone who knew his way around the water.

"Mr. Beecher, Allie," George said. "What happened?"

"That's what we're trying to figure out," Mr. Beecher said.

"Did either of you hear gunshots last night?" Rex asked as he stood.

"No," I replied. "Mal would have barked."

"It might be a body dump," George said as he squatted down to take a look. "There's not a lot of blood here." He squinted up at us, his dark black gaze serious. "Probably killed somewhere else and moved here."

"Why here?" I asked.

"People know you walk this alley," Rex said. "And with your reputation . . ."

"What reputation?" I put one hand on my hip and held Mal with the other.

"Of finding dead men," George said.

"Mal finds them," I pointed out. "What does that have to do with anything?"

"They probably killed him, brought him back here, posed him to look like he was sleeping, and left him here for you to find."

"Are you sure he didn't kill himself?" Mr. Beecher asked.

"No gun around," Rex said, taking in the scene.

"It could be under the Dumpster," I pointed out.

"Jack Sharpe was right-handed," George said. "The Dumpster is on his left."

"So it is Jack Sharpe," Mr. Beecher said. "I thought so."

"I'm going to have to rope off the crime scene until Shane can get here," Rex said. Shane was the local crime scene investigator and Jenn's boyfriend. "George, take a look at Mr. Benjamin. He lost his breakfast and might be in shock. Allie, keep Mal away from the body. You and Mr. Beecher should go sit on the steps to your apartment until I can square away the scene."

"Yes, sir," I muttered.

"Come on, Allie," Mr. Beecher said, taking my elbow in his hand. "This is the best adventure of my life."

"Well, Mal and I wish it wasn't a normal occasion in ours," I said as we scooted past the ambulance. Dirk Benjamin sat in the back of the ambulance. George had draped him in a blanket and was checking his pulse. I remembered seeing my first dead body. It didn't make me sick, but it did put me into shock.

Mr. Beecher pulled another treat for Mal out of his pocket as we settled onto the steps to my apartment.

"I don't know why Rex leapt to the conclusion that the body was left for me to find."

"It was my first thought, too," Mr. Beecher said.

"Why?" I asked. "You walk down this alley twice a day. The body could have been there for you to find."

"Then they were successful, as I did find it, too," he said. "But most likely it was left for you."

I rolled my eyes. "You can't rule out Doud's Market or Mackinac Gifts, their owners and patrons," I said. "It's a stretch to say that it was left for me."

"Not much of a stretch," Rex said as he approached, his latex-gloved hand holding the corner of a piece of paper. "They left you a note."

Easy Butterscotch Fudge

11 oz. butterscotch baking chips
16 oz. vanilla frosting—any brand premade

Line an 8x8-inch pan with wax paper.

Microwave the butterscotch chips in a glass bowl until melted. Check every 15 seconds—takes about one minute. Mix with the vanilla frosting. Scoop into pan, even out, and chill until hardened, about an hour. Cut into pieces. Store in a covered container.

Chapter 2

"They left me a note?" I stood, surprised and dismayed. "Where did you find it? What does it say?"

"It was in Jack's hand," Rex said. "Did you know Jack?"

"No," I said, and shook my head. "No." I peered around Rex to get another look at the dead man. "He doesn't look familiar."

"The killer must know you, then," Rex said. "This note was addressed to you." He held up a blank note card with my name typed across the front. *Allie McMurphy*. "I don't like it," he said.

"What does it say inside?"

"kf3," Rex said and he studied the paper. "What does it mean?"

"Is it a code?" I asked, and studied the paper over his shoulder.

"Sounds like chess to me," Mr. Beecher said. "An opening move."

"Chess?"

"Yes," Mr. Beecher said. "The white knight opens."

"Oh, that's creepy," I said, and got chills up and down my arms. "What do you think it means?"

Rex frowned at the paper. "I hope it doesn't mean that the killer is playing games." His warm gaze studied my face. "Do you play chess?"

"No," I said. "Not really. I mean, it's been a while. I used to play with Papa Liam, but I haven't in years." Papa Liam was my father's father and the last owner of the Historic McMurphy Hotel and Fudge Shop. Papa had died this spring, leaving the family business to me. "I have to admit, it's very easy to beat me."

"I play," Mr. Beecher said with a twinkle in his dark blue eyes. "I happen to be the island's reigning champion."

"Is there a chess players group on the island?" I asked.

"Of course," Mr. Beecher said. "Now most players gather at the senior center, but we do have some young ones who play at the high school."

"It wouldn't necessarily be an older person who wrote this note," I said. And wrapped my arms around my waist. I looked at Rex. "Why would they want to play a game with me?"

"I don't know." Rex's mouth was a thin line. "Is there anyone who you've upset recently?"

"What? No," I said. "Why would you think I upset anyone?"

"No reason," he said. "I'm trying to understand why your name is on the front of this note card."

Shane walked up carrying his evidence kit. He wore a navy-blue windbreaker with CSU on it and a ball cap. His glasses framed concern in his eyes. "Hello, guys and dolls," he said. "What do we have here?"

"A dead guy," Mr. Beecher said. "I'm pretty sure it's Jack Sharpe."

"Who is Jack Sharpe?" I asked.

"Jack is a stable hand at the Jessops' stables," Rex said.

"Oh, man," I said, and covered my mouth with my palm. "Does this have anything to do with Trent? I mean, he and I are not on the best terms right now."

"I thought you two were dating," Mr. Beecher said with one eyebrow raised.

"We broke up," I said, and did my best not to look at Rex. I had just broken up with Trent Jessop. Trent was very wealthy and his business obligations and family obligations had come between us. Then there was Rex. Since our kiss at Frances's wedding reception, things had gotten a bit awkward between us. I know we needed to talk, but I wasn't sure what I felt or what to do. I think he was letting things settle in my mind. I think I was letting things settle in my mind.

"Ah," Mr. Beecher said.

"What does that mean?" I asked, and studied the older man.

He shrugged. "It means perhaps the killer didn't know you weren't dating."

"You think the killer might have gone after Jack Sharpe because he worked for Trent and therefore I'd get involved in the investigation?"

"He made sure you were involved with that note," Mr. Beecher said.

I held Mal close to my chest. "I feel terrible for Jack Sharpe and his family. No one should ever lose their life like this. It's such a waste. How old was Jack?"

"He was in his fifties," Mr. Beecher said. "I knew him well enough to say good morning, but that's all. Jack usually kept to himself. I believe he was in Mr. Devaney's English class in high school. You should ask him."

"If he was in his fifties, it would have been before Mr. Devaney's time, wouldn't it?" I asked. Mr. Devaney was my handyman at the McMurphy Hotel and Fudge Shop. He had recently married Frances, my general manager. The couple were off on an extended honeymoon. Both were retired teachers and in their seventies.

"Douglas Devaney started teaching here right out of college," Mr. Beecher said. "His family was from Traverse City and he grew up visiting the island."

"So I suppose he could have had Jack Sharpe in his class. Why did Jack work at the stables? I thought most of the stable hands were young guys looking for work over the summer breaks."

"Jack grew up on the island," Mr. Beecher said. "He wasn't much for school. In fact, his main ambition was to enjoy fishing. He worked enough to afford to pay rent on a small cabin. He spent most of his free time out on the water. Sometimes he'd get paid as a tour guide for other fishermen who wanted to fish the area."

"He was one of Trent's regular guys?" I asked. Trent's family owned one of the biggest stables on the island. Cars were not allowed, except for the ambulance and fire truck. People took horse-drawn carriages, rode bicycles, or walked everywhere they went. Horses were in big demand on the island.

"As far as I know," Mr. Beecher said. "I see him . . . or saw him, most days when I walk by the stables. Seemed like a nice enough guy."

"Did he have any family? Wife, children, girlfriend?"

"He was a confirmed bachelor," Mr. Beecher said. "I think fishing was his first love."

"Is this going to take long?" I asked Rex the moment I noticed he was free. "I've got a business to get back to and fudge to make."

"You can go," Rex said. "I'll be by later to get your statement. I'm sure you know how this works."

"I do," I said, and stood, putting Mal down on the ground and attaching her leash. "I won't speak to anyone about what I saw."

"Good," Rex said with a short nod. "Mr. Beecher, if you don't mind, I need to take a statement from you."

"Sure," he stood as well. We had been seated on the back stoop of the McMurphy, waiting for Rex and his men to get the things they needed from the crime scene. Rex had taken the note into custody, but I remembered the chess move. A little research might tell me more about the chess move. Of course, that didn't mean I could research what a killer meant by it.

"I'll see you later, Mr. Beecher," I said, and walked Mal inside the McMurphy.

"Where were you?" Jenn asked when I got in and let Mal off her leash. "You've been gone an hour."

"Mal found a dead body," I said with a deep sigh. "I can't talk about it until I give Rex a statement. He was kind enough to let me come in as long as I promised not to say a word to anyone."

"Oh, my goodness! Are you okay?" Jenn asked. "Is Mal okay?" She picked up Mal and gave her a squeeze.

"We're fine," I said, and checked the mail that sat on the receptionist desk. Frances Devaney was the hotel manager from way back and I had been happy to keep her on after Papa Liam died and I took on the ownership of the Historic McMurphy Hotel and Fudge Shop. The reception desk was Frances's normal perch, but as I mentioned before she was currently on her honeymoon with my handyman, Douglas Devaney. That meant that all of Frances's and Mr. Devaney's work was divided between myself, Jenn, my assistant manager, and my assistant candy maker and chocolatier Sandy Everheart.

Unfortunately, it was after Labor Day and my college intern had gone back to school. That meant we all had extra work. Thankfully, with the official tourist season finished, things in the fudge shop and the hotel could slow down a bit into fall.

I sorted the mail into bills, personal notes, and advertisements. The advertisements went straight into the recycle box next to Frances's desk. "Has it been busy?"

"Nicely steady," Jenn said. "Where did Mal find the body this time? It looks like they didn't take your clothing for evidence. I bet that's a first."

"It is a first," I said with a wry smile. "I didn't get close enough to the body. Well, I shook his shoulder to ensure he was dead, but that's it."

"It was a guy? Anyone I know?"

"Darn it," I muttered. Then I looked Jenn in the eye. "I really can't tell you."

"Oh, right, like I'm going to impede the investigation." Jenn pouted.

"You know with my luck I'd start to tell you and Rex would show up and arrest me."

"Rex will never know," Jenn said.

The bells on the front door rang as the door opened and Rex stepped in.

"I told you," I said, and gave Jenn a friendly smack

on the arm. Mal barked and jumped out of Jenn's arms and went over to jump up on Rex for her pets.

"That man is uncanny in his ability to walk in at the right moment," Jenn said low. Then she brightened and smiled at Rex. "Officer Manning, what brings you to the McMurphy, as if I didn't already know."

"Jenn," I said, and sent her a look of distress.

"What? He's a friend of yours," she said. "Of course he came to see you."

"Hello, Jenn," Rex said as he walked through the hotel lobby. Mal followed on his footsteps. My calico cat, Carmella, snuck out from her hiding place under one of the lobby's wing-backed chairs. Everyone loved Rex—even my animals. Rex was one of the few people Mella would risk having to play with Mal to come see. The cat jumped up on the receptionist desk and purred in Rex's direction. He reached out and absently stroked the cat's back. "Allie, do you have time to give a statement?"

"Sure," I said. "I didn't expect you to get to me so quickly."

"I've got my guys canvasing the area. Right now the only witnesses I have are you and Mr. Beecher. I've already gotten his statement."

"Let's go to my office," I said, and waved him up the stairs. The McMurphy was a Victorian hotel in the middle of Main Street on Mackinac Island. It was four stories. The lower level held the fudge shop in the right-hand corner as you entered. To the left was a small area for Wi-Fi usage and gatherings. Behind the fudge shop was the lobby and reception area. I had remodeled the downstairs before I opened the McMurphy for the season, reclaiming the hardwood floors. I'd had the walls painted and wallpapered with a pink-and-white-stripe vintage paper that matched the original. The hotel rooms were on the second and third floors and reachable by stairs that went up the side behind reception. There was also a very old elevator that took guests up to the second and third floors in case they had special needs and couldn't navigate the stairs. My office and apartment were on the fourth floor.

Rex knew both well as after a few murder investigations, he'd visited both my office and my home.

"Come on in," I said, and opened the door to the owner's office. The walls were surrounded by bookshelves and in the center of the room were two large oak desks that faced each other. One was mine and the other was where Jenn worked. Jenn wasn't just my assistant manager. She also planned events on the island and did most of her planning in my office.

I pulled some ledgers off a chair next to my desk. "Please have a seat."

"This is an official investigation, Allie," he said.

"It doesn't mean you can't sit," I said, and waved toward the seat as I took my chair. "You sit with me when you call me into the station for an official investigation."

"Point taken," he said, and sat. The man wasn't super tall, maybe five foot ten, but he was built like an action hero. Sometimes the way he looked at me made my breath catch. He studied me for a minute.

"What?" I asked breathlessly.

"You told Mr. Beecher you weren't dating Trent Jessop."

My heart rate picked up. "I'm not. We're not."

"Does he know that?"

"Why does that matter?"

"Because I want to take you out," Rex said, his tone soft and sincere. "But I can wait until you are absolutely sure there's nothing between you and Jessop."

"I . . . um . . . we . . ."

He sent me a small smile. "I don't have any intention of rushing you," he said, and pulled out his notebook and pen. "Let's talk about the body you found."

"Okay," I said, confused by his ability to change subjects so quickly. "But wait, did you just ask me out?"

"When I ask you out there will be no doubt," Rex said. "I want you to be sure that you're ready to date me and aren't just experimenting to see if you can live without Jessop."

"I don't experiment," I said, and stuck my chin up. "Why would you think I would do that?"

"I have two ex-wives," he said dryly. "I've had my share of rebound relationships."

"You want a relationship?"

"When we go out, I intend to make it last," he said, and shifted in his chair. "That means no ghosts in the closet. No back and forth about it."

"I see." I blinked. My mind was stunned by his words. Rex was above all a serious kind of guy. I would have to remember that.

"Tell me what brought you out for your walk this morning," he said.

"Mal," I said. "We went on our usual morning walk."

"So you took your regular route?"

"Yes," I said. "Pretty much every morning we go down the alley. Mal does her business and then we walk behind the Main Street stores. It's usually less crowded."

"Where did you come across Mr. Beecher?"

"He usually walks down the alley as well," I said. "I see him regularly." I tilted my head. "Do you think the killer might be targeting him and not me? I mean, he walks that way twice a day. Everyone knows this. Plus, he plays chess. I don't play chess."

"Your name was on the front of the note card," he said.

"Oh, right." I sat back and slumped.

"How did you come upon the body?"

"I was talking with Mr. Beecher about the proposal to pay for a side of Main Street to be included in the background shots for the mystery pilot that is being filmed on the island."

"What proposal?"

"Jenn said that the production company is taking bids. Whichever side of Main comes up with the most money will be the side they film their credits and backgrounds on."

Rex frowned. "That's ridiculous."

"I agree."

There was a knock on the office door. Jenn stood in the hall with Dirk Benjamin beside her. "Hey, kids," Jenn said. "Someone here to see Rex." Then she whispered, "It's Dirk Benjamin."

"Hey, Rex, man, sorry, dude," Dirk said, and strode in. The man was pure Hollywood with a toothpaste-commercial smile and muscles from here to eternity. "I lost you back there. But I'm here now."

"Right." Rex seemed less than thrilled.

"So what are we doing?" Dirk asked as he stepped into the room, filling the space.

"Yes," Jenn said with a nonstop grin. "What are we doing?"

"I'm getting a witness statement," Rex said, and stood. Surprisingly, he stood toe-to-toe with Dirk. I think I read somewhere that Hollywood preferred leading men under six feet tall. Still somehow my first impression of Dirk was that he was tall. Weird. "I don't think you need to be in on this."

"Oh, he can be in on this," Jenn said. "Right, Allie?"

"I guess so," I said.

"Good, see, the little lady said I could be in on this." Dirk grabbed Jenn's office chair, turned it around, and sat down on it backward so he could put his mighty forearms across the back of the chair. "Go on, dude, do your thing," he encouraged Rex.

Rex's eyes narrowed, but he sat down. "Where were we?"

"You were asking me how I found the body," I said as helpfully as I could.

"Right." Rex looked at his notes. "You were talking to Beecher about the filming."

"Yes," I said. "When Mr. Beecher asked where Mal was—" I looked at Dirk. "Mal is my puppy."

At the sound of her name, my dog came running in. She went straight to Dirk and jumped her front feet up onto his thigh.

"That's Mal," I said.

"So you're the famous body finder," Dirk said, and rubbed Mal between the ears. "She's a cutie."

"Thanks."

"Beecher asked you where Mal was," Rex said to get me to finish my story.

"Yes," I said, and nodded. "I looked for her and found her a block or so up from us sniffing around the Dumpster behind Doud's Market and Mackinac Gifts. I called to her, but she wouldn't come."

"That's not like her," Jenn said. "Mal is really well trained."

"Then what happened?" Rex said, and gave Jenn a look for interrupting.

"I went to get her and realized that she wasn't sniffing trash but a person. I asked him if he was all right, but he didn't answer. I then bent down to shake his shoulder but he was stiff. It was clear he was dead. I called 9-1-1."

"Did you see anyone else in the alley?" Rex asked.

"No," I said.

"Could you tell how he died?"

"No," I said. "He looked like he was sleeping. His back against the building and his hat over his face."

"He was staged," Rex said, and made a note.

"How awful," Jenn said, and put her hand to her mouth.

"You should have seen it," Dirk said. Old Rex here—"

"Officer Manning," Rex corrected him.

"Right, dude, this guy goes up to the dead guy and lifts the hat off him with a pen. It exposed a bullet hole right above the eyes. There was blood and brains everywhere."

"Oh, my!" Jenn said.

"Okay, let's not get too carried away," Rex said. "Allie, did Mal see anything else?"

"Not that I was aware of," I said. "I picked her up and held her until you came along."

"Right. Then that's all I needed for now," Rex said. "You know how to get ahold of me if you come across anything else."

I stood and sent him a quick smile. "I will."

"Cool," Dirk said, and stood. "Now what, boss?" He hooked his thumbs in his belt loops. "We go find the bad guy?"

"Something like that," Rex said.

"Dude, you have the best job," Dirk said.

"Excuse me," Rex said. "Let's go, Dirk."

"Bye, Dirk," Jenn said as she ogled him on the way out.

"Bye, Jenn, is it?" he asked, and kissed her hand. He winked at me and grinned.

"Oh boy," Jenn said, and fanned her flushed face.

"I thought you were in love with Shane?" I teased her.

"Oh, I am, but I think Dirk is on my list."

"What list?"

"The one where you get a free pass if he ever looked my way," Jenn said with a smile.

"I think I'll pass," I said, and shook my head. "He isn't the brightest bulb in the box."

"Who cares when he looks like that," Jenn said. "Now tell me, were there really brains everywhere? How did you handle it?"

"Dirk lost his breakfast," I said, and sat at my desk. I watched as Jenn carefully returned her chair to its place under her desk. "You are never going to clean that chair again, are you?"

"Nope," Jenn said, and sat in it. "Oh, it's still warm."

This time I rolled my eyes. "Hey, who's watching the front desk?"

"I have a bell set up," Jenn said. "There's a sign to press for service."

"And the room keys behind reception?"

"All locked up," she said, and lifted the master key

in her hand. "Sandy is in the fudge shop and we are all set right and tight."

"You know, Shane's on the island working the case," I said. "Are you going to meet him for lunch?"

"If you don't need me, that would be great!" She smiled wide. "Who knows, we might see Dirk." She scrunched her shoulders and wiggled side to side like a little girl with a crush.

"Jenn!"

"What? A girl can't have a crush?"

I had to laugh. How Jenn could think of two guys at once was beyond me. I had enough trouble with dating to make any judgments.

Chapter 3

Later that afternoon, I sat at Frances's desk after checking in new guests. Thanks to Jenn's good publicity, we still had both hotel floors open and almost filled. I had to give her credit for keeping the business running at the end of the season. We would be full for the weekend with the Butterfly House fundraiser as well.

The doorbells rang and a porter came in with a giant bouquet of mixed fall flowers. "Wow, those are lovely," I said.

He glanced around the flowers. "These are for Allie McMurphy," he said.

"That would be me," I said, and took the flowers. I fished a tip out of the receptionist drawer and tipped the porter. I read the card on the way to the reception desk. It said:

To my darling, Allie. These are to let you know
I'm thinking of you. Love always, Trent.

Oh, boy.

Trent and I had broken up after I caught him kissing my cousin Victoria. She claimed she didn't know I was dating Trent. He claimed the kiss didn't mean anything between old friends. I told him I needed a break to think about our relationship.

Then things got messy.

I was a bridesmaid at Frances's wedding and Rex was the groomsman assigned to be my partner. Rex asked me to dance and things got a little close, ending in a kiss. My timing has always been bad. It seemed that Trent had shown up uninvited to the wedding reception to "surprise" me and saw me kiss Rex. It was all a tangled mess.

I have to admit that I wasn't any good at dating. I'd spent my high school days in the kitchen. I gave up a chance to go to the prom for the opportunity to watch a lecture and cooking demonstration by one of my favorite chefs. College was a blur of occasional dates mixed with work as an apprentice in a candy shop. Frankly, I concentrated so much on learning everything I could to run the McMurphy that I never went through all the drama most people wade through in early dating years. I suffered for it now.

"Gorgeous flowers," Jenn said as she came downstairs. "Who are they for?"

"Me," I said, and placed them on the reception desk for everyone to enjoy. "From Trent."

"Oh," Jenn said, and then read the card. "Ooh!"

"Right?" I sat down on Frances's tall stool. "What am I going to do?"

"Well, honey, you are in a place a lot of women would envy. You have two gorgeous men who want to date you. Bask in it."

"What? No," I said, and shook my head. "Basking is not the right thing to do here."

"Then how do you feel about Trent?"

"What's not to like? He's gorgeous, rich, and a great kisser," I said sadly. "Except that he is not around a lot.

He's got businesses in Chicago to attend to as well as businesses here on Mackinac Island. I've seen less and less of him as the summer goes on. Once the ferries stop for the winter and his businesses here close, I'll see even less."

"If you love him, you could close the McMurphy on the off-season. Lots of people do it. I'm going back to Chicago in a couple of weeks. You could come stay with me."

"You've decided to go back to Chicago for sure?" I said, surprised at how disappointed I felt.

"Yes," she said. "You know I was only here for the season."

"I know, but I had hoped that you might decide to stay. You've got some good business going here on the island."

"I have a chance to work with Antoinette in Chicago. She is the *it* girl in event planning there right now. If I can work for her for a year or two, I can snag some really wealthy clients and improve my résumé."

"Right," I said, and sighed. "What about Shane?"

"Shane and I are okay," she said. "He understands that I have ambition. There's no reason we can't still see each other. I can come visit here and he can come visit there. We'll work it out."

"I don't know if I'm up to working things out like that in a relationship." I put my elbow on the desk and rested my cheek on my palm. "I've spent my whole life preparing to live and work and be at the McMurphy full-time."

"I blame that on your Papa Liam," Jenn said with a frown, and crossed her arms over her chest. "Just because he liked being here with your grandma, doesn't mean he should have raised you to think this is the only life for you."

"I know there are other ways to live," I said. "I grew up in Detroit. Went to college with you in Chicago. I don't want those other ways."

"And what about Rex?"

"Rex? Is handsome, sexy, a local—but he's been married twice before" I sighed. "One ex-wife can be labeled a mistake, but two? I don't know." I shook my head. "If I date Rex and things go bad, it will affect the entire island. Remember how it split everyone apart when Trent and I were on the outs due to his grandfather being found dead in my utility closet? I'd hate to think of what would happen if I dated Rex and then we broke up."

Jenn laughed out loud. "Girl, you are way over-thinking this. Nothing is as serious as you think. It's life, enjoy it and play around a bit. Okay?"

I sat up straight. "Enjoy it," I said. "I wonder if anyone told Jack Sharpe that."

"Jack Sharpe?"

"The guy Mal found dead in the alley. Do you know him?"

"I don't."

"I understand he worked in Jessops' stables and spent a lot of time fishing."

"See, a man who knew how to play," Jenn said.

"Except he's dead now."

"But that has nothing to do with you, right?"

"I wish," I said, and sighed. "Rex thinks his killer might be trying to bait me somehow."

"Why?"

"They found a note in Jack's hand and it had my name on it."

"Oh, dear, I certainly hope they don't think you killed that man."

"No," I said, "thank goodness they don't think I killed him. But Rex fears his killer might be trying to play a game of cat and mouse with me. He thinks Jack was killed somewhere else and left for me to find."

"What was in the note?" Jenn asked.

"The opening to a game of chess." I went to the closet in the hallway under the stairs and pulled out a chessboard. "I don't play chess. Do you?"

"No," Jenn said.

"Well, Mr. Beecher told me the move was the white king's knight."

"That's creepy," Jenn said, and watched as I set the game up on the coffee table between the couches near the elevator.

"I think he wants me to make some sort of move."

"Like what?"

"I don't know," I said. "Mr. Beecher said he plays chess. I've asked him to come visit and discuss opening moves with me."

"I certainly hope the killer doesn't think you're going to kill anyone to find him."

"Me too," I said as I felt my eyes widen. "I don't think he expects me to kill. I think he wants me to figure out who he is. So when Mr. Beecher comes I'm going to get the names of all the members of the chess club."

The doorbells rang and I looked up to see Liz McElroy walk into the McMurphy and make a beeline for me. Liz was the lead reporter of the *Mackinac Island Town Crier*. She was also a dear friend. Liz was tall and slender with dark brown curly hair and intelligent eyes. Today she wore a pale blue camp shirt and a pair of khaki cargo pants. "Hello, ladies."

"Hi, Liz," Jenn said. "What brings you by?"

"Murder," Liz said. "Allie, I heard your pup found another body this morning. There sure are a lot of killings going on this season."

"I don't know what it's all about," I said.

"I understand it was Jack Sharpe you and Mal found in the alley behind Doud's and Mackinac Gifts."

"You heard right," I said. "There isn't really much to tell. Have you talked to Mr. Beecher?"

"Not yet," Liz said. "Did he see what happened?"

"He was with us when Mal found Jack."

"I'll make a note to interview him as well," Liz said, and poured herself a cup of coffee from the small coffee bar I kept stocked in the back corner of the lobby.

"He'll be here soon," I said. "If you want to stick around."

"I will, thanks," Liz said, and walked up to the desk. "Gorgeous flowers."

"Thanks," I said.

"Trent bought them for her," Jenn butted in. I sent her a look.

"Really?" Liz said with interest.

"That is not fodder for the *Town Crier*," I said, and stubbornly set my chin.

"Don't worry, I won't write about your flowers in the paper . . . yet," Liz said, and sipped her coffee. "This is merely friendly banter."

"I know better than that," I said. "You are always telling me everything is on the record. But right now, my love life is off-limits."

"Too bad," Liz said. "These are pretty flowers."

The doorbells rang again and I shooed the girls off to the lobby while I registered new guests. They

were the Biltmores and they were in for the week. I
put them in room 305, took them up to the room,
showed them the small suite with a king-size bed and
small couch. "The porters will bring your luggage
up from the docks and I'll set it inside your room,"
I said. "There is a great bar across the street if you
want something to eat. It's on the water with some
spectacular views."

"Thank you," Mrs. Biltmore said. "You look so
much like your Grandma Alice."

"Thanks," I said with a quick smile. "I'll be around
if you need anything." I closed the door behind me
and went down to the lobby. Usually it was Frances
who dealt with checking guests in and out. I mostly
worked in the fudge shop, while Frances managed the
hotel aspects of the McMurphy. With Frances gone
this week, I was getting a real feel for hospitality.

When I got back to the lobby, Liz and Jenn were
talking to Mr. Beecher. They all sat on the two couches
facing each other. A chess set was between them
and Mr. Beecher was telling my friends how to play
the game.

I checked on the porters. They were five minutes
out. Most island guests arrived by ferry. The ferries
placed the luggage on the docks where each piece
was tagged depending on the hotel the guests were
staying at. Then porters would pile the luggage into
bike carriers and bike them to various hotels. We
usually got our guest luggage first because we were
so close to the docks.

A quick glance told me that the ladies were busy
with Mr. Beecher. Mal sat in the old man's lap. Mella
stretched out on the back of the opposite couch, her
tail twitching. Billy Zellor came in with his arms full

of luggage. I had him put all he carried into the space behind the reception desk where I would sort it and lug it up to various rooms. Frances usually filled the guest rooms on the second floor with guests before she opened up the third floor. Now that I had luggage to haul up to the guest rooms, I understood why.

"Hey, Allie, come over here for a minute," Jenn said, waving me down.

I walked over to the group. "Hi, Mr. Beecher," I said. "Sorry I wasn't able to get to you right away. It's been a little crazy here without Frances and Mr. Devaney."

"That's quite all right," Mr. Beecher said. "I was telling Liz what happened and why the chessboard is so important."

"Do you think the killer is a member of the chess team?" I asked.

"Maybe," Mr. Beecher said. "I doubt it's anyone who's a regular. Those people are salt of the earth. That said, we do have one or two newbies."

"Just because you're new to the island doesn't make you a killer," I said.

"I'm not quick to judge," Mr. Beecher said. "You ladies have proven to me that great people can be new to the community."

"This summer taught us that longtime residents can be murderers," I pointed out.

"Point taken," Mr. Beecher said. "I'll get you a copy of the club roster. They meet every Thursday at the senior center. You ladies are welcome to come join us."

"I think they'll all know I'm not any good at the game," I said with a shake of my head. "I don't know the first thing about it."

"I know the names of the pieces," Jenn said. "My father taught me."

"I was a member of the chess club," Sandy said as she stuck her head out of the fudge shop. "Won several tournaments until they got mad and kicked me out."

"Wow, Sandy," I said. "You amaze me." Sandy was an expert chocolatier who learned her craft in New York City. She had come back to the island to help her ailing grandmother. Fortunately for me, she'd arrived after all the local hotels had hired for the season. When I stuck a HELP WANTED sign in the window, she had come for an interview. I'd looked at her credentials and knew she was a rare find. I didn't have enough of a budget to pay her what she was worth, but we came to an agreement. Sandy could start her chocolatier business out of my fudge shop in exchange for helping me with the fudge.

This was the week after the season was officially over. Traditionally we stopped giving fudge demonstrations and only sold fudge. Without the twice daily demonstrations, I had more time on my hands, that is, if Frances and Mr. Devaney were here. With the happy couple gone, Sandy was still doing a lot of work for me in the fudge shop. It might not be the official season but we still had a lot of foot traffic looking for world-famous Mackinac Island fudge.

"Come out here," I said. "We can use your help."

"Does this have to do with finding the dead guy?" she asked as she wiped her hands on her apron and came closer. Sandy was young and pretty with copper skin, high cheekbones, and a fat braid of black hair that ran down her back.

"How did you know?" I asked. Sandy had been

working and I hadn't spoken to her about everything that had gone on today.

"I hear everything," she said simply. "Is that the opening move on your note?" She nudged her chin in the direction of the chessboard.

"Yes," I said. "The killer has picked the white side."

"He's using a man's death as the symbol for moving the king's knight?" She frowned. "Seems grand."

"Too grand," I said. "Why would he think Jack was anyone's knight? Does he think that Trent is the king? Because Jack worked for Trent."

"It might not be that symbolic," Mr. Beecher said. "Anyone who kills a man in cold blood is not all together sane."

"Okay," I said with a sigh. "Should I go to the chess club meeting? I mean, if I show up and show how bad I am at playing chess maybe he'll stop this madness."

"You think he's going to kill again?" Liz asked. I could see her reporter's ears perk up at the thought.

"I certainly hope not," I said.

"We need to find out who might have wanted Jack Sharpe dead and why," Jenn said.

"I think we should leave that to Rex, don't you?" I asked.

"You can do that," Liz said, "but, if this killer is trying to engage you in a game of wits, chances are it will only make him madder if you don't participate."

I cringed at the idea. "Do you think one of us will be in danger?"

"I don't know," Liz said. "Do you want to wait and find out?"

"Mr. Beecher," I said. "Can Sandy and I come to the next chess club meeting?"

"Sure," he said with a smile lifting his short, white

beard. "I'd suggest you let Sandy here school you on the game first. It won't do for you to show up and not play."

"Okay," I said, and looked at Sandy. "Can you stay for dinner and teach me some basics?"

"I have to take care of Grandma tonight. I can come tomorrow afternoon."

"Thank you," I said, and gave her a hug.

She stiffened, then patted me on the back. "I'll go easy on the club members," she said to Mr. Beecher.

"Now, don't you do that," he replied. "These folks can do with some good competition."

Sandy raised an eyebrow. "I'll do my best to give them some."

I raised both of my hands. "Please go easy on me. I have no idea what I'm doing. I understand you need to see four or more movements ahead of your opponent. I'm not that kind of clever."

"You will be," Mr. Beecher said, and stood. "Don't sell yourself short. You've outsmarted a few people in the past. You might find you're really good at the game."

"I'd rather be making fudge," I said, and tried not to pout.

Mr. Beecher laughed. "I think we'd all rather you were making fudge. That said, I'm going to get me a piece."

"I'll cut you a quarter pound of whatever you want," I said. "On the house."

"On the house?" His eyes lit up.

"As long as you help me hone my chess skills."

"Deal," he said, and rubbed his hands together with glee. "I'm thinking dark chocolate."

"I've got several dark chocolate flavors," I said.

"Why don't you come over here and pick out whatever looks best to you."

We walked into the glass-enclosed candy-making kitchen. The fudge shop had originally been pretty open to the rest of the lobby, but with the addition of a cat and a puppy to the McMurphy, I'd paid to have the shop enclosed with glass walls so that people could still gather around the kitchen and watch us make fudge. But it kept the pets safely away from the hot sugar. It also helped lower my insurance since the kitchen was now closed off to anyone but the staff.

"I'm thinking that dark chocolate cherry walnut is just the flavor for me," Mr. Beecher said.

I cut and wrapped a nice quarter-pound piece for him. He took the boxed piece and slid it into a pocket hidden inside his suitcoat.

"Do you want a bag?" I asked.

"No, the pocket will do," he said, and patted his pocket, then leaned in toward me. "I can't let the competition see me with your fudge. They might think I'm picking favorites."

"Aren't you?" I asked with a lifted eyebrow and a smile.

"Now only you and I need to know that, young lady," he said. Then he put on his fedora. "I've got to get home to my Sheila," he said.

"There's a Mrs. Beecher?"

He winked at me. "She's going to really enjoy that fudge."

Then I watched him walk out the back door and disappear into the alley. I don't know why I'd assumed he was a bachelor. Maybe because he always walked alone. I made a mental note to learn more about my neighbors. People had a tendency to surprise you.

Chapter 4

It was after dinner and I had Papa Liam's chess board set up in my living room. I'd spent the rest of the day checking guests in and out. Cleaning rooms, making beds, and generally ensuring my guests were comfortable and safe. The people coming in for the Butterfly House fundraiser all wanted to talk to me about the murder that happened at the Butterfly House and how I solved it.

I finally had to have Jenn start handling the customers. The last thing I wanted was to relive those terrifying moments. Now Jenn was working and I was studying famous chess moves online. I played through several classic opening moves trying to see what chess players saw when they looked two or three moves ahead. Unfortunately, all I was successful in doing was giving myself a headache.

My cell phone rang and I picked it up. It was Trent. "Hello?"

"Allie." Trent said my name and a wave of missing him washed over me. "Did you get my flowers?"

"Yes," I answered, and curled up on the couch. "Thank you."

"We haven't talked since Frances and Douglas's wedding reception."

"I know," I said. "I wanted to let you know that I didn't plan that kiss with Rex. It just happened. I think it was the romance of the wedding."

"I don't want to talk about that," he said gruffly. "I know we aren't dating."

I swallowed hard. "That's right."

"I want you back," he said softly. "I miss you. I love you. What will it take to get you back?"

"I don't know," I said.

"I meant it when I said that Victoria kissed me. It didn't mean anything."

"Our problems run a little deeper than Tori," I said. "You are always gone on business."

"I can fix that," he said. "I can work remotely."

"I don't know if I want to be responsible for you compromising your family business. Your mother and sister already don't care for me. Now that the season is over your entire family is in Chicago. You can't stay on the island just because of me."

"I want to stay for you," he said. "You are what I want and I'll do whatever it takes to get you to understand that."

"You think that now," I said. "But what if, ten years from now, you look back and think of all that you missed? All the business deals that might have gone a different way had you been there. What about your mom and your sister? I'm sure you want to live closer to your family."

"I want you to be my family," Trent said sincerely.

My fingers clutched the phone. "Trent, don't . . ."

"I know what I want," he said firmly.

"There seems to be a lot of that going around these days," I said.

"Do you know what you want, Allie?" he asked.

"I know I want to make the McMurphy my life. I don't want to just live here during the season like some fudgie. I want to make fudge year-round and take the off-season to do repairs and enjoy the different seasons on the island. It's a simple joy I never knew. My father moved my mother away to Detroit before I was even born. I missed growing up here."

"I understand," he said softly. "I'm willing to be where you are."

"But you haven't been," I said. "I won't ask you to change that."

"You don't have to ask me," Trent said. "I can help you, Allie. I know a lot about business and the island."

"I know you do," I said. "There's no doubt you are successful, Trent." I paused. "Can I ask you something?"

"Anything."

"Where are you right now?"

"I'm in my penthouse in Chicago," he said. "I can be on Mackinac in the morning."

"I'll be working in the morning," I said, and sat back and closed my eyes.

"You can't tell me that you don't miss me."

"I miss you," I said. "I've been missing you a lot lately."

"I'll be there in the morning."

"I'm busy," I said, and sat up straight. "Frances and Mr. Devaney are out on their honeymoon."

"It was nice of them to wait until the end of the season," he said.

"Yes," I agreed. "Right now I don't have time for anything but the McMurphy."

"And Rex?"

"What is that supposed to mean?"

"You know what it means."

"Have a good night, Trent," I said, and hung up the phone. I didn't have a clue what I was going to do with Trent or with Rex for that matter. I tried to put the problem out of my mind. Sometimes these things had a way of working themselves out. Most of the time it meant I ended up alone.

The next morning, I was up at 5 a.m. making fudge. The thing about the off-season is that you didn't do demonstrations and without demonstrations you didn't draw in the crowds to taste the product and impulse buy. So my production schedule was cut down by a third. I knew that spring and fall were the downtimes for the fudge shop. When the holidays came around, I planned on ramping up my online sales. The off-season was nice. All you did was make a few batches of fudge and when that was gone you were done for the day.

Our hotel guests received a free pound of fudge when they stayed with us. So I calculated that into my batches. But now that the summer season was over there weren't as many guests. In fact, if it weren't for the butterfly museum fund-raiser I might have closed for the rest of the week. But the fund-raiser made the McMurphy an official weekend hotel and people had paid for packages where they would stay two or three nights at the hotel and attend the festivities.

It meant the McMurphy was two-thirds full. Jenn came down around 7 a.m. and made fresh pots of coffee for the coffee bar and set out the daily newspapers. The butterfly group's package included doughnuts and other continental breakfast foods. Jenn set things out on the buffet that Mr. Devaney had set up in the hotel for the fund-raiser. We had paper plates, plastic silverware, paper napkins, and coffee cups with sleeves set out.

"That fudge smells so good," Jenn said as she brought me a fresh cup of coffee.

"Thanks," I said. "With smaller batches, I've been experimenting with new flavors. This one is a toffee and nut fudge. I've got a coconut, cherry, and pineapple fudge in the case. The standard regular chocolate fudge, dark chocolate fudge, peanut butter fudge, and then blueberry walnut."

"I'm surprised I haven't gained ten pounds this summer just smelling your fudges," Jenn said.

I slid the last batch into the tray, put the tray in the candy counter, and closed the doors. "You always look like a million bucks."

Jenn wore skinny jeans, a flannel shirt, and work boots. "Thanks, but not today. I'm going to go help with some setup for the fund-raiser ball."

"That's Saturday night, right?"

"Yes," Jenn said. "But we are going to open the ballroom on the third floor of the art museum for the dance. It's been closed for over a year and they've stored some things in there. So today I'm meeting with Blake Gilmore and some of the others who are working on the fund-raiser. We're going to clean the stuff out and then wash the walls and scrub the floors. Do I look like a washerwoman?"

I laughed. "You look like a model out on a fall shoot. You know you can always come help me clean up the guests' rooms once you are finished with the ballroom."

Jenn laughed. "No, thanks, I have a feeling I'm going to be tired by the time I come home."

"It's all right," I said. "I've got Mal to help me. Don't

I, Mal?" I spoke to my small fluffy white pup. She barked an enthusiastic reply.

"All you have to do is push her around like a dust mop and the rooms will be clean," Jenn teased.

"Speaking of Mal, I need to take her out on her walk. Can you handle things by yourself for a short while?"

"As long as you don't find another body and take four hours, we'll be fine."

"Shush, don't jinx me," I teased her. I hung up my apron and put Mal on her leash. Then I snagged a heavy flannel jacket from the hooks along the back hall and we stepped out into a cool morning. The sun was barely up and the streets were unusually quiet. One of the best things about Mackinac was the lack of combustion vehicles. It slowed things down. The air was fresh and exhaust-free and people expected it would take a while to get around.

Mal did her business and then we went for a walk. This time we walked down Main Street toward the elementary school and along the bike path that wound its way around the outer edge of the island. The trees had started to turn fall colors of red and orange. The pines danced along the bright blue sky while the lake rocked back and forth lapping at the rocky shore. There was something simple and beautiful about living on an island. I knew the winters could sometimes be hard, but I didn't want to ever be a snowbird. I thought that one day my children would grow up on Mackinac and enjoy all the things the state parks offered.

"Good morning, Allie." I heard a call from behind me and turned to see Mrs. O'Malley and Mrs. Morgan riding up behind me on fat-tired cruiser bikes.

"Good morning," I called.

Mrs. O'Malley was short with a round face and black hair in a pixie cut. I often spoke with her when I visited the senior center to deliver fudge and get all the latest island gossip. Mrs. Morgan had snow-white hair that was covered with a silk scarf. Both ladies wore jackets and jeans. They stopped beside Mal and me.

"I heard you found another body," Mrs. O'Malley said.

"I read Liz McElroy's column online last night," Mrs. Morgan said. "She tells quite a story. Poor Jack."

"Did you know Jack Sharpe?" I asked.

"Honey, we know everyone who's ever lived on the island longer than a season," Mrs. O'Malley said. "Jack lived here his whole life. Not that he had much of a life. The man was always out on the lake fishing. All he cared about was fishing."

"You know he rarely even brought any fish back home to eat," Mrs. Morgan added. "He said it wasn't about a food source, but the thrill of fighting with the creatures."

"I understand he worked at the Jessops' stables," I said. "Did he work there his entire life?"

"Ever since he got out of high school," Mrs. Morgan said. "Jack didn't have much ambition and he was happy to be who he was. His poor mother wanted to tear her hair out. She brought this beautiful healthy boy into the world and he didn't have the where-withal to even give her grandkids."

"Do you have any idea who would want to kill him or why?"

"No, we have no idea," Mrs. O'Malley said. "There's no scuttlebutt about any skeletons in his closet. As far as we knew he was only one of two places—in the stables or on the lake."

"Where did Jack live?"

"He rented a small place for the longest time, but a couple of years ago he moved. You see, his family owned a little cottage up by the airport. Not much to look at," Mrs. Morgan said. "Just a tiny two-bedroom place. When his mother died, he moved in there."

"Who gets the property now that Jack is dead?"

"Well, I suppose that would be his niece, Nell," Mrs. O'Malley said.

"Does Nell live on the island? Is she his only relative?"

"Nell lives in Grand Rapids," Mrs. Morgan said. "She's a teacher down there in one of the colleges."

"Nell's his only relative. Jack had a brother, Barney," Mrs. O'Malley said. "Barney moved to Grand Rapids. He met and married a gal down there. Nell is their only child. Is she coming up to take care of funeral arrangements?"

"I don't know," I said. "I imagine she might."

"They weren't that close," Mrs. Morgan said. "She might just have him cremated and stored up here until next summer."

"I don't know why she wouldn't come," I said. "The island is gorgeous this time of year."

"She's a teacher," Mrs. O'Malley said. "It might be too much for her to come all this way."

"What do you ladies know about the chess club?" I asked.

"Not much," Mrs. Morgan said. "They meet at the senior center once a month or so. It's after lunch and I'm usually taking a nice nap about then."

"I used to play chess," Mrs. O'Malley said. "It's been a while but I used to hold my own a few years ago."

"You mean fifty years ago," Mrs. Morgan said with a laugh.

"Seems like yesterday to me," Mrs. O'Malley grumbled.

"Are you wanting to join the group?" Mrs. Morgan asked.

"Oh, I don't know," I said. "I'm just learning chess. I'd rather wait to see if I am any good at it."

"All it takes is practice, my dear," Mrs. O'Malley said. "You're smart. You'll get this figured out."

"I started reading some of the how-to books, but frankly, it's awfully confusing."

"Don't read those books," Mrs. O'Malley said. "They'll fill your head full of things other people have done. The best way to play chess is like you, not mimicking others. It will keep your opponent on their toes."

"Thanks," I said with a smile. Mal started pulling on her leash. "Got to go," I said, and let Mal pull me back toward town. "Come visit me anytime."

"We will, dear," Mrs. O'Malley said. "I'm looking forward to more fudge."

"I'll come around the senior center soon," I said. "I promise to bring some fudge—with nuts."

"My favorite," Mrs. Morgan said. I let Mal pull me back toward town. The sky had started to cloud up and the smell of rain filled the air.

There was one thing I learned from the ladies. Whoever killed Jack Sharpe wasn't his niece, Nell.

Chapter 5

"What are you doing?" I asked Mal as she stopped along the route and dug at a flower garden in the front of one of the giant vacation cottages on the island. She dug harder. I finally reached down and scooped her up in my arms. "Stop that." The last time Mal dug in a flower garden she dug up pieces of a shredded human body. I wasn't in the mood to find another dead person.

Mal looked over my shoulder and barked. I turned to see what or who she was looking at. There in the hole that Mal had dug was a sock. I approached it with trepidation. Pulling the bit of clothing out of the hole, I studied it in the light. Mal's tail wagged like she had done a great thing. "It's a sock, Mal," I said. "A plain white gym sock." Luckily, there were no other marks on the sock. Mal had dug up socks before and it didn't turn out so well for the person who lost the sock.

I put Mal down and stepped away from the hole. Instead of moving on with me, Mal went back to the hole and started digging. This time she found more than a sock. She found a flesh-covered big toe. "Darn it," I said, and pulled out my phone. I had Rex on speed dial and dialed him up.

"This is Manning," he said.

"Rex? I found something—well, Mal found something and it looks like a human toe."

"Where are you?" he asked. I could hear worry in his voice.

"I'm across the street from the school," I said.

"I'm headed out your way. Are you in danger?"

"I don't think so," I said, and glanced around. "There doesn't seem to be anyone else out here."

"Stay on the phone with me," he ordered.

"Okay," I said, and hugged my waist with my free arm and looked around. "There was a sock, but it only looks like this one toe is missing. Do you think it's a copycat? Mal found toes in a sock previously."

"I won't know until I see it," Rex said. "I'm heading down Main. Can you see me yet?"

"Not yet," I said, and looked down the street. Usually Main was wall-to-wall tourists, but not today. It was mid-week and thankfully the streets were practically deserted. "Should I look and see if there are any other body parts?" I asked as I peered down the hole.

"Don't touch anything," Rex said. "I signaled for dispatch to call Shane out there. Let's let him and his fellow lab guys do any further digging."

"Okay," I said.

"I see you," he said.

I looked down the road and saw him approaching. He waved his hand and I waved back. I noticed he still had his shadow—Dirk Benjamin. I guess the man wasn't put off by the dead body. The actor must be really into studying for his part. Mal barked and pulled sharply on her leash, tugging it out of my hand. "Mal!" I called after her. She ran straight to Rex and Dirk.

Rex picked her up and brought her back to me. "Shane is on his way."

"Okay," I said, and took Mal from him. "Bad doggy." I doubt it did any good, but Mal was so smart it was hard to punish her.

"Hey, Allie," Dirk said, and shoved his hands in the back pockets of his already tight jeans. "Rex says you have more evidence."

"Mal discovered something under the bushes," I said.

"Is this where Mal was digging?" Rex asked, and peered into the depression.

"Yes," I said. "First she pulled out this gym sock." I handed him the sock held between my forefinger and thumb to try to keep from contaminating it further. "I didn't think anything of it until she went back in and dug up that."

I pointed to the dirty digit in the dirt.

"Whoa—is that a toe?" Dirk asked. This time he seemed more curious than sick over the find.

Rex hunkered down and pushed the digit with the back edge of his pen. "She didn't put it in her mouth, did she?"

"No," I said. "She just dug in the ground and then poked it with her nose so that I would see it."

"I don't know anatomy well," Rex said. "But it looks like a man's big toe."

"I'd say it looks like a dude's toe," Dirk said. "Cool."

"I thought so too," I said. "It's kind of big and there isn't any polish on it."

"I figure it probably belongs to Jack Sharpe," Rex said. He dug the pen around the hole. "I'm not seeing any other parts."

"Dude, let's hope that toe came from the dead guy and not someone else," Dirk said as he hunkered down next to Rex to examine the find.

"I don't remember Jack missing any body parts," I said with a frown.

"He had on shoes when you found him," Rex said, and stood. "The ME reported there was evidence he'd been redressed."

"So he was missing his toe?" Dirk asked.

"I can't confirm it yet," Rex said. "Not until I have an official report."

"Right, so like the ME has to send his official report your way," Dirk said with a grin. "Like in *CSI*—that's a television show. Do you guys get that up here?"

"We have cable television," I said.

"Most people are too busy enjoying the parks and outside recreation to watch a lot of television," Rex said.

"Whoa," Dirk said. "Dude, we're filming a television show. You guys are going to watch that, right?"

"Sure," I said when it looked like Dirk was going to panic. I patted his considerable bicep. "I'm sure there will be premiere parties and watch parties every night it's on."

"Cool," Dirk said, flashing a toothpaste grin.

"Was he tortured?" I asked, turning back to Rex and the toe. "Did the killer cut off Jack's toe to try to get him to tell a secret? Or as proof of life for a ransom?"

"I don't know," Rex said. "We never heard anything

about a ransom. I think whoever did this wanted you and Mal to find the toe. It's too similar to another case you and Mal helped solve."

"Wait, you solved a case of a missing toe?" Dirk asked, his blue eyes wide.

"There was a lot more than a toe in that case," I said. "There was a wood chipper involved."

"Awesome!" he said, his grin spreading. "I'll mention that one to the writers. Maybe they can do an episode with that."

"Trust me, it wasn't that great," Rex muttered.

"So you think the toe is part of the chess game this guy thinks he's playing?" I asked, and hugged Mal until she squeaked.

"Is there a note anywhere?" Rex asked, and scanned the ground nearby.

"I didn't find one," I said. "How would he know that Mal and I would walk out this way? I mean, we rarely go much farther than the alley or the police station."

"Maybe he's stalking you," Dirk suggested.

"I'd notice if I was being stalked, wouldn't I?" I asked Rex.

"Yes, in most cases of stalking you would know. Look, this guy could have buried this toe long before he killed Jack and stuck him in your alleyway."

"Why would he have done that?" I asked.

"There's no telling," Rex said.

"Maybe he thought you'd find the toe first," Dirk suggested.

"You think he killed Jack and buried the toe here hoping I'd find it? And when I didn't. . ."

"He put the whole body where you were sure to come across it," Rex said. "Maybe."

I shivered. "So he's trying to get my attention?"

"He or she," Rex said. "We don't know who yet."

"Huh, dude, I didn't think of a woman killer," Dirk said.

"We don't want to make any assumptions this early in an investigation," Rex said.

"Do you think a woman did this to Jack?" I asked.

"That would have to be one cold, angry woman," Dirk said. "I've known a few."

Rex sent Dirk a look. "I agree it's most likely a male did this," he said, and raised his hand in a *stop* motion. "But, we can't rule anyone out at this point."

"Cool," Dirk said. He shifted his pose for a moment and readjusted his expression. "We can't rule anyone out at this point." He repeated in a perfect imitation of Rex.

"Wow," I said, amazed.

"Was that supposed to be me?" Rex asked.

"No, no, dude," Dirk said, and held up his hands with a short shrug. "I'm just practicing. You know? Warming up for the show."

"Here's Shane," Rex said, and waved Shane down. Shane was a tall, skinny man with geekish dark-rimmed glasses. He wore his usual uniform of navy blue with CRIME SCENE UNIT written in big white letters on his back.

"Cool, the CSI dude," Dirk said, and took a step closer to me and Mal. "I like watching this dude work."

"What do you have?" Shane asked. He looked from Rex to me and back to Rex. Shane knew me pretty well between the crimes I had solved and the fact that he dated Jenn.

"Body part," Rex said. "Mal dug it up but didn't taste it." He held up the sock. "She also dug this up but Allie touched it so we don't know if it has any valid evidence or not."

"Why did you touch it?" Shane asked me as he hunkered down and opened his evidence kit. He gloved up and took the sock, carefully placing it in a bag.

"Yeah," Dirk said. "Even I know not to touch evidence."

"Mal kept digging at it," I said in defense. "I didn't think it had anything to do with a crime scene. We're on the way to the beach. It could have been simply a lost sock."

"But it wasn't," Shane pointed out.

"No, it wasn't," I said with a sigh. "With the toe, it's part of a crime scene."

We watched in silence as Shane worked the scene. Rex grabbed a roll of yellow DO NOT ENTER tape from the crime scene kit and strung it up in a six-foot perimeter. I stayed just outside the tape and pulled Dirk over next to me. Foot traffic on the island was so light that Rex really didn't need the tape. I think he wanted distance between his scene and the hunky actor. I wondered if Rex felt a little intimidated by Dirk's Hollywood good looks. He shouldn't have; Rex was handsome in a more masculine way. Besides, it was nice to talk to a man who didn't use the word "dude" in every sentence.

"I don't see any other human remains," Shane said after working for thirty minutes in the silence.

"Wow, it really was only the toe," Dirk said. "Creepy."

"Can I go?" I asked. "Mal and I need to get back to

the McMurphy. We have visitors for the Butterfly House fund-raiser."

"Yes," Rex said. "You and Mal are free to go."

"Great," I said enthusiastically. "I get to go home wearing my clothes and shoes. Do you know how rare that is?"

"Wait, what?" Dirk sent me a sly grin. "You usually walk away naked?"

"Not naked," I said, and blushed. "I usually have to go to the clinic and go through a crime scene exam. Jenn usually brings me a clean set of clothes. No, I don't go anywhere naked."

"Too bad," Dirk said with a naughty wink.

"I wouldn't say it's rare for you to get to keep your clothes," Rex said. "But it's good to see you not having to go to the clinic."

"Shane might not be as happy as you about it," I said teasingly.

"Why not?" Rex asked.

"He can't see Jenn when she brings me the appropriate clothes."

"I'm seeing Jenn tonight," Shane said. "We're going to dinner."

"Oh, I thought she was busy with the fund-raiser," I said. "People start coming in tonight for tomorrow morning's open house at the Butterfly House."

"She has things well in hand," Shane said, and stood. He pushed his glasses up on his nose for a second and studied me. "Did she say anything to you about leaving Mackinac?"

"Yes," I said, and drew my eyebrows together. "She said you two had an understanding."

"Yeah," he said, and frowned. "I was kind of hoping she'd change her mind."

"Me too," I said.

"There's another message here," Rex said.

"Dude, like at the other crime scene?" Dirk asked, and ducked under the crime scene tape.

"What? Where?" I asked, and Mal and I followed Dirk under the tape.

Rex hunkered down and studied the trunk of the bush where Mal was digging. "Look under the branches."

Shane, Dirk, and I squatted and tried to look where Rex was looking. There on the base of the bush, carved into the trunk were the words "knight to f-6."

"What does it mean?" I asked.

"It's an opening move for black," Shane said. He looked at me and then Rex. "There may be more than one toe buried on the island."

"What do you mean?" I asked.

"It's an opening move with black's knight," Shane said. "He may have other lesser moves hidden for you to find."

"Dude!"

"It means the killer is into chess," Rex said as we all stood. "That's all it means. It most likely has nothing to do with Allie."

"Except that we both know I've solved a body parts case before," I pointed out. Then I turned to Shane. "The first note was written out to me. Do you think he's waiting for me to make a move?"

"Let's not make any assumptions," Rex said, and crossed his arms over his chest. "What we have is someone not in their right mind playing a game only they can comprehend."

"Do you think anyone is in danger?" I asked.

"At this point everything is speculation."

"The thing to do is to figure out who this killer thinks your players are," Dirk suggested. "The winner of chess kills the opponent's king, right? So if they are playing chess, then you must be the king."

"Okay," I said slowly.

"If you are the king, then you need to protect your queen," Dirk said. "Any idea who your queen is?"

"Jenn," I said, and felt a frisson of fear run down my spine. I grabbed my cell phone and dialed Jenn's number.

"Hey, Allie, what's up?" Jenn asked when she picked up the phone.

"Are you all right?" I asked. "Where are you?"

"I'm fine. I'm at the McMurphy working the reception desk. It's been a little crazy here. We sure could use your help."

"I'll be right there," I said. "Just do me a favor, okay?"

"Sure, what?"

"If you see or feel anything suspicious, please call me right away."

"Now you're scaring me. Are you okay?"

"Yes," I said. "Mal dug up another sock and a toe."

"Oh no," Jenn said. "Was there a dead body?"

"Not that we know," I said. "Rex told me that the ME sent along a note that Jack Sharpe wasn't intact. Rex thinks the toe belonged to Jack."

"Wait, I thought he was shot."

"He was," I said. "But it looks like they tortured him before they did him in. We think they might have cut off the toe and buried it in a sock under a bush in the path Mal and I sometimes take when we walk down to the shore."

"Wait," Jenn said with a long sigh. "I thought you solved the case of the body parts."

"It might be a copycat," I said.

"Oh, that's not good."

"No, it's not," I said. "We've been through so much this season. I'd hate to think that someone might try to re-create it all."

"If they do re-create all of them, that most likely means they are local and have been watching you since your Papa Liam died. There's no way they would know all of the cases you've worked on otherwise."

"True, I guess that is a way to narrow down the killer," I said. "Do you think they killed Jack for a reason?"

"Are you looking for motive?" Jenn asked. "I haven't heard anything about Jack other than he likes to fish and he worked in the stables to support his fishing habit."

"I know," I said with a frown. "I haven't heard anything that would be a good reason for someone to want to kill him."

"You girls don't need to worry about solving this," Rex said. "I've got my full team on it."

"I know," I said, "But a little extra help never hurt."

"Allie," he said, his tone a warning.

I simply smiled at him. "It's all going to be all right."

"Yes," he said. "It is. Let me do my job."

"Come on, Mal," I said to my puppy. "Let's let the police do their jobs and get back home." I walked down Main Street.

I could hear Jenn giggle on the other end of the phone. "What are you laughing at?" I asked.

"You," she said and I swear I could imagine her shaking her head. "There's no way you're going to leave this one to Rex."

"No way," I echoed. "This is personal. I want to make sure that none of my family or friends get hurt again. That's why I wanted you to be careful until I get back to the McMurphy. Shane said that the chess moves they found at this site showed the killer's second move—or maybe his first. We don't know for sure yet what order the moves were made in. Either way, Dirk suggested I might want to keep an eye on who the killer might think my players are."

"Players?"

"You know, knight, rook, bishop, queen," I said. "If this is a chess game, then I have to figure out who my pieces are and how to keep them safe."

"Oh, am I your queen?" Jenn asked.

"Yes," I said as I wove my way through the little bit of foot traffic on Main Street. "The problem is the whole island knows it."

"You think the killer will try to hurt me?" Jenn asked.

"Let's make sure he can't," I said.

"On that we can both agree," Jenn said.

I made my way back to the McMurphy with no further incidents. I arrived to find Sandy in the fudge shop kitchen making a sculpture that resembled Stonehenge.

I took Mal's halter and leash off her and let her free, then walked into the fudge shop. "Hey, Sandy, is that Stonehenge?"

"Chocolate-henge," Sandy said with a straight face. "It was commissioned by the island Wiccans. They are celebrating the harvest and thought it would be fun to have a centerpiece."

"That's weird," I said, and studied the circle of standing rocks she was creating.

Sandy shrugged. "I don't judge. I make what people ask for and let them worry about what it means."

"Right, well, listen," I said. "Mal and I found another sock and toe buried under the bushes on Main. Rex said that the toe most likely belongs to Jack Sharpe."

"Is that good news?"

"It means that no one else has been murdered," I said. "So, yes, good news, I suppose. Although there was another message."

"What did it say?" Sandy asked. Her expression was mild concern. Something I'd learned about Sandy was that she didn't show as much animated emotion as I did. But that didn't mean she wasn't paying attention.

I repeated the message. "It's suggested that the killer may be eyeing the people closest to me as pieces in a giant game of chess. What is your take on it?"

"If that is true then Jack Sharpe was a knight in the killer's game," Sandy said. "His first move was a classic knight opening and now he has moved a pawn."

"I need to learn this game," I said.

"Funny, but it was an opening I learned when I first learned chess," Sandy said. "Perhaps the villain doesn't know chess well either."

"If he doesn't know chess, then why message me with chess moves?" I wondered out loud.

"Perhaps he's trying too hard to be clever," Sandy

said. "Perhaps he's simply deluded. He did kill a man and presumably cut the man's toe off."

"Right," I said. "Thanks for the reality check."

She simply looked at me. "Crazy people are far less devious than they think."

"I'll keep that in mind."

"It's the quiet ones you have to watch."

That made me smile. Sandy was indeed quiet.

"If the killer thinks that the people close to me are chess pieces, that means you could be in danger."

"Would he think of me as a pawn?"

"I doubt it," I said. "You are too important to me."

"Then a bishop, perhaps," Sandy said. "I have a few moves before I need to worry. If the killer plays a true game."

"Here's my doggy," Jenn said, as she entered the lobby and picked Mal up. She brought her toward Sandy and me. "Are you okay?"

"I'm fine," I said.

"Mal found another clue," Jenn said. "You should hire her out as a private investigator." She picked up Mal's paw. "Marshmallow McMurphy, PI."

"Only if they pay well," I teased.

"Allie puts everyone to work," Sandy said.

"I do, don't I?" I laughed and the girls laughed with me. Jenn and I walked out of the fudge shop and Mella wound her way around our legs. I picked the cat up. "If Mal is a private investigator, how am I going to put you to work?"

"She's in pest control," Jenn said. "You can hire her out as a good mouser."

"There you go," I said. "Sounds like the McMurphy will always be able to pay its bills."

We laughed. It was nice to joke a bit after all the serious things that had been happening lately. Sandy's reminder that I may not be the only one who doesn't know how to play chess took some pressure off me.

I had more important things to think about than playing a game. Like Jenn leaving for Chicago in a week. How was I ever going to replace her?

Easy S'more Fudge Bars

Crust:

  1 premade graham cracker pie crust

Fudge Filling:

  2 cups semisweet chocolate chips
  1 (14 oz.) can sweetened condensed milk

Marshmallow Topping:

  1 (7 oz.) container marshmallow fluff

Heat oven to 400 degrees F.

Bake pie crust about 5 minutes, enough time
  to warm the crust and crisp it up a bit.
  Remove from heat.

In a glass bowl melt the chocolate chips—stir
  every 15 seconds (takes about a minute).
  Add the sweetened condensed milk. Stir until
  well combined.

Pour fudge into the pie pan and smooth.

Spoon marshmallow cream over top.

Turn oven to broil. Broil bars until the
  marshmallow edges take on a golden hue.

Remove from heat and chill. Cut into thin
  slices and enjoy!

Chapter 6

The mayor showed up at the McMurphy about ten the next morning. I had just checked out the last person leaving for the day and was behind the reception desk. "Miss McMurphy," Mayor Andrews addressed me as she walked into the McMurphy.

"Mayor Andrews," I said, and walked out from behind Frances's desk. "What brings you into the McMurphy?" I think it was the first time the mayor had ever been in the McMurphy this season.

"I've come representing a group of shop owners on your side of the street. We have a nice friendly competition going on about what side of Main Street will be in the opening shots of the pilot being filmed."

"I heard," I said. "Can I pour you a coffee?"

"Yes, cream, please," Mayor Andrews said. Sylvia Andrews was in her late fifties. She had brown hair cut in a shoulder-length bob. A sharp nose and narrow eyes accented a thin face with high cheekbones. Today she wore loose-fitting jeans and a white blouse. The mayor had picture-perfect makeup and hair that was so full of product a hurricane couldn't budge it. "I heard a rumor that you refuse to buy into the costs associated with the filming."

"That's true," I said, and handed her a paper cup with a heat sleeve. I had filled the cup with my best dark roast and half-and-half. "I don't think the businesses should have to pay for the production company to film Main Street."

"I've been working for years to get film crews back on Mackinac," the mayor said, and sipped her coffee. "We had a huge bump in tourist dollars when they filmed *Somewhere in Time*. But that was decades ago. With today's thirty-second attention span we need to keep Mackinac in the public eye. I thought you would have seen the value just in the fudge-off you were a part of this summer."

"I did see quite a bit of business from that show," I said. "But I didn't pay them."

"The complaints my office got were that you and the Grand Hotel and others were unfairly highlighted in that show," she said. "This competition will see that all of the businesses on the island have as much chance to be highlighted."

"Look," I said, and raised my hand. "I didn't ask to be a part of that show. I was drafted. So any complaints people might have, have nothing to do with me. The fact of the matter is, Mayor, I have a tight budget since I did the remodel on the McMurphy this spring. I'd rather spend my money on further improvements than some off chance that a show will get beyond a pilot."

"I understand," Mayor Andrews said. "But I hate to see you not be a team player. I understand you've been working hard to integrate yourself into island society. Pitching in will go far in helping the members of the Chamber of Commerce feel like you care about the island."

"I wouldn't be here if I didn't care about the island," I said.

"Then I'm sure you will agree that filming Main Street will go a long way to helping sustain the tourist business. Especially with a weekly television show starring Dirk Benjamin."

"He seems to be a big draw," I said.

"I understand they're in negotiations with Bella Hand for the main female role," Mayor Andrews said. She eyed me speculatively. "They say Bella will play a bed-and-breakfast owner who is an amateur sleuth."

"Gee, does she make fudge?" I asked, tongue in cheek.

"Look, this is serious business," Mayor Andrews said with a slight scowl on her face at my antics. "If the producers pick your side of Main Street, they will be looking at various businesses to re-create internal sets. They could pick the McMurphy as Bella's home. That would bring a lot of tourism to the entire island and especially added dollars to the McMurphy."

"I think the McMurphy is fine the way it is," I said. "We've had a record season. I'm almost at capacity even though the season is over. I seriously don't have the room to accommodate any more business."

"You're thinking small, Allie," the mayor said. "With added income and revenue, you could add on to the McMurphy."

"We both know I'd have to get any new additions to the McMurphy approved by the historical committee. They don't like changes to Main Street."

"I have a considerable sway with the committee, Allie," she said, and sipped her coffee. "I could see that the expansion gets approved."

"Right now all I want is to get approval to use my flat rooftop as a deck for events. People can look out over Main Street, and the view of the straits is gorgeous. I think you can see quite a bit of the island up there."

"A rooftop deck? What are your thoughts for its use?"

"I was thinking parties, reunions, wedding receptions, and other things like that," I said. "In fact, we could use it for a variety of fund-raisers for projects on the island."

"Hmm, I can see what I can do to get the committee's approval," she said. "As long as you understand that you need to be a team player."

"But if I pay the two grand you want for the producers, I won't have any money for the rooftop deck," I pointed out.

"If you don't help in the Main Street promotion, you may not get any permits for quite a while," she said. "I've got two years before I run for office again."

I narrowed my eyes. "Is that a threat?"

"Merely an observation," Mayor Andrews said. "I'm sure you'll come around and help out your fellow Main Street shops."

"I'll give it more thought," I said. The bells on the door rang and a couple came in pulling suitcases. "If you'll excuse me, I've got guests to attend to."

"Don't take too long," the mayor said. "The committee is meeting with the producers this evening. Shooting begins on Monday."

"What if I put in my two thousand dollars and the other side wins anyway?"

"Then your money will be returned," the mayor said. "And you'll have the satisfaction of knowing that you did everything you could to help the producers make the right choice."

"Sounds like a gamble," I said. "I'll let the committee know by this afternoon." I went over to check in Mr. and Mrs. Wilhoite. Their room wasn't ready yet since it was early, but we were able to put their suitcases in a locked closet space and let them go enjoy their day on the island.

Sandy came in to work on her chocolate features and I left her in charge of the fudge shop. I went up to the second floor to clean the rooms. Usually Frances and Jenn did the room cleaning. We had talked about hiring a full-time maid, but there wasn't money for that in the budget yet.

It took me about thirty minutes to properly clean a room. With six rooms per floor and two floors it was six hours' worth of work a day. But it was satisfying work. I changed sheets and made beds and thought about the mayor's proposal of the possibility of adding another floor of rooms. It would mean I would have to give up the roof deck, tear out my office and apartment, put in more rooms, and then add a floor with a new apartment. It also meant more stairs to climb to get up to the apartment from the back alley.

I didn't like it. The McMurphy was built to accommodate a certain number of customers. Just enough to not overwork the family and still make a living. Of course, I can always take out the fourth-floor apartment and put in rooms, but my father grew up in the owner's apartment and I wanted my children to experience that kind of life. That is, if I ever had children.

I couldn't imagine Trent's family letting their grandchildren grow up above a hotel and fudge shop. I know he thinks we could work things out, but I wasn't sure of a future without living at the McMurphy.

"Hey, Allie," Jenn said as she stuck her head into the last room I was cleaning. "Are you in here?"

"Yes," I said as I exited the in-room bathroom. "I'm finally finished with the rooms."

"Did you stop for lunch?"

"No," I said as I exited the room with a bucket and cleaning supplies. My hands were in yellow rubber gloves. "I miss you and Frances."

"I finished prepping for the opening on the fundraiser," Jenn said. "I'll be able to help more tomorrow."

"Thankfully, we have two rooms I don't need to clean due to no guests. It saved me an entire hour." I glanced at the time and felt a frisson of panic. "Darn it, I need to get dressed and out to the committee on paying the producers."

"I thought you had decided not to play," Jenn said as she followed me up to the apartment. I dumped the cleaning tools just inside my apartment and headed to my bedroom to wash up.

"Mayor Andrews stopped by this morning and made noises that if I didn't play I might not get the permits to make the roof deck."

"Oh, that's not right," Jenn said. "Are you really going to let her push you like that?"

I pulled off my polo and black slacks and washed up before tossing a sundress over my head. A quick addition of minimal makeup and I was as ready as I could be for the committee. Jenn sat on my bed and watched me.

"What are you going to do? If you pay for the production company to film in front of the McMurphy, you won't have any money to fix the roof."

"I think the production company should pay me to film my exterior," I said. "I'm going to say just that at the meeting."

"Oh boy," Jenn said. "That's going to be an unpopular move."

"It's the only move for me," I said as I slipped into sandals and headed downstairs. "Are you here for the afternoon? Can you watch Mal and take care of the McMurphy?"

"I'm all yours," she said.

"Thanks." I grabbed my purse and headed out the back. The meeting was at the administration building two blocks behind the McMurphy. I got there as the meeting started and grabbed a seat next to a man I hadn't met yet. "Hi, thanks," I said as he moved stuff to let me sit next to him. "Allie McMurphy," I introduced myself.

"Mike Hampton," he said, and shook my hand. "Are you for or against this crazy thing?"

"Against," I said. "I think they should be paying us to film on Main Street, not the other way around."

"That's a pretty unpopular stand," Mike said.

"What brings you here?" I asked.

Mayor Andrews hit the gavel. "Ladies and gentlemen, let's get started." The meeting flowed around me as I listened to all the arguments for and against. I noted Mike seemed to be in the "for" column although I still had no idea what part on Main Street his business was on. Mackinac Island was a small community but I was still fairly new and trying to place people with their businesses.

I did a quick search with my phone and stood up. "Mayor Andrews," I said.

"Yes, Ms. McMurphy." She allowed me to speak.

"A simple search of how production companies work shows me that the production company pays the city a permit fee to close streets and film. Nowhere do I see that people pay the production company to film their businesses."

"Are we being scammed?" Berta Flatbush asked from across the aisle.

"I just checked with my sister in Chicago," Mrs. Aimes said from in front of me. "She tells me that the production company pays the city when they want to shoot a movie."

"I demand to know what is going on," Phil Rosenthal said from my right. "Are we competing for the right to film in front of our businesses or not?"

"Now, now," the mayor said, and slammed her gavel. "Calm down, everyone. This is not a scam. Think of it as a friendly competition."

"Who gets the money?" I asked.

"The island Chamber of Commerce," the mayor said. "When the production company said they couldn't shoot both sides of Main Street equally, it was decided that the Chamber would auction off one side of Main Street to be filmed."

"So it wasn't the production company asking for cash?" I clarified.

"The winner of the auction will receive full rights to film their side of the street along with full exterior shots of their property to run in the opening montage for the show," the mayor said. "Ladies and gentlemen, it is a competition. The film rights committee decided that the auction was the only way to fairly divide this resource. All proceeds will go back to the Chamber of Commerce to help promote Mackinac Island tourism."

"That was clever," Mike said as he leaned in so that only I could hear.

"What?"

"That clarification move you did," he said. "Everyone came here thinking they had to pay to get the film crew to shoot their side of Main Street. Now they see they don't."

"I wasn't trying to be clever," I said. "I wanted the mayor to clarify what was going on."

"Well, I'm not opposed to winning the bid to have my business filmed," Mr. Thompson said. Thompson owned the bed-and-breakfast on the other side of the alley behind me. At one time his grandfather and my grandfather had built a pool house between the two properties and guests from both places used the enclosed pool. But over time Henry took a dislike to the McMurphy and soon banned my guests from the pool house.

"You're not located on Main Street," Mrs. Aimes pointed out. "You are on Market Street."

"That doesn't matter, does it, Mayor?" he asked. "It seems to me that a high bid is a high bid. Winner takes all."

The mayor pondered the problem for a moment and then pounded her gavel. "Winner takes all," she declared.

"I bid five thousand dollars," Mr. Thompson said.

The room erupted into complaints.

The mayor pounded with her gavel. "I have a bid of five thousand dollars. Do I hear five five?"

"Six thousand," Mrs. Aimes said.

"Seven thousand," Mr. Thompson said.

"Ten thousand," Mrs. Aimes said. "As long as you include dinner with Dirk Benjamin."

"I bid fifteen thousand," Mr. Thompson said.

"He is nuts," I said to Mike.

"It's the thrill of the hunt," he said.

"I bid twenty thousand dollars," Paige Jessop said as she walked into the meeting. "They will shoot in front of the stables and wherever we want around town."

Mr. Thompson opened his mouth but no sound came out.

"Twenty thousand once," the mayor said.

Mr. Thompson's mouth gaped again.

"Twenty thousand twice," the mayor said. "And sold to Paige Jessop."

I felt relief course through me. I wouldn't have to spend any money and Thompson still didn't get to have filming on Market Street.

"And that's how you get things done," Mike said.

"Paige is good at that," I said. We got up to leave. "I'm sorry, I didn't catch where you work."

"I'm retired," Mike said. "I came to see what was going on in town."

"Oh," I said. "Where are you retired from?"

"I retired from Applewhite and Birch in Chicago," he said. "I was in advertising for years."

"That's a fun business," I said.

"It is cutthroat," he said.

"Do you miss it?"

"The cutthroat part?" he asked. "Or the creative?"

"Both," I said with a laugh.

"I spend my time painting," he said. "So my creative is good."

"If you're selling those paintings, that can be pretty cutthroat," I said.

"I don't sell my paintings," he said. "But I have other ways of sparking my interests."

"Oh, do you fish?" I asked as we stepped outside.

"I prefer more urbane hobbies," he said.

"Right, you are from Chicago," I said. "Do you have a place in the city?"

"I do, but right now I prefer the island," he said.

"I studied in Chicago," I said. "But I prefer to live on the island. My family history is here. Do you have family on the island?"

"My grandparents owned a cottage and left it to me when they died. We Hamptons have lived on the island for nearly as long as your family, Ms. McMurphy."

"I'm sorry we haven't met sooner," I said, and shook his hand. "I'm working on meeting everyone on the island."

"Allie, do you have a minute?" Paige called to me from the administration building door.

"I've got to go," I said. "So nice to meet you." I turned to Paige. "Paige, I thought you were in the city for the rest of the year."

"I came out because I'm worried about Trent," she said. "And well, other things."

"Wait—how did you know about the auction?"

"Mother," she said. "She wanted me to be sure that only Jessop properties were featured in the filming."

"Of course," I said.

"I didn't mean to offend you," she said. "You weren't bidding."

"I'm saving my money for other things," I said, and

crossed my arms over my chest. I promised myself I wouldn't be defensive. Paige was well-bred and looked as if she spent her whole life in a spa. She was dressed with cool casualness that belied the expense of her clothing. It was well-heeled comfort. I felt a bit shabby in my sundress and sandals.

"I wasn't going to bid against you," she said. "You're practically family."

That made me smile wryly. "Trent and I broke up."

"Trent is over the moon for you," she said, and put her arm through mine and turned me toward Main Street. "Come on, let's get a coffee and talk about things. I've never had a sister before."

"Neither have I," I said as I let her lead me along. "But I would prefer you don't make any assumptions about my relationship—or lack thereof—with your brother."

"Okay, so I might have gone too far with the whole sister thing," she said, and steered me forward. "Let's have coffee anyway. There's some things I want to talk to you about."

"Like what?"

"Like how my family feels about you and Trent."

I sighed long and hard. This was a conversation I was hoping to avoid. I guess it was best to tackle it head-on.

Chapter 7

We got coffee from a little coffee hut on the corner and sat in the sunshine. There was sidewalk seating with black wrought-iron café tables and chairs. With the tourist season pretty much over, there weren't too many people wandering about. Being on a side street helped.

"I hope you didn't come all this way to try to talk me into fixing my relationship with Trent," I said as I wrapped my hands around the paper cup filled with a chai tea latte.

"My mother sent me, actually," she said, and sipped her drink. "We wanted to ensure we were a big part of the filming for the pilot. She heard the mayor was trying to build a rivalry between sides of Main Street." She shrugged. "We own businesses on both sides so it only made sense that we put forth the effort to win the bid."

"I understand that," I said. "I'm glad this isn't about Trent and me."

"I wanted to have coffee to check in with you. I haven't had much time to get to know you."

"You are busy with your family businesses," I said. "So am I."

She blew out a long breath. "My father has announced plans to retire next year," she said. "He's been grooming Trent to take over as president of Jessop Enterprises."

"No wonder he's been so busy."

"Trent's been pushing back," Paige said. "The family is worried. Trent has been a real trooper, always doing what was best for the family. That all changed after he met you."

"I'm not going to take responsibility for your family squabbles," I said.

"Good," Paige said. "I thought that's how you felt."

"It's none of your business, but the main reason I broke up with Trent was that we want different lifestyles. I've spent my life prepping to make the Mc-Murphy my home and business."

"Trent hasn't been the same since he wasn't invited to Frances's wedding," Paige said. "He's distracted and moody. Mother wanted me to check with you and see if you had any idea why."

"You should ask him," I said.

"I'm worried that he's obsessing over you because you broke up with him. Trent is used to getting his way in relationships. You're the first woman to break up with him. He's usually the one to move on."

"Well, I certainly am not going to take him back so that he can focus on the family business."

Paige laughed. It was like a sweet clear bell sound "Oh no, Allie," she said, and touched my hand. "I'm not here to ask you to take Trent back."

Okay, I have to admit that stung. I knew I wasn't on

the same social level as they were, but it didn't mean it didn't hurt to hear.

"I'm here to let you know that my family supports whatever decision you make. We really admire you. You've taken your family business by the horns and are doing quite well for not having any real experience."

"Wait, I worked as a candy maker for years as I put myself through college."

"See? You are quite the go-getter," she said, her eyes sparkling. "We Jessops admire people who pull themselves up by their bootstraps. It's how we made our fortune."

"Why are we having coffee?" I asked, and sat back.

Paige leaned into the table. "Because I want to be your friend. I don't care whether you date Trent or not. I admire what you've done here and I think we can be great friends."

"But you live in Chicago," I had to point out.

"Father wants me to run the Mackinac Island businesses so I'm going to move into the cottage full time."

"Oh," I said. "Oh, congratulations! I know you will be great at running things."

"Thanks," she said. "I wondered if we could meet for lunch once a week. That way I can pick your brain on how to manage a Mackinac Island business. I'd like you to be my mentor."

"Seriously?" I sat up straight. Paige had an Ivy League education. She wanted to have me as a mentor.

"I'm very serious," she said. "It was Mother's idea that I contact you. She really thinks you have a good grasp of what you want and you are innovative in how you do it. For instance, I have no idea how you managed to snag Sandy Everheart, but her chocolatier business complements your fudge shop wonderfully. You two are doing a shared business concept, right?"

"Yes," I said. "I'm also sharing business space with Jenn. She is running an event-planning business."

"But I heard that she is going back to Chicago," Paige said. "Are you going to replace her?"

"It's off-season," I said. "With the decrease in fudge sales, I can do most of Jenn's work."

"You plan on adding an event-planning business to your workload?"

"I don't think I need to worry about event planning," I said. "Jenn can do a few hours a week from Chicago for next season."

"Ah, I see," she said. "You really do plan for everything."

"Well, welcome to island living," I said. "To female entrepreneurs." I lifted my cup in a toast.

"To a great working relationship," she said and we touched cups.

"Speaking of work," I said, and stood. "I have to get back. Frances and Mr. Devaney are still on their honeymoon."

"Thanks for meeting with me," Paige said. "When is a good time to get together for our first lunch?"

"You will probably need a week to get moved in and settled," I said. "How about a week from Saturday? We can get together for lunch at the Nag's Head."

"Perfect," Paige said, and made a note on her phone. "I'll send an email reminder."

"Thanks," I said. "And good luck working with the production company on the pilot shoot. It will be a real business boom if the pilot gets picked up and they use your exteriors. People love to come see where things are shot."

"The Grand still gets people who come see the places they shot that old movie *Somewhere in Time.*"

"Speaking of the Grand," I said. "I'm surprised they didn't have a representative at the meeting vying for screen time."

"They don't have to," Paige said. "They fend off requests to film on their property all the time."

"I understand that the show is about an amateur sleuth who owns a hotel. Dirk Benjamin plays the local policeman who is at odds with the heroine. Dirk has been following Rex for at least two days now."

"Oh, I bet Rex loves that," Paige said with a laugh. "I'm going to have to visit Rex and tease him."

"Are you sure you're not going to check out Dirk up close and in person?"

"Frankly, I'm not impressed. I've met Dirk before at a fund-raiser in Chicago. He is handsome enough, but not very bright. It will be interesting to see how he portrays the policeman."

"Maybe the sleuth will talk circles around him," I said. "It will be fun to see how the script plays out. I'm guessing no matter what happens, Rex won't be happy."

"But the mayor and the film committee are happy," Paige said. "They should be as they are twenty thousand dollars richer."

"I'm certain you'll get a good bang for your buck," I said. "Even if it only goes one season, things last forever on the Internet."

"That's what I'm hoping for," Paige said. "Thanks for agreeing to mentor me."

"My pleasure," I said, and meant it. Maybe this day wasn't going to be a total loss after all.

Chapter 8

"Allie McMurphy," Mrs. Allen said as I walked past her fudge shop on my side of Main Street. "I cannot believe you let that Jessop girl outbid our side of the street to win the film rights."

"Hello, Mrs. Allen," I said. "How are you this afternoon?" Sometimes it helped to fight fire with a cool, cheerful attitude.

"I'm not happy, not happy at all," she muttered. "I had plans for them filming my fudge shop. I was hoping they would use it for an interior shot on the series. People would come from all over to see that—especially with Dirk Benjamin as the lead."

"The Jessops own the bar across the street from your fudge shop," I pointed out. "Also they own the stables just a block down Main Street from you."

"So?" She shook her head.

"I'm sure the characters will have to walk from the fudge shop to the stables at some point in the script. That means they are going to film right in front of your fudge shop. They may even feature it."

"They might?"

"You never know," I said with a shrug. "You could get filmed and not have to pay a cent for it to show off your shop."

"Huh," she said as the thought stopped her short.

"You're welcome," I said, and continued to the Mc-Murphy. I pushed through the doors and listened to the jangling bells. Mal came scrambling toward me, putting the brakes on a few feet away and sliding into my shins. "Hello, Mal," I said and she stood on her back legs and begged for me to pick her up. "How was your afternoon?"

I picked up the dog and stuck my head into the fudge shop. It was empty. The kitchen was clean and a few pounds of fudge still sat in the enclosed candy counter. But it looked like Sandy was done for the day.

The lobby was empty as I made my way to the stairs. Jenn came flying down them, practically bowling me over. "Whoa," I said. "What's the hurry? Have I made you late?"

"You were gone a long time," Jenn said, and hurried down the stairs, tucked in behind Frances's reception desk, and gathered up a wayward pair of blue pumps. "I'm going to be late for my dinner date with Shane." She stood and wiggled the blue knit jersey dress down to a descent half-thigh height. "How do I look?"

"Like a million bucks," I said. "I didn't know you were going anywhere special tonight. I would have gotten back sooner."

"It's not that special," Jenn said with a halfhearted shrug. "I'm simply going to be telling him my plans for leaving next week. I'm hoping looking sexy will help soften the blow."

"I think it might have the opposite effect," I said. "He might throw you over his shoulder and take you home with him."

She stopped short and thought about it a moment. "That might not be a bad thing." She dug lipstick out of her purse and looked into the reflection off the glass wall as she applied it. "I could use a little caveman in my life right now."

I shook my head. "I thought you had an event for the fund-raiser tonight."

"That's tomorrow, silly," she said. "Tonight is for me and Shane."

"He asked me about you today," I said.

"Did he?"

"I think he knows you're leaving us."

"Of course he knows," she said. "I never made a secret about it. I just need to tell him my moving date. I'm hoping we can still see each other on weekends and holidays." Her shoulders dropped. "I'm going to miss him." She looked at me and it looked like she might tear up. "I'm going to miss you, too."

"It's okay," I said. "I know I can't pay you what Antoinette will pay you. And you'll get a lot of experience and contacts in Chicago." I hugged her and she hugged me back.

"I'm thinking if I leave you might have a better chance at a serious love life," she teased me with a squeeze. "I won't be in the way."

"You are never in the way," I said. "There is always room for you at the McMurphy."

She straightened and dashed tears from her eyes before her makeup could run. "I'm not leaving yet."

"That's right," I said. "Tonight is for you to go out

on the town with your fella and have a good time. Don't worry about the McMurphy. I'll set up a bell for any late stragglers."

"There shouldn't be any," she said. "I checked in the last registered guest an hour ago."

"Even better," I said. "Oh, guess what?"

"What?"

"Paige Jessop asked me to mentor her on being a Mackinac Island small business owner," I said, and felt my chest rise in pride.

"Wow," Jenn said. "Why? I mean, I know why someone would ask you to mentor them. My question is why would Paige be interested in running an island business?"

"I guess her father is retiring and split the business. Paige will take care of island things and Trent will take care of the rest."

"Oh," Jenn said, and touched my arm. "That means Trent won't be coming back to the island."

"It's okay," I said, and lifted the corner of my mouth in a half smile. "We broke up. Remember?"

"That's not what those flowers said," Jenn said, then tsked her tongue.

"It's all pretty straightforward now," I said. "Trent will be spending most of his life off the island. I'm looking for more in a relationship than an occasional how-do-you-do? I'm glad to know things in Trent's life are working out for him."

"Oh." Jenn looked sad. "I was rooting for you two as a couple."

"Yes, well, I was hoping it would last more than a few months, too. But after Victoria"—I shrugged—

"I guess I must rely on the old saying, things happen for a reason."

"Speaking of things happening, I have to run," Jenn said, looking at her watch. "We're meeting for drinks first."

"Enjoy," I said, and picked up Mal and squeezed the puppy to my chest. Soon Jenn would be gone and I would be on my own for the winter. I hated to see her go, but it was a good first season. I think I actually won a few locals over.

I put Mal down and went up to my apartment. Jenn was right, all our reservations had come in for the night. That meant they shouldn't need anything from me. The fudge shop was closed down and locked. I had a buzzer that ran from the reception desk to my apartment if anyone needed anything. It was going to be a quiet night.

I made soup and a sandwich for dinner. It was strange to be alone in the apartment. From the beginning I'd had Frances helping me out and then Jenn came and filled the house with motion and laughter. There wasn't a night when I didn't have someone over for dinner or drinks. Now that Frances and Mr. Devaney were gone and Jenn was moving out, there were going to be a lot more quiet nights.

I supposed I could do something about them. I could call Trent. For that matter I could let Rex know I was looking for company. But I decided instead to enjoy the peace and quiet of being alone. Mella curled up next to me on the couch. Mal played with a bone at my feet. I opened my laptop and checked my emails. There were already people booking for next season. I had a single man book for next week. With the Butterfly fund-raiser gone and the season over there really wasn't much to bring in tourists except for the weekends.

I pulled up my budget worksheets and checked on the business side of running the McMurphy. I'd made a small profit this season. It was enough to get me my roof update in the spring as long as the permits came through. I wondered if the mayor would act on her threat to hold up my permits because I didn't join in on the bidding for film rights. The whole thing seemed kind of crazy to me.

There was a knock on the kitchen door leading out to the alley. Mal jumped up barking. It was the sound she made when she was certain there was an intruder. I went over and peered out the peephole. I'd had one installed after someone had left a threatening note on my back door. I had one camera near the back door of the McMurphy. I meant to have cameras in the alley, but it was an expense I hadn't budgeted for yet. It was on my list.

There didn't appear to be anyone at the door. I pushed the door open slowly and stepped out onto the landing. Whoever had knocked must have run down the stairs and out of the alley fast. It was difficult for anyone to move that fast. I looked around to see why anyone would have knocked. Mal sniffed at my feet. I saw a note attached to the door. Frowning, I went back inside to grab a tissue. Then I took a picture of the note on my phone and carefully removed it from my door. Inside the kitchen, Mella jumped up on the counter and wound her way around my arms.

I set the note down on the counter and studied it. It was printed out in thirty-six-inch font.

Make your move or someone else will die.

"Well, that's not good," I said to the dog. I dialed Rex.

"Manning," he said gruffly.

"Hi, Rex," I said.

"Allie, what's the matter?"

"Why do you think anything is the matter?"

"Because you don't call me unless something is wrong," he said gently.

"I guess that's true," I said with a sigh. "I don't know how much is actually wrong, but there was a knock at the door."

"Did you check the peep before you opened it?"

"Yes," I said, and rolled my eyes. "When I looked out there was no one there. Mal and I stepped out. I looked around but there wasn't anyone even in the alley."

"A ditch and run?" he asked.

"There was a note on the door. I took a picture and then removed the note with a tissue."

"What does the note say?"

I read him the note. "Do you think there will be another murder?"

"Stay put," he said. "I'll come by and check it out."

"Okay," I said, and moved Mella before she could walk on the note. Rex was at the back door within ten minutes. I opened the door before he could knock. "Come on in," I said. Mal barked and jumped up on Rex, her stub tail wagging hard.

Rex reached down and gave Mal a rub on her ears. "Hello," he said as he entered the kitchen.

"Thanks for coming," I said. "I left the note here on the counter."

He went straight to the note and studied it.

"What do you think?" I asked. I picked up Mella and petted her to soothe my nervousness of having Rex in my tiny kitchen. He took up a lot of room.

"It could be a threat," he said, and leaned over the note again. "It could also be a prank. It's hard to tell."

"What do you suggest I do?"

"You already did the best thing you could do," he said, and pulled an evidence bag out of his uniform pocket. "I'll collect this and we'll keep it in case something else happens."

"Do you think I'm in danger or worse, one of my friends might be in danger?"

"We can step up our patrols of the alley and check in with you twice a day," he said, and leaned his slim hip against my kitchen counter. "I wish there were more we could do to keep you safe, but without proof that this is a credible threat there is little I could legally do."

"You mean beside move in," I said, and then stopped and realized what the implications of what I said were. My eyes grew wide and I looked at him. "You know what I mean."

"I do," he said. "Does this mean you're over Jessop?"

"I had coffee with Paige this afternoon," I said. "She told me that their father is about to retire and has Trent set to take over the majority of the family businesses. I haven't talked to Trent, but I bet he's going to be busy."

"That doesn't work for you, does it?"

"Right now the McMurphy is my number one priority," I said. "It would be nice to be with someone else who made Mackinac a number one priority."

"I would think you would want to be the number one priority." He crossed his arms over his chest as if to keep his hands off me. I felt the heat from his body and wondered what it would be like to lean into him.

"I'm not used to being a number one priority," I said with a half shrug.

"You would be my number one priority," he said boldly.

"I can't," I said as fear thundered through me. "I need more time and space. I haven't talked to Trent and—"

He gave a short nod. His mouth was a thin line. "I can wait."

"I—" I didn't want to lose them both, but I wasn't ready to choose. Not yet. "Thank you," I said. "It's just I really count on you. I don't want to lose that."

"You won't," he said. "I promise you that. No matter what you decide."

"You'll always come when I've got a clue or a threat?" I sent him a half smile.

"I'll always be there."

"I'll hold you to that."

It was his turn to smile. "Good."

"Okay."

"I'll take this note to Shane and log it in. I don't know if it means anything but I'd prefer you call me should anything else happen."

"I will," I said.

He patted Mal on the head, then picked up the

bagged note. "You take your time," he said. "I'm not going anywhere."

I held the door as he stepped out. "I have a question."

"What?" He was mere inches from me. His eyes were impossibly blue and ringed in black lashes.

"Is it true that your wives left you because you wanted to live on the island?"

His mouth made a firm line. "That was my second wife, Mandy. She thought the island was great during the summer months. Winter drove her off."

"And your first wife?"

"I had a lot to learn about being married."

"I don't think winter is going to scare me off," I said firmly.

"That's what she said," he said softly.

"I'm not her."

"No," he said with a shake of his head. "You're not either of them."

"Thanks."

"You're welcome." He leaned over and kissed my cheek, leaving a warm spot on my skin. Then he turned and hurried down the stairs and out into the alley.

I picked up Mal and buried my face into her warm fur. Rex was a man of his word. He would wait as long as I needed. Until he found another woman who was dedicated only to him. Why did the idea of someone else dating him bother me so much?

Dark Chocolate Coconut Fudge

2 cups dark chocolate chips
1 (14 oz.) container sweetened condensed milk
2 tablespoons coconut oil
1 teaspoon vanilla
1 ½ cups coconut flakes (reserve ¼ cup and toast for topping)

In a double boiler, gently melt the dark chocolate chips and mix in the sweetened condensed milk until well combined. Remove from heat. Add coconut oil, vanilla, and coconut flakes, stir until combined.

Butter and line an 8x8-inch pan. Pour chocolate in prepared pan. Top with toasted coconut. Chill until firm. Store in a covered container. Enjoy!

Chapter 9

I sat up straight in bed. Someone was screaming. Mal barked and went racing out of the bedroom. "Jenn?" A quick glance at the time told me it was 2 a.m. I jumped out of bed, grabbed my silky bathrobe, and pulled my arms through the sleeves. The door to Jenn's bedroom was open. She wasn't in bed. The screaming continued.

Then someone else was yelling. This time it sounded like a man. The door burst open. It was Jenn. "We have a problem."

Fear ran down my spine like lightning. "What's going on? Are you all right?"

"I'm fine," Jenn said. "Mrs. Dennis in room 216 is not fine."

"Oh no," I said, and followed Jenn out of the apartment. Mal ran in front of us barking as we hurried down the stairs. The screaming and yelling were coming from the second floor. "What is going on?"

"I'm not exactly sure. I heard the screams and went to investigate and got told to get you," Jenn said, and we both hurried down the stairs to the second floor.

"I don't understand—"

Another blood-curdling scream came from room 216. Guests had all tumbled out of their rooms and into the hall. Room doors were left open. Almost everyone had been sleeping.

"What's going on?" Mr. Ramsworth asked as we came around the corner.

"Please, everyone," I said. "Let me through. Jenn, make some hot cocoa for our guests."

"Got it," Jenn said, and began to herd the other guests downstairs. "I've called the police. They are sending officers over."

"Great." I entered room 216 worried. Mrs. Dennis stood in the center of the room wearing her nightgown. She had curlers in her hair and looked white as a sheet. "Mrs. Dennis," I addressed her. "Are you all right?"

"No, no, no," she shouted. Her eyes were wide as could be.

"I told her to stop screaming," Mr. Dennis said. He must have been the one yelling.

"What is it?" I asked.

She pointed toward the half-open window. There on the sill was a pool of blood. My throat seized up. Where was it coming from?

"Okay," I said. "Please sit down."

She opened her mouth to scream again, but I distracted her by pulling her to the chair by her arm. "Sit!" I used my best teacher voice.

Mr. Dennis sat on the side of the bed. He appeared to be fine, but dazed and upset.

"Are you okay?" I asked him. "Is that your blood?"

"No," he said gruffly.

"No, you're not okay or no, it's not your blood?"

I touched his shoulder and tried to get a good look at him.

"No, it's not my blood," he said, and cleared his throat. "I'm okay."

"You don't look okay," I said. "Put your head between your knees." I grabbed the comforter from the top of the bed and covered his shoulders. "Try to slow your breathing."

"There's something swinging in the window!" Mrs. Dennis shouted, her voice rising at the end of the sentence.

"I'll take care of it," I said. "The police are on their way." I grabbed a second blanket and placed it around her shoulders. Then I guided her to the bed to sit next to her husband. "Please help him breathe."

Once I got Mrs. Dennis to concentrate on something other than the bloody window, I turned to investigate. We were on the second floor with a view of the alley. The room was situated below my office on the fourth floor. The window was partially open, allowing the blood to seep into the sill. I opened it all the way and stuck my head out to see what I could see. The streetlight in the alley showed me that it was a headless chicken that hung by its legs from a thin piece of baling string.

"Allie? What's going on?" I looked down into the alley to see Officer Brent Pulaski.

"Someone is sending a threatening message," I said.

He shone his flashlight at the hanging foul. "Is that a chicken?"

"Freshly killed," I said. "I've got blood everywhere."

At those words, Mrs. Dennis screamed again. I

stuck my head back into the room and went to her. "It's okay," I said. "It's okay. It's a chicken."

She opened her mouth as if to scream and I clapped my hands to distract her. "Okay, let's go downstairs," I said, and carefully bundled the couple up to get them out of the room. "Jenn," I called down the stairs as I walked Mr. Dennis down. We stopped on the landing to see the crowd of guests that had formed in the lobby areas. Officer Pulaski and Officer Lasko came in through the front door. Jenn handed someone a mug of tea and looked up at me.

"Let me help," she said, and ran up to the landing. She took Mr. Dennis's arm and urged Mrs. Dennis to follow.

"They need a new room," I said to Jenn. "Give them 314. It's an upgrade," I reassured the couple. "There's a nice sitting room."

"I don't care about a sitting room," Mr. Dennis grumbled.

"I want a different hotel," Mrs. Dennis declared loudly.

"You might as well stay," Office Pulaski said gently. "We need to get your statement and investigate. That's going to take a while."

"Jenn will make you comfortable," I reassured the couple. "I've got to help the officers investigate what is going on." It was at that moment that I wish Mr. Devaney and Frances weren't out of town. I could use a good handyman and customer relationship manager right about now. I had no idea how I was going to clean up that mess.

"What room is it?" Officer Megan Lasko asked briskly. Officer Lasko and I had a bit of history. For some reason, she didn't like me and was not afraid to show it.

"I'll take you," I said. We left Jenn and Brent downstairs calming the Dennises and other guests. I took her into room 216. It was a small room near the stairs with a queen-size bed and an en suite bathroom that included a shower. There was a window on either side of the bed. Unfortunately, the one between Mrs. Dennis and the bathroom was now covered with blood.

"Did you touch anything?" Officer Lasko asked. She took out her flashlight and studied the bloody windowsill.

"I was careful," I said. I frowned at the blood that pooled on the carpet under the window. I was going to have to rip out the flooring in this room before I could rent it again. I supposed I could try to clean it out, but people would know and look at it suspiciously.

Officer Lasko stuck her head out the window and looked around. She pulled back inside. "He had to have put a ladder up to reach this. It's too far to reach from your fire escape."

"I don't like that," I said.

"Do you have video cameras on the alley?"

"I put one in, but only by the back door."

"You might not want to be so cheap and get a system that covers all your walls."

"I'll add that to my budget," I said wryly.

"Any idea who would want to do this?" she asked.

"There was a threatening note left on my back door earlier this evening," I said with a frown. "Rex came out and took it."

"I'll see if the two things are connected. Did you catch the perp on your video?"

I winced. "I didn't check."

She raised her right eyebrow at me. "You didn't check?"

"I—"

"Should have checked that. I'm surprised that Rex didn't think to do that." She wrote something in her notebook.

"Me too."

"Without the threat, I can't really say if this is more than a prank." She stuck her head back out. "Could be high school kids messing around."

"I don't know any high school kids," I said. "Except for the neighbor. But he's been at his father's below the bridge for the last month or so."

"What about the guests in this room?" she asked. "Do they have any connection to anyone on the island?"

"I don't know," I said. "You're going to have to ask them." I hugged my waist.

"We could call CSI out here to document everything, but it will cost you."

"Cost me?"

"There's no real crime here," she said with a shrug. "Vandalism at best. After a while the taxpayers are going to get tired of paying for all your little crime scenes."

"My little crime scenes?" I repeated. "I don't make crime scenes."

She tilted her head and studied me. "There's no proof anyone did this."

"What? You think I scared my guests and ruined my windowsill? Why? What purpose would it serve?"

"It gets Officer Manning's attention," she said. "It seems you're pretty fond of that."

"I don't need to go that far to get Rex's attention," I said.

She wrote some things in her notebook.

"I'll get my camera and document everything myself," I said.

Brent popped his head into the room. "That is one bloody chicken," he said, and moved in to get a closer look.

"It's a prank," Officer Lasko said with a dismissive tone.

"Mrs. Dennis didn't feel as if it were a prank," Brent said. He stuck his head out to check it out. "I would guess that it was a two-man job. Someone to hold the ladder and someone to hang the chicken in the window."

"How is it attached?" I asked.

Brent stuck his upper body out the window and flashed his light on the side of my hotel. "They jammed a huge nail into the siding."

"They couldn't have done that in the middle of the night," I said as I stuck my head out. "I would have heard that—or at the least Mr. and Mrs. Dennis would have heard them pounding."

"You think they did it earlier and came back?" Officer Lasko looked unconvinced.

"We have a lot going on," I said as I pulled back into the bedroom. "It would have to be someone who knows when we're busy inside. And someone who knows when we come and go outside in the alley." I frowned. "They would have to know that Mr. Devaney isn't here. There's no way he would have let something like that go on the back of the building."

"So either someone who works for you did this—"

"What? No!"

"Or someone who knows how you do things," Brent said.

"It's a small island," I said. "I suppose it wouldn't be that hard to figure out what a good time to do this would be."

"I still think it's a prank," Officer Lasko said. "Have you seen any kids hanging around?"

"No," I said. "Mal would alert me if anyone was hanging around."

"Well, I don't think there is any real threat here," Officer Lasko said. "Let's go and let these people get back to their night's rest."

"Will you at least create a report?" I asked.

"Yes," Brent reassured me. "I'll stop by in the morning with your report number."

"What do I do with that?" I asked as I ushered them both out of the room.

"Let us know if you get any further threats or pranks," he said. "We'll put it all together and keep an eye on threat levels."

"What does keeping an eye on things do?"

"Usually dissuades kids from pulling any further pranks," Officer Lasko said. "I'm sure our coming out here tonight will scare the kids who did this enough that they won't be back."

"Thank you, officers," I said as we went down the stairs and into the lobby where the rest of my guests huddled.

"Jenn is putting the Dennises up on the third floor," Mrs. Adams said. "Can the rest of us go back to bed?"

"Yes," I said. "It's safe. It seems that it was merely a childish prank. Someone hung a dead chicken and caused it to swing in the window. I'll leave floodlights on for the rest of the night. Thank you all for your patience with this. There will be a free full breakfast buffet in the lobby in the morning. Plus, a second pound of fudge when you check out." That announcement seemed to satisfy most of my guests.

They went back to their rooms, some muttering about hysterical guests. I don't blame Mrs. Dennis for being upset. I don't think she needed to be quite so vocal. For a while I was scared something worse had happened.

I waited for the lobby to empty and all the guests to go back to their room. Meanwhile, I cleaned up after the impromptu hot cocoa party. Jenn came wandering back downstairs. She was still dressed from her date.

"The Dennises are safe and sound in their new room," Jenn said. "I think we've calmed down Mrs. D enough that she won't give us a bad Yelp review."

"That says something," I said. "I promised everyone a full breakfast buffet in the morning."

"Are you going to cook?" Jenn asked.

"I thought you'd cook," I said with a grin.

"I'll go pick up bagels and fruit if you cook eggs and bacon," Jenn said.

"Sounds perfect," I said. "I'll make bacon and sausage and an egg casserole. We can keep everything heated in our chafing dishes. Luckily, there aren't that many guests."

"Most of them will be up early for the fund-raiser events," Jenn said.

"I don't think we need to have anything available after eight a.m.," I said.

"Not even doughnuts?" Jenn's expression was disappointment.

"For you, I'll have doughnuts," I said. Then I waggled my eyebrows at her. "Got home late?"

"I had a nice date," she said with a sly smile.

"So you and Shane are okay?"

Her face went sober. "He is not happy with a long-distance relationship."

"I'm sorry," I said.

"It's okay," she said, and put her arm through mine, turning us to the staircase. "He'll come around."

"I certainly hope so," I said. "For your sake."

"Let's go to bed, missy," she said as we walked up the stairs. "The morning will come early now that we are providing breakfast."

"Let's not make a habit of it."

Chapter 10

I think breakfast kept my guests happy. At least no one demanded to change venues.

"I heard you had an interesting night last night," Sandy said as she readied the fudge shop for her morning chocolate work.

"The police think it was kids pulling a prank," I said. "But I need to get more cameras around the McMurphy. The prank is going to cost me use of the room until I can afford to replace the flooring. Not to mention cleaning the windowsill."

"Mr. Devaney knows what to do to save you and clean it up," Sandy said.

"I wish he were here," I agreed. "But he's not and I'm not bothering them on their honeymoon."

"I know a guy," Sandy said.

"Who?"

"My cousin Billy," she said.

"Does your cousin do custom cleaning?"

"He has been known to clean up a blood spill or two."

"Really? Is he in crime scene cleanup?"

"He's a butcher," she said, and went into the fudge shop to work.

I leaned against the wall and watched her for a moment. "I suppose a butcher would know how to clean up blood. Is he expensive?"

"I can get him for a good price," she said as she pulled out her chocolate.

"Sold," I said. "I plan on putting in new flooring anyway, but if he can take care of the mess, I'll pay whatever he asks."

"Don't ask him what he wants. Tell him what you'll pay him," she said as she pulled out the kettle to warm the chocolate.

"Got it," I said. I turned on my heel and went upstairs. Since Jenn was busy with the fund-raising event, and Frances was gone, I was the only one doing maid duty for the day. That meant I was wearing a kerchief over my hair and pink rubber gloves when Dirk Benjamin knocked on the doorjamb of the room I was cleaning.

"Hello?"

"Yes?" I said as I walked out of the bathroom with a toilet brush in my gloved hand. "Oh, hello," I said. I was a bit horrified to be seen looking like a cleaning woman. The scent of pine cleaner wafted around me.

"Allie, right?" he asked. He looked like a dream. His broad shoulders were clad in a soft denim shirt. The sleeves were rolled up to reveal strong forearms. He had on tight jeans that were worn like a cowboy. He had to know what impact his green eyes and charming smile had on a girl's heart rate.

"Yes," I said. "Sorry, I was cleaning."

He crossed his arms in front of his chest. "I thought you were the owner."

"It's a small business," I said. "My manager is on her honeymoon along with my handyman. That leaves me to do the cleaning."

"The room looks great," he said, looking around. "Wow, fudge maker, small business owner, and amateur sleuth. Is there anything you can't do?"

"Oh, now you're sweet-talking me," I said, and worked to hide my blush. "What do you want?"

"Why would a compliment mean I want something?"

"Most of the time, it does," I said, and crossed my arms, mirroring him. "What do you need, Mr. Benjamin?"

"Oh, wow, call me Dirk," he said. "I want to be friends."

"Dirk," I said. It was so strange to call someone as famous as Dirk by their first name.

"Can we be friends?"

"Sure," I said. "I'd shake your hand, but . . ." I waved my gloved hand.

"How about I take you out to dinner tonight?" he asked.

"What?" I was caught off guard.

"I'm asking for a dinner date," he said.

"As friends, right?"

"For now," he said, smiling, and I swear there was a twinkle in it.

"Okay," I said. "What time?"

"Eight o'clock," he said. "I don't think you'll need the gloves."

"Eight o'clock," I repeated. "No gloves."

"Oh, and I tend to draw attention."

"Do you think?" I teased.

"You might want to wear something killer," he said. "In case pictures happen."

"In case pictures happen? How do pictures happen?"

He put his hands in the front pockets of his jeans and shrugged. "I'm a celebrity."

"Yes, I guess you are."

"You don't mind being seen with me, do you?" he asked, and winked.

I couldn't stop the blush that rushed up my cheeks. "No, I don't mind."

"Good!" He rubbed his hands together. "I'll see you at eight."

"See you then," I said, feeling a little dazed. I wiped the sweat out of my eyes with the back of my pink rubber glove. What had I just done? It was three in the afternoon. That meant I had five hours to figure out what I was going to wear on a dinner date with a famous actor. I pulled off the gloves and texted Jenn. Dirk Benjamin just came in and asked me to dinner.

What! came the texted reply. What did you say?

Yes, I texted.

When?

Tonight at 8, I texted. I need help figuring out what to wear.

I'll be done here at 5, she texted. I look forward to the challenge.

"Yes," I said out loud as I put away the cleaning supplies. Jenn had more of a wardrobe than I did. She also could make anyone look like a million bucks at any budget. Speaking of budgets, I didn't have one. I also didn't have access to a shopping mall. That meant I had to look Hollywood-ready with what was in my closet or Jenn's. Lucky for me we were the same size.

"Allie," a man's voice called my name.

I turned to see a man my height. He had broad shoulders and heavy arms. His face was round with high cheekbones and a strong nose. He wore a white T-shirt and white cargo pants. His black hair was pulled back into a low ponytail. "Yes?"

"Ben Everheart."

"Oh, you're Sandy's cousin?"

"She said you had a bloodstain you wanted cleaned." He put his hands in his pockets and studied me.

"Yes," I said. "Come with me." I took him up to the room and waved toward the window that was still open. "Someone hung a headless chicken outside this window. As you can see, it made a mess."

He walked over and studied the blood-and-feather-splattered window, as well as the dried puddle of blood on the windowsill and where it ran down the wall and pooled on the carpet. He squatted down to see how wet the carpet was.

"I figure I'm going to have to rip up the carpet and replace it. I'm worried about the windowsill and the wall."

"Hmmm," he said.

"What do you think?" I hugged my waist and waited. Like Sandy, Ben wasn't prone to saying a lot.

"I can fix this," he said after long moments of silence.

"Great," I said. "How much?" I wanted to ask him what he was going to do, but I knew that I was expected to trust him. I'd worked with Sandy enough to know that while she might not talk a lot, she always came through.

"Not much," he said.

"Okay," I said, and frowned. "When can you start?"

"In a couple of days."

"Right," I muttered to myself. I really didn't have a lot of choice. I supposed I could hire a crime scene cleaner from the Lower Peninsula, but that would be a lot of time and money and then there would be no guarantee it would be any better. "Okay," I said, "Thank you."

"In the meantime, try hydrogen peroxide," he said. "It will work up some of the mess in the carpet."

"Got it," I said.

"Don't wait."

"I won't." I had a bottle upstairs in the bathroom. Ben walked out of the room and down the stairs. I stood at the landing and saw him stop and say something to Sandy. Then I turned and went upstairs to grab the peroxide. Another trip down to the room and I poured peroxide on the stain and blotted and scrubbed. It sort of worked. I could see where the rag I was using was absorbing some of the blood. But after fifteen minutes of hard work it didn't look any better.

"Try a hot blow dryer."

I looked over my shoulder to see Rex standing in the doorway. He had on his full police uniform. His hat was tucked under his arm. "A blow dryer?"

"Or an iron," he said. "Heat the peroxide and it works."

"Oh, okay," I said, and stood. "There's a blow dryer in the bathroom."

He beat me to the door and came out with it. The blow dryers we had were small handheld appliances that had seen better days. "Maybe you need to try an iron instead."

I took the blow dryer from him, plugged it in, and hit the spot. Some of the stain did disappear. But there was still a lot of bloodstain left. I turned off the appliance and sighed.

"Looks like a nasty prank," he said, and stuck his head outside the window to see where they had hung the chicken.

"Ben Everheart came by," I said. "He's going to help me with the cleanup."

"Ben's a good guy," Rex said. "Have you called your insurance company?"

"My insurance company?" I drew my eyebrows together. "Is this something I should claim?"

"It probably will hit your deductible, but should anything else happen you'll have that paid for."

"Huh, that's a good idea."

"I assume you documented everything."

"Yes," I said. "Officer Lasko told me to document things. She said that it wasn't important enough for the county to pay Shane's salary to come out."

"There is some truth in that," Rex said, and crossed his arms over his chest.

"I figured so. I took pictures and samples."

"Samples?"

"Yes," I said. "I took pieces of the bloody carpet, rope, etc."

He grinned at me.

"What?"

"You can't use it because it wasn't officially collected."

"Oh." I felt a little deflated. "Well, I can still get estimates from my insurance."

"Yes," he said. "You can. Any idea how they got it up in the window?"

"They had to have used a large ladder," I said. "Come look at it from outside." He followed me out of the room and down the stairs, out the back door. Rex was an ex-marine. He put his hat on the moment he stepped outside.

"Did you find any evidence of a ladder? Where they set it up? How they got it here?"

"I didn't," I said, and drew my eyebrows together. "They should have left some mark from the ladder, right?"

He went over the ground under the window. There was a tiny patch of grass, but mostly gravel alley. "Yes, with any weight on a ladder, it should leave footmarks."

"You mean the ends of the ladder that sort of swivel and have the flat end?"

His smile widened. "Yes."

"I can see how we should have that." I glanced around. "Do you think they might have wiped their prints?"

"It must have been what they did," he said. "I'm not that sure kids would think of that with a prank. Most kids who do something like this are in too big of a hurry to worry about wiping away evidence."

"Do you think it has anything to do with the killer?"

He focused his gorgeous blue eyes on me. It made my heart rate pick up. It wasn't fair that he had eyes that pretty and an action hero physique. "You think this is related to the murder? Why? Did you find a note?"

"No, I didn't find a note. That's weird, right? I

mean, even if it were kids they would have left a note. Wouldn't they?"

He shrugged. "Not necessarily. Do your cameras cover this area of the building?"

"No," I said with a sigh. "No one had harassed my guests before. I thought having one focused on my back door was good enough."

"And now?"

"I need to call the company. I'm going to get one up on all four corners."

"You have people on either side of you," he said.

"Wait, do you think they used the roof of the photography shop?" I glanced at my neighbor. "They could have come from there and crossed over to my roof and lowered the chicken down." I frowned. "It would explain the lack of ladder prints, but it doesn't make sense. Why choose a second-floor room and not a third-floor room? Wouldn't the third floor be easier from the roof?"

"I don't like the idea of anyone on your roof," he said, and squinted as he looked up. "It is too difficult to hang the chicken from the roof. If they went from the roof they should have targeted your apartment or the third floor at best."

"I still can't figure out why they targeted that room," I said. "You don't think it was Mr. and Mrs. Dennis who did it, do you?"

"I heard she was screaming."

"She brought everyone out of their rooms. And demanded that they change hotels. It was quite the scene."

He squinted at me. "What perks did you give them?"

"I moved them to the third floor in a suite room."

"Was it a big price upgrade?"

I frowned. "A hundred dollars, plus I brought in a hot breakfast for everyone in the hotel. But I don't think they were swindling me. Mr. Dennis said he would be fine with the room. It was Mrs. Dennis who was hysterical. I don't think you can fake that."

"Something doesn't add up, but I don't think it has anything to do with the murder," he said. "No need to worry."

"Okay," I said as we walked back into the Mc-Murphy.

"Hey, Allie, why aren't you getting ready?" Jenn said as she saw me walking in. "You only have a couple hours."

"What are you getting ready for?" Rex asked.

"She has a dinner date with Dirk Benjamin," Jenn said.

I swallowed hard and gave Rex the side eye. "He wants to talk to me is all," I said, trying to make it seem like less of a deal.

"But you need to look fabulous," Jenn said.

I winced. "He said I might want to look good in case we're photographed."

"I'm dressing her to the nines," Jenn said. "I've got a pair of six-inch stilettoes calling her name."

"Now that is something I'd like to see," Rex said. He had taken his hat off when he entered the building and his close-shaved head looked hypermasculine. Next to Rex, Dirk seemed almost too pretty. I studied him carefully.

"You realize that I am only having dinner with him because he wants to be friends, right?"

"Whatever," he said. "It's your choice."

Ugh. I wanted to pull my hair out. I hadn't thought about what Rex would think if I went to dinner with Dirk. Truthfully, all I had thought about was that Dirk Benjamin had asked me to dinner. Me. I never thought what it would mean to my messy love life.

Chapter 11

"You look amazing," Jenn said, and clapped her hands.

I studied the mirror and pulled at the hem of the hot pink dress Jenn had loaned me. We might be the same size but clothes looked very different on me than they did on Jenn. As I pulled down on the hem, the bodice dragged down exposing way too much cleavage. I pulled up the cleavage and the hem shortened. "This is never going to work."

"Are you kidding me?" Jenn put her hands on her hips. "It's perfect. You have legs for miles even if you did turn down my five-inch heels."

"Three inches are tough enough," I said as I practiced teetering on the pointed heels of the pumps. "I'm used to solid flat shoes."

"All you need now is a little bling as frosting." She hung a statement necklace in twisted silver and pearls around my neck. Placed a set of silver bangles on my wrist and handed me dangling pearl earrings.

"I don't know," I said as I put the earrings into my pierced-ear holes. I shook my head and felt the weight of the pearls tugging on my earlobes. "It seems a bit much."

"Only because you never wear jewelry," she said, and pulled a long length of hair away from my dangling earring. "Remember, you are going to be photographed. You want everyone to ask who that gorgeous woman with Dirk is."

I made a face. "I don't feel like myself."

"You still look like you, only . . . sexier," Jenn said. "You would look even better if you had taken my advice and put on the false eyelashes."

"I think a cat eye is sufficient. The outfit is a bit showy so the makeup should be understated."

Jenn sighed and crossed her arms. She studied me with a tilted head. "I suppose you'll do."

"Maybe I should just call Dirk and tell him I can't," I suggested as I yanked on the hem of my dress.

"Oh, no you don't," Jenn said. "When Dirk Benjamin asks a girl to dinner, that girl goes and is giddy about the opportunity."

I rolled my eyes. "I'm going to call him." I'd taken three steps toward my phone when there was a knock at the door.

"It's him," Jenn said with more enthusiasm than I had.

"Drat," I muttered as I teetered behind her.

Jenn opened the door. "Oh, it's you," she said.

I looked around her to see Trent on the other side of the door. "Is Allie here?" he asked, and looked around Jenn to spot me in the hot pink dress. "Allie? You look . . ."

"Amazing," Jenn said, and crossed her arms over her chest.

"Of course, amazing," Trent said, and shot Jenn a

look. "I was going to say you look like you are going out. Am I interrupting?"

"Oh, no," I said, and scooped up my phone. "I was just canceling my plans for tonight."

"No, you're not," Jenn said, and grabbed my phone out of my hand and leapt away. I gave her the stink eye. She knew there was no way I could chase her in these shoes.

"Where are you going?" Trent asked.

"Nowhere," I said, and reached for my phone. "I thought you had business in Chicago."

"I came to see you," Trent said.

"Paige told me that your father is retiring," I said as I grabbed for my phone yet again. Jenn easily waved it out of my reach.

"Yes," Trent said. He gave me a look that had me blushing. "That is a killer dress."

I straightened and adjusted the hem. "It's Jenn's dress."

"But it's all you inside," he said, and took a step toward me.

"Hey, kids, what's up?" Dirk stepped into the apartment through the open door. He was wearing expensive dark jeans that hugged his every curve. His wide shoulders were encased in a cotton button-up shirt. He rolled his sleeves three-quarters of the way to show off his well-muscled forearms. He took a look at me and his grin widened. "You look amazing."

"Thanks," I said. I tried to find something to do with my hands so I would stop nervously tugging at everything.

"Hi, Dirk Benjamin," Dirk said when he spotted Trent. He held out his hand.

Trent, as cool as ever, shook his hand.

"Trent Jessop," he said. "I take it you're here to pick up our Allie."

I cringed a little at the tone of Trent's voice. I half expected him to put his arm around me when he said, "Our Allie." I took a slight step sideways to prevent it. I wasn't anyone's anything.

"Dirk has asked me to dinner," I said, and picked up my purse. "We're going to talk about my experiences with murder and how he's going to portray the head of police in the pilot they are shooting."

Trent raised his eyebrow. "You're in the pilot?"

"I'm the star, dude," Dirk said, and did a little dance that ended in a fake punch to Trent's shoulder. The move made him look silly and I could feel how uncomfortable the entire room got. "Yeah, well, Allie, are you ready to go?"

"Yes," I said, and walked toward the door. Dirk put his hand on my elbow and walked out with me.

When we got down the stairs, he guided me to the front door.

"Have fun," Jenn said from the top of the stairs. I looked over my shoulder to see Trent leaning against the wall watching us with a predatory look. "Don't do anything I wouldn't do," she teased. "Oh wait, that covers pretty much everything. Have fun."

"We plan on it," Dirk said, and opened the front door for me. The bells on the door jangled at the movement. I stepped out into the cool air of the night. It was still early and that meant there were plenty of people around. "So, that guy, Trent, is he your boyfriend?"

"Was," I said as he steered me to a horse and carriage. "Where are we going?"

"I made reservations at the Grand Hotel."

"Wow, nice," I said as he helped me up into the carriage. I wished desperately to have not borrowed the dress from Jenn. Unfortunately, my wardrobe consisted mostly of white polos and black pants.

"After you," he said.

The carriage shifted as he got up and sat beside me. I couldn't help but notice the people who stopped and stared. They took pictures. I tried not to look too awkward, but I felt awkward.

He took my hand and kissed the back. "Relax," he said. "It's not so bad."

The carriage driver took off down Main Street. It was hard to ignore the flutter of the crowds and the phones raised as people took pictures. "I'm not good at this," I said, and caught myself giving a nervous laugh.

"It's okay," he said, and winked. "I was horrible at first. You'll get used to it."

"Will I?" I asked. "That implies that I'll be seen with you in public more often."

He shrugged his wide shoulders and leaned back. "I told you, I want to be friends. You're friends with Rex, right?"

"Yes," I said.

"I'm playing him in the show. I want to know more about the dynamic between you and him."

"There's no dynamic," I said, and drew my eyebrows together. The carriage finally turned off Main Street up to the Grand Hotel. "We're friends."

"You count on him a lot, right?" he said. "I mean, for your investigations."

"I call him if there's trouble," I said. "So, yes, I suppose I do count on him."

"Cool," he said, and grinned at me with that movie star grin. "See, I want to be that kind of friend."

I took a deep breath and let it out slow. "It's hard to be friends in a fishbowl," I said, and waved toward the crowds who talked, pointed, and took pictures.

"That's why I have dinner reservations at the Grand," he said. "Those guys are great at making sure I have privacy."

"You've been staying at the Grand?"

"Sure," he said with a nonchalant shrug. "It's where the entire film crew will be staying."

"I'm sorry," I said. "I'm not up on island gossip. I know you're shadowing Rex. Did I hear right? They picked the female lead?"

"Sure," he said. "Bella Hand. She came in this morning for filming."

I winced. "Is that her real name?"

"I don't know," he said. "I hear she's a looker. That's important to viewers. More important than her real name."

"Why aren't you taking her to dinner?"

"Who, Bella? We'll have time for that later. Right now, I'm still doing research."

"We're going to dinner at the Grand so that you can grill me for your research?"

"Sure, well, I mean, I hope we can be friends, too."

I felt myself relax. "Won't we make a scene at the restaurant?"

"See, that's where I've got this all figured out. My man Humphries has me hooked up."

"Humphries?"

"The manager," Dirk said. "I told him I wanted some privacy and he set us up with this cool place."

"The side porch?" I asked. I had heard that you could rent the smaller side porch for private gatherings.

"Even better," he said as we arrived in front of the Grand.

"Mr. Benjamin," a bellhop said as he opened the carriage door. "Welcome back."

Dirk hopped out of the carriage and it rocked on its springs. Putting out his hand, he helped me down the step and onto the ground. I yanked at the hem of my skirt. Dirk took my hand and put it in the crook of his arm. "Humphries has a place set aside for dinner," he told the bellhop.

"Right, sir," the bellhop said. "Follow me." He dashed ahead of us, rounding the corner of the building. "Mr. Humphries, Mr. Benjamin and his date are here."

"Thank you, Adam" Mr. Humphries said. He was a short man stuffed into a tuxedo. His hair was blond and combed over. There was gray at the sides. "Mr. Benjamin, Miss . . ."

"McMurphy," I said as Mr. Humphries shook Dirk's hand.

"Yes," he said, and looked down his nose at me. If that was possible since I was four inches taller than he was. Mr. Humphries was so short he made Dirk look like a hulking giant. "Please come this way. I've set you up in a private dining space."

Dirk held my hand in the crook of his arm and walked me across the lawn. The ridiculous heels I wore kept getting stuck in the grass. They sunk in about two inches with each step. Finally, I started walking on tiptoes to keep the shoes on my feet.

"I wanted to have them set us up in the gazebo that was featured in that old movie *Somewhere in Time,* Dirk said. "Gotta respect that Chris Reeve, you know?"

"I guess that's true," I said. "But it's not at the Grand."

"Yeah, I learned that. For some reason they moved it."

"The film company willed it to the state of Michigan, so they moved it to the governor's mansion. That way it's available for all."

"Well, I wanted to take you to dinner in the gazebo," he said, and patted my hand. "But Humphries couldn't snag it at the last minute. Some sort of wedding or something."

We approached a white tent that was strung with white fairy lights. Humphries lifted the opening. "After you, ma'am," he said, and I stepped into the stunning tent. In the center was a table set for three with fine china and various goblets from water to wine for each course.

"This is great, thanks, my man," Dirk said, and clapped Humphries on the back.

"Yes, sir," he said, and didn't react to the manhandling. "Your servers this evening are Sasha and Rick." He pulled out my chair for me and I sat. The ground was soft green grass and my heels sunk into the ground as he adjusted my seat for me. He opened my napkin for me and placed it in my lap. He did the same for Dirk. Then with a wave of his hand, he stepped back. Two young waiters stepped up and filled our glasses with water.

"I preordered everything," Dirk said. "I hope you don't mind."

"I—"

"Humphries assured me it would dazzle my companion," Dirk said. "We'll start with the white wine and the first course."

"Very good, sir," Humphries said.

"Sounds like I'm in good hands," I said, and tried not to be disappointed that I didn't get to order for myself. "Who is the third chair for?"

"Ah, you noticed that, did you?"

"Yes," I said as the waiter with blond hair poured a lovely white wine.

"Jeffery Jenas will be joining us," Dirk said.

"Jeffery Jenas?" I knew I looked as perplexed as I felt. So far the whole night was odd.

"The show's writer," Dirk said. At that the tent curtain opened and Humphries showed another man in. "Ah, Jeffery, please come in. I've ordered your favorite wine."

Jeffery Jenas was tall and thin. He wore a loose short-sleeved shirt that was open at the collar and a pair of worn jeans. His blond hair hung in his eyes. "Great, thanks," he said, and took the empty chair. "Jeffery Jenas," he said, and held his hand out to me.

"Allie McMurphy," I said, and shook his hand.

"Yeah, I know," he said. He picked up the glass of wine that had been poured for him. "I've been following your story all summer."

"I'm sorry?" I said.

"Jeffery's been on the island since May," Dirk said. "He's been following your sleuthing."

"Thanks for all the great plot ideas," he said, and toasted me with his wineglass before taking a second gulp.

"I don't want to seem rude," I said. "But why haven't I seen you before? It's a small island. We should have run into each other at some point."

"I've rented a room in the Sigmunds' cottage on Mission Point," he said. "Been writing a lot." He finished his wine and raised his glass for the waiter to bring him more. "I've been by your fudge shop a couple of times, but then so have a lot of tourists."

"You mean fudgies," I said. "We affectionately call non-islanders fudgies."

"Right," he said, and raised his glass to toss down more wine. Then he leaned in toward me. "So, how's the latest investigation going?"

"I'm sorry?"

"You know, the dead guy in your alley. Everyone knows you're investigating. How is that going?"

"I'm not investigating," I said, and drew my eyebrows together. "I've left that up to Rex Manning and our friend here." I waved at Dirk.

"Dude, investigating is kinda boring," Dirk said, and sipped his wine as they brought us our first course. "It's a bunch of waiting for test results and looking at notices on the computer. Not a lot of action there."

"Which brings me back to you, Ms. McMurphy," Jeffery said, and waved his wineglass at me. "I understand you use the senior citizens to help you with your investigations."

"I do?"

"You do," he said with a sincere nod. "The word is that you go from finding a body straight to the senior center to get the dirt on people. I want to write that into the series. Tell me why you decided to ask the seniors at the center."

"Oh, I know that one," Dirk said. "The senior gossip line is fast and they usually know when anything is amiss on the island." He turned and grinned at me. "I'm right, aren't I?"

"Yes," I admitted. "They are plugged into the community. Are you writing senior characters?"

"Nobody wants to watch old people on their televisions," Jeffery said, and shoved the first course into his mouth.

"There are lots of good older characters on television," I argued.

"We want the show to be a success," Jeffery said with his mouth full. "It's why they got Dirk involved. People can't wait to see his mug on their televisions."

"People also like good writing and a solid mystery," I said pointedly. Then I turned to Dirk. "Not to diminish your appeal."

"Hey, no worries," he said, and sat back as the waiters removed our plates and poured the next course of wine. "I love a good puzzle."

"Like my Papa Liam," I said. "As for me, I'd rather spend my days making fudge than solving puzzles."

"Could have fooled me," Jeffery said.

"Excuse me?"

"I'm just saying your reputation precedes you."

"I think she makes a sexy sleuth," Dirk said. "You're writing her as a sexy sleuth, right?"

"You're writing about me?"

"I told you," Dirk said. "He's a genius."

Chapter 12

"Tell me this, fudge maker," Jeffery said. It was well into dinner and he was on his fourth glass of wine. "How strategic are you in your sleuthing?"

"I'm sorry?"

"I bet you have an idea who the latest killer is, don't you?"

"I don't really think I'm strategic." I had stopped eating at this point in the dinner. The waiters didn't seem to notice, removing my plates and placing new ones in front of me with alarming regularity.

"I bet you are three steps ahead of the killer, aren't you?" He waved his glass at me.

"Are you?" Dirk asked me. "Because it would be cool if you were."

"I'm not allowed to talk about an ongoing investigation," I hedged.

"That hasn't stopped you from discussing the other cases," Jeffery said, nailing me with his gaze. "This guy's into chess, isn't he? Are you going to play his game?"

"How do you know that?" I asked.

"I have my insider information," he said.

"She found a toe the other day," Dirk said. "It was disgusting."

"Whose toe was it?" Jeffery asked.

"There is some thought it probably belonged to the victim," I said. "But test results haven't come out yet."

"And didn't you find another body that was cut up into pieces?"

"Did you?" Dirk asked as he followed the conversation between Jeffery and me like he was watching a tennis match.

"Earlier this spring," I said with a shrug. "It wasn't my best day and it was actually my puppy, Mal, who found it."

"So the killer is copying the murders you already solved."

"I certainly hope not," I said.

"It's a cool concept," Jeffery said. "I'd write that into a television show."

"Hey, maybe you should work with Allie to solve this new murder," Dirk said.

"I'm not solving the murder," I said.

"I heard the killer wasn't really giving you much of a choice," Jeffery said.

"Where did you hear that?" I drew my eyebrows together.

"I heard that he has made threats. I also heard that he hung a headless chicken in one of your guest's windows."

"First off, we don't know if it is a he or a she who murdered Mr. Sharpe," I said. "Second, we don't know if there is any connection between the prank at the window last night and the killer."

"There was a prank last night?" Dirk asked.

"Someone hung a freshly killed chicken in the window of one of my guests," I said. "It made a terrible mess, but everyone is safe. There is no proof that it had anything to do with the murder."

"How did you know about the prank?" Dirk asked Jeffery.

The writer shrugged. "I'm into all the gossip." He shoveled fruit and cheese into his mouth.

I leaned back, impressed. "You go to the senior center?"

"I've got my connections," he said. "I'm renting a room from Mrs. O'Connor. She knows pretty much anytime someone passes gas on the island."

"Then she knows who killed Mr. Sharpe," I said with a tilt of my head.

"Now that is something she hasn't caught wind of yet," he said with a mouthful of food, and pointed his fork at me. "She is waiting for you to figure it out. Or at least start asking questions so she and her friends can follow along with your train of thought."

"Do you play chess, Mr. Jenas?" I had to ask.

"Sure, why?"

"The killer seems to think I'm playing chess with him."

"Oh, I remember that from the notes at the scenes," Dirk said, his eyes lighting up. "I did a Google check of the moves in the notes. It's from some famous game with Bobby Fischer."

"Seriously?" I asked, and leaned toward him. He pulled out his phone and hit the browser.

"See, I put in Nf3 Nf6 and it comes up Robert James Fischer," he said, and showed me his phone.

"Crazy," I said. "I wouldn't have thought to Google it. But then I'm not good at chess."

"Don't you play?" Jeffery asked, and drew his eyebrows together as if confused.

"I played some as a kid, but nothing serious," I said.

"Crazy," he said, and snagged a petit four off the dessert plate. "I'd have thought you were good at the game."

"Why?"

"You figure out the killers," he said, and raised one eyebrow. "It means you think one step ahead of the criminal . . . or so your reputation says."

"Criminals aren't known for being smart," I retorted.

"You should teach her," Dirk said. "I bet you know a lot about the game."

"I've got episodes to write," he said, and sat back.

"It's okay, I have signed up for lessons at the senior center." I didn't like the man too much. He seemed rude and his manners were horrible. But I didn't want to insult Dirk. "Thanks for thinking of me," I said to Dirk.

"Well, dinner was tasty," Jeffery said, and stood up. "Thanks for inviting me." He pocketed a couple of tarts and clapped Dirk on the back. Then he looked me in the eye. "I'm looking forward to seeing how you solve this one. See you later, Ms. McMurphy."

"Good-bye, Mr. Jenas."

"Well, that went well," Dirk said with a smile, and waved the waiter down. "Can we get some coffee?"

"Yes, sir," the waiter said, and disappeared.

"Thank you for dinner," I said. "I've certainly had an interesting time."

"That Jeffery, he's a genius," Dirk said. "I'm looking forward to reading his screenplays."

"How many is he writing?" I asked as the waiter filled a china cup with coffee and placed it in front of me.

"He has the first seven episodes written," Dirk said, and added sugar to his coffee.

"I thought you were filming the pilot," I said, and added cream to my coffee. I was glad I hadn't done much more than sip the glasses of wine that were served for dinner. I didn't want to embarrass myself with this handsome man.

The dynamic had shifted subtly after Jeffery left. The tent seemed more intimate. The fairy lights twinkled behind him and I was strangely aware of my own skin.

"We are," he said with a nod. "But I have a few connections. I happen to know that since I signed on, the network has agreed to a ten-episode season."

"Well, congratulations," I said, and toasted him with my coffee cup. I took a sip and studied him over the lip. "Will you be filming all the episodes here on Mackinac?"

"We're shooting as many exterior shots as possible," he said. "Then we'll shoot the rest in the studio and they'll put it all together with television magic."

"Oh," I said, feeling a touch of disappointment. "I guess you won't be here that long, then."

"About three weeks," he said. "Shooting starts Monday. Then you'll be lucky to see me. It will be all fourteen-hour days, morning shoots, night shoots and such." He paused.

"What?"

"I'm going to miss shadowing Rex Manning. It's been a real eye-opener."

"I'm sure Rex is going to miss having you around, too," I said with as straight a face as I could keep.

He leaned forward. "Do you think he will? I mean, I think I've learned a lot from him. I'm hoping to channel a bit of that swagger he has." Dirk settled for a moment and then his facial muscles rearranged to match Rex's expression. "I'm telling you, Allie, you need to leave the investigations to me."

I couldn't help the laugh that escaped from me and Dirk grinned with pride. "That was Rex dead-on."

"Thanks," he said. "I've been practicing."

"Are you going to imitate Rex in the series?"

"Oh, no, that wouldn't work," he said with a shake of his head. He put his coffee cup down. "An actor studies his character. There should be a shade of the man but not an imitation. I thought I'd keep my hair, for one." He ran his hand through his thick, blond waves.

"I agree," I said. "The hair has to stay."

"It's my signature thing," he said. "So then, what do I imitate to capture the character?" He placed his hands on the tabletop, fingers splayed. "I will imitate how he holds his hands—loose and yet always ready to take action when the moment arrives." He raised his hands. "That's a detail that I can take on. People will recognize it without understanding where it comes from."

"That's brilliant," I said.

He sent me a crooked smile. "Thank you."

"You're welcome," I said, and saluted him with my coffee cup. "This has been a lot of fun, but I should get home. I have to be to work at five thirty a.m."

"Even with it being the off-season?" he asked.

"I have Internet sales I need to get out," I explained.

"That and my hotel manager is still on her honeymoon. The extra work of cleaning the rooms and checking people in and out of their rooms takes time."

"So you don't usually clean the bathrooms," he said with a twinkle in his eye.

"No." I felt the heat of a blush rush up my cheeks. "But it is my hotel and it's good for me to see every room at least once a week to see if it's being cleaned properly or needs any upkeep."

"Beautiful, smart, and humble," he said, and stood. "Come on, my friend. Let's give people a photo op and take you home via an open carriage."

"Oh," I said, and stood. And took his arm. "Can we not? I'm not really one for all the attention."

"Now, that is a lie," he said as we walked out. I had to remember to keep my heels out of the ground. "I understand you were part of a reality television show earlier this summer."

"I got roped into that," I said.

"And I suppose you were roped into every single investigation they have attributed to you," he said and his hand tightened on my hand for a brief second. "You are more than a simple fudge maker. I am convinced you are beautiful and brave and deserve the reputation you have received." His gaze was warm on my face and I felt the heat of a blush rise up.

"Well, if I protest to that then I sound silly, now don't I? You have me quite boxed in." I patted his arm as I clung to him, trying to keep my heels out of the grass. "Truth? I don't want to look as if I'm using your fame to further my fudge business."

"Ah, propriety is everything, then?"

I laughed at that. "If that were the case I wouldn't have given in to the desire to have dinner with you."

He nodded as he waved down a carriage. "Let's go back to your place in an open carriage. I promise not to think any worse of you."

"How can I say no to a man who provided such a lovely dinner?" I let him help me up into the carriage. Somehow in the middle of the dinner, I'd forgotten the shortness of my skirt or the low cut of my bodice. Climbing into a public open carriage brought me back to reality. I tugged hard on the skirt to keep it from exposing too much thigh.

"You look amazing," he said as he climbed in beside me. "I really appreciate you making me look good."

I smiled at him. "Is that what this is all about?"

He leaned in close. "Everyone knows you are only as good as your last photo."

"I thought that was as good as your last movie?"

"Not in this Instagram world in which we live," he said, and pulled his phone out of his pocket. "Come on, let's take a selfie." He pulled me close and snapped a quick photo. "See? You look amazing."

The photo had me looking at him with my head turned so that what people got was the side of my face and a direct shot of my cleavage. I did have to admit that I looked dazzled. Even if it all felt a bit staged.

Chapter 13

"You have to tell me everything," Jenn said as I opened the door to my apartment. I had her shoes in my hands and walked on bare feet. Mal raced to the door and jumped up, begging for me to pick her up.

"There isn't much to tell," I said, and picked up Mal. I gave her a quick pat and walked the shoes over to Jenn. "Thank you for lending me these. They certainly aren't practical for walking across lawns."

"You walked across the lawn? Where? What happened? Oh, did he have a romantic picnic planned?" Jenn took the shoes from me. I'd stopped downstairs and had wiped the dirt and grass off the heels.

"Not a picnic per se," I said. "He had a private tent put up on the lawn of the Grand Hotel."

"Nice," Jenn said, her eyes growing wide. "What did you eat? How could you eat sitting next to Dirk? Did he kiss you? Was it all terribly romantic?"

"There were fairy lights," I said, and walked to the bedroom. I put Mal down and Mella jumped up on the bed. I ran my hand along her back and over her tail, enjoying the feel of her soft fur.

"And?"

"Wine," I said, sitting down on the bed. "There was so much wine—five courses' worth."

"You must be thoroughly relaxed. Did he kiss you?" She was on the edge of the bed hugging her shoes.

"No, he didn't kiss me. It was actually a business dinner," I said, and stood pulling off the dress. I placed it in the hamper and slipped on a bathrobe.

"A business dinner in a private tent with fairy lights and five courses of wine?" Jenn looked incredulous.

"He invited the show's writer," I said, and walked into the bathroom to wash the makeup off my face and brush my hair.

"Is the writer a woman or a man?" Jenn asked with narrowed eyes. She followed me into the bathroom. Mal danced around our feet.

"What has that got to do with anything?" I asked as I scrubbed my face with a soapy washcloth.

"It could still have been considered a date if the writer is a woman," Jenn suggested.

"What?" I drew my eyebrows together. "No, no, no. It wasn't a date. I knew it wasn't going to be a date. Remember? I told you he wanted to be friends."

Jenn pouted. "Then why did I dress you? That was my best outfit, you know."

"Because Dirk said to dress sexy as people would be taking pictures," I said.

"So it was all for show?"

"All for show," I said. "The man is all about Dirk. Do you know he said his career was only as good as his latest Instagram picture?"

"Seriously?"

"I feel sorry for anyone who lives by their image," I said, and moved into the kitchen to make myself a cup of tea. "We all get older."

"Yes, well, tell that to some of those Hollywood actresses. Seriously, they never seem to age."

"It's all fake," I said, and put a kettle on. "You know what? I'd rather be real, wrinkles and all." I pulled a blue mug down from the shelf and popped a tea bag inside.

"Well, darn," Jenn said, and sat down hard on the bar stool. She put her chin in her hand. "I was hoping you would start dating Dirk."

I let out a loud laugh. "Why?"

She shrugged. "I might have thought it would be cool to tell people in Chicago that I was best friends with Dirk's girlfriend."

I patted her arm and poured the boiling water into my teacup. "Sorry to disappoint you."

She brightened. "No worries, I can still tell everyone I met Dirk and am best friends with a friend of his."

I passed her the tea mug and got a second mug down, pouring a new cup of tea for myself. "Now, that is the Jenn I know and love. Tell me, how is the fundraiser going?"

"It was a complete success," Jenn said and we walked into the living area and sat down on comfy chairs. Jenn wore yoga pants and an oversize T-shirt. "We raised over twenty-five thousand dollars."

"Wow, that's a lot of money," I said. "Tori will be so happy."

"The Butterfly House is going to expand," Jenn said. "This was such a success that they are going to consider doing it again in two years."

"Not next year?"

"They don't want to cause funding burnout."

"Makes sense," I said. I tucked my feet up under me. "So I have you all to myself for a while longer?"

"I wanted to talk to you about that," Jenn said, and blew over the top of her tea to cool it. "I'd like to stay another week. That way you are covered while Frances is gone and then I'll help cover the first week she is back in case they decide to vacation longer."

"Thank you," I said, and tilted my head. "What does Shane think?"

"He's a bit miffed right now," she said, and sipped her tea. "I'm kind of hoping an extra week or two will calm him down. He'll see that just because there is a lake between us doesn't mean we can't continue our relationship. I really think he'll like Chicago."

I shook my head. "It's harder than you think," I said. "It's part of the reason I broke up with Trent. Long distance is just no fun."

"I know," she said, her eyes welling with tears. "But I have to believe it will work. This Chicago job is a once in a lifetime deal. If I don't go and do this, I will always wonder what if."

I put down my teacup, reached over, and hugged her. "I'm sorry. I support you." I looked her in the eyes. "You know how great you are, don't you? Shane would be a fool not to know that."

She sniffed and reached over to grab a tissue. Wiping the tears from her eyes, she fumbled her teacup. "I'm going to miss you," she said. Mal put her front paws on Jenn's lap. Jenn laughed and rubbed the pup's ears. "Yes, I'm going to miss you, too."

"Mal and I want you to stay," I said. "But we also

understand why you must go. Just know that you will always be welcome here."

"I'm not going anywhere for another week," she said. "So, no more crying tonight. Tell me about the writer. Was it a gorgeous woman? A handsome man?"

"A rather slouchy, rude man who drank a lot and talked with his mouth full," I said, and picked up my teacup to sip some more. "His name is Jeffery Jenas and apparently, he has been renting a room in the Sigmunds' cottage on Mission Point since May. You have a better ear to the community. Did you know that there was a writer staying at Mrs. O'Connor's place?"

She pursed her lips and drew her eyebrows together. "I think I heard Mrs. Tunison say something about Mrs. O'Connor's boarder. I thought it was some old dude. No one ever sees him out in public."

"Apparently, he's been writing the first half season of scripts," I said. "That has to take a lot of work."

"And I imagine a lot of staring out the window," Jenn said with a smile. It was good to see her mood lighten.

"I felt bad because we hadn't met," I said. "But if you didn't know him, then I feel much better."

"What are you saying?" She played as if she was affronted.

"I'm saying you know everyone. It's what I love about you, your ability to make friends so quickly."

"Thank you," Jenn said. "Tell me about this writer. Why did Dirk bring him to dinner?"

"He wanted me to give Jeffery ideas since I've solved a few murders."

"What did this Jeffery think of this?"

"I don't think he was too impressed," I said, and

shrugged. "Jeffery seemed to think I would be good at playing chess because I've outwitted murderers."

"But you don't play chess," she pointed out.

"That's what I told him. He was surprised."

"Wait, doesn't the killer want you to play chess with him?" Jenn asked.

"Yes," I said. "Dirk put the moves the killer placed on the notes into his search engine and discovered they were moves from an old Bobby Fischer game."

"Okay, that's freaky," Jenn said. "Are you going to the senior center tomorrow to take lessons?"

"Yes," I said. "I'm joining the chess club. I'll stink at it, but it might help put me in the mind of the killer."

"Did they ever determine if the chicken was a prank or a threat?" Jenn asked.

"Rex is leaning toward prank," I said. "I've got to remember to get more outside cameras."

"You should just go with a security system," Jenn said. "That way they put up the equipment and they monitor everything. It should save you on insurance."

"Papa Liam was so against a security company. He used to say it was against everything that Mackinac Island stands for. After all people come here to experience another place and time."

"Well, that was your grandfather," Jenn said, and got up and placed her teacup in the sink. "He was not a young woman running a business by herself."

"I'll look into it," I said. "You're right. Papa isn't here anymore."

"Oh, honey, I'm sorry," Jenn said, and came over to give me a hug. "I didn't mean to dredge up your grief. I know it hasn't been six months since he died."

I hugged her back. "Sometimes it seems as if he died so long ago and yet it was only yesterday that

I was talking to him on the phone. He was telling me what a great first season we were going to have and all the things we were going to do." I sighed long and hard. "Sometimes when I sit in his chair I think of all the things that he could have helped me do this season."

"But you did a wonderful job," Jenn said. "You remodeled the McMurphy and you have increased occupancy and I happen to know that your fudge sales are up by a third over last year."

"It's been a lot of work," I said. "But I think he would be proud of what I've accomplished."

"Yes," Jenn said. "He would be very proud."

"Well, enough maudlin thoughts," I said, and rose. "I'm going to bed. I've got fudge to make in the morning and chess lessons to take."

"Good night, Allie," Jenn said.

"Good night." I picked up Mal and brought her into the bedroom with me. Mella liked to hang out in the living room. I usually cracked my bedroom door at night so she could come and go as she wished.

"Did you ever follow Bobby Fischer's career?" I asked.

Sandy sat across from me in a corner of the senior center. She was currently kicking my behind at chess. We'd played three games and she was able to beat me in less than ten moves each time. The good news is that I seemed to be getting better with each game.

"The great Mr. Fischer?" she said, and studied the board. "Certainly, everyone followed him back in the day. The man was a master."

"Do you remember the winning game against Donald Byrne?"

"October 17, 1956," she said. "Yes, I do remember now. Why?"

"I did a search of the moves that the killer placed on the notes and it goes back to that game."

"Interesting," she said. Then she moved her queen. "Checkmate."

"Darn it," I said.

"If it helps, you are getting better. You need to look at least three moves out," she said. "Try to anticipate my next move and what you will move and then my countermove."

"That's a lot of guessing," I said.

"But you know me. I've worked with you almost the entire season," she pointed out. "You should be able to predict how I think."

"I'm not sure I can predict how I think let alone anyone else."

"That's not true," she said, and reset the board. "You have figured out who killed who. You are cleverer than you realize." She opened the game by moving her knight. "Now, go."

I rested my cheek in my hand and studied the board. I realized that she had opened each game exactly the same. Instead of moving a pawn I mirrored her knight move.

She leaned in and studied the board. Then she moved a pawn two spaces. I mirrored her again. She looked up at me and then moved a second knight.

It was clear that my strategy was not going to work. I studied the board and mapped out the next three steps. I hoped to exploit her quick move. She frowned and moved her bishop. I moved again, abandoning my mirror strategy for a more aggressive approach. I took her pawn. Then I took her castle. Then I took another pawn.

She no longer watched me. Instead she watched the board. I felt the thrill of figuring out what she might do and how I would respond. I was pressing her. I got too cocky.

"Check," she said.

I studied the board. To save my king I would have to give up my queen. I made the move.

"Checkmate," she said.

"Darn," I said.

"You're getting better," she said. "You—"

"Got too confident," I said, and sat back.

"Yes," she said. "Do you want to play again?"

"No," I said with a sigh. "I have some work to do. Thank you for taking me on and teaching me."

"Of course," she said, and put the game away. "The rest of the club has gone on to lunch." I looked around to see that they were indeed serving lunch in the other side of the senior center.

"Shall we do this again next week?"

"You should play that girl whenever you have a chance," Mrs. Tunison said. "The only way to learn something right is to play the best." She squeezed Sandy's arm. "So good to see you back in the club. We've missed you."

"I thought perhaps you were glad to be rid of me," Sandy said.

"Well, it is nice to win once in a while," Mrs. Tunison said. "But you have been missed."

"I'll be back next week," Sandy said. She glanced at me. "I've got a sculpture to do."

"The fudge shop kitchen is yours," I said. "I got my Internet orders out this morning."

"You have cut back production for the shop?"

"The last of the guests from the fund-raising event check out today. We will have a near empty building the next couple of nights. I do have a guest coming in on Monday but that's it."

"It will be good for things to slow down," Sandy said. "There will be more time for you to plan for the winter and next season."

"How are the winters on the island?" I asked. "Papa Liam used to close from November through May. I was considering staying open."

"Most places close," she said. "I think the Christmas holiday is becoming popular and you may have guests until the New Year. But most people won't go through the bother of coming to Mackinac from January through April."

"Is it because of the harsh weather or the isolation?"

"Yes."

That answer took me aback. In his later years Papa Liam would winter in Florida. Maybe I needed to think about where I would go when the tourists all fled and the weather became too much to handle.

Chapter 14

"Allie! Allie McMurphy!" I turned to see a woman come out of the senior center.

"Yes?" I drew my eyebrows together.

She hurried to me. "Oh, goodness," she said, and held her chest as she tried to get her breath back. "I was afraid I would miss you."

"What can I do for you?" I asked.

"It's Mrs. O'Connor," she said, and shook my hand. "I heard you had dinner with that handsome boy, Dirk Benjamin."

"I did," I said.

"And my boarder, Jeffery," she continued as she inhaled deeply and blew it out. "Sorry, it's hard to catch my breath."

"I understand that Mr. Jenas has been renting a room from you since May," I said. "I'm surprised I hadn't heard about him or the mystery show before this week."

"Oh, it was all hush, hush," she said. "They made me sign an agreement not to say a word. It was difficult at times. Especially after I found out that Jeffery was carefully following your exploits." She paused and looked around, then leaned in to me. "For a while I thought perhaps he was stalking you. But that can't be, can it?"

"Certainly not," I said, and patted her hand reassuringly. "I've never met him before last night. I don't have any idea why he would want to stalk me."

"He's a writer," she said. "You never know what they are thinking, especially ones who write mysteries."

I smiled. "I'm sorry we haven't met before." The older woman was about five foot four and stocky. Her hair was gray and curled tight around her head. Today she wore denim dress pants and a short-sleeve button-up shirt in a cherry pattern.

"Oh, well, I've been quite busy, you know. I have been standing in as head baker at my grandson's bakery."

"His bakery? Which one?"

"There is only one good bakery on Mackinac Island," Mrs. O'Connor said, and lifted her chin in pride. "Todd's Cakery. Todd is my grandson. I taught him everything he knows."

"Is that on Market Street?" I asked.

"Yes, the very one," Mrs. O'Connor said. "Have you tried the blueberry scones? It's my award-winning recipe."

"I'll have to check them out," I said.

"You should do that."

"If you've been working in the bakery, then perhaps you've met my best friend, Jenn Christensen. She has been acting as my assistant manager and event planner this season."

"Oh, yes, the pretty one with the great head for planning. She came in several times this season picking up treats for meetings or ordering cakes and such for events."

"Has your grandson ever ordered chocolate sculptures from Sandy Everheart? She is very good at the art. I bet there are many things she could do with cake toppers."

"I'll be sure and let him know," Mrs. O'Connor said. "But you know what I really wanted to do was flag you down and ask you to get a cup of coffee sometime. I feel as if we are practically family, what with Jeffery watching your sleuthing so closely."

"I would like that," I said, and stopped as a thought occurred to me. "Did Mr. Jenas know Mr. Sharpe?"

"The dead man?" She wrung her hands. "No, I don't think so. Jeffery spends a lot of time in his room." She frowned. "Except when he's out walking."

"Walking?"

"He goes for long walks twice a day. I thought he was walking the path around the outside of the island." She frowned. "But I never really paid that close attention to where he was going. I suppose he could have been into fishing like Mr. Sharpe. Why? Is Jeffery a suspect?"

"I can't say," I said.

"What makes you ask?" She raised a gray eyebrow. "Is he a chess player?"

"You know, I don't really know. What I do know is he asked me if I was a chess player."

"Really?"

"Yes, he seemed surprised when I said no. I found that a little weird. I mean, who imagines they know someone well enough to guess what kind of board games they like to play?"

"Maybe he was thinking about all your successful sleuthing."

"Then wouldn't he have asked if I was good at the game Clue?" I shook my head. "Or maybe think I like to watch mystery shows on television. Why think I know chess?"

"Well, the man is a mystery. Why, the most I can get out of him is a hello and a good-bye with an occasional, 'Mrs. O'Connor, where do you keep the spare towels?'"

I laughed at that. "Perhaps he uses all his words when he's writing."

She laughed at that. "You are a lot of fun, Allie. I'm sorry it has taken this long to be introduced."

We turned onto Main Street just a block from the hotel. The crowds were thinner than during the season, but that didn't mean things weren't still hopping.

"Allie!" I looked up to see Trent calling my name.

"Oh, your handsome boyfriend wants you," she said, and winked at me. "I don't know how you juggle two good-looking men."

"Dirk is just a friend," I reassured her. "Please call me at the McMurphy when you want to set a time for coffee. Okay?"

"I certainly will," she said. "It was nice to meet you. Stay safe. There's a killer on the loose, you know."

"I will." I waited for Trent to get closer and watched Mrs. O'Connor hurry up the right side of the street. I assumed she was going up to Market Street to the bakery. I was pretty sure her home on Mission Point was in the other direction.

"I heard you were at the senior center," Trent said, and walked up to give me a kiss on the cheek. "I brought you flowers." He pulled his arm around from behind his back and showed me a bouquet of flowers.

"They are lovely," I said, and took them and smelled them. "I thought you were heading back to Chicago."

"I had a couple of free days so I thought we could spend some time together."

"How's Paige?" I asked. "We had coffee the other day. She told me about your father retiring."

"She's fine," he said. "The stables are keeping her busy." He flashed his gorgeous smile. I swear the man practiced in front of a mirror until he perfected the toothpaste smile.

"I'm still surprised your father put Paige in charge of the island businesses. They all seem a little rough. What with the bars, the stables, the mulch and land-scaping."

"Paige lives for the local flair," he said, and put his arm through mine as we walked back to the Mc-Murphy. "So what are you doing for dinner tonight?"

I stopped and pulled my arm out of his. "Trent, we broke up. Remember? There's a little problem of you living and working in Chicago. I told you I don't want to be second to your career."

"Oh, come on, Allie. I promised I'd see you more often. There are many people who make long distance work. You have to want to make it work."

"See, that's where I'm not so sure. I mean, what if I don't want to make it work?"

"Seriously?" He ran his hand through his hair. "How can you say that? After all we've been through."

"That's just it," I said. "We've been through a lot for only a few months. Maybe that's not such a good thing."

"Allie, love," Dirk called from the block in front of

us. He walked up and picked me up and twirled me. "You look amazing." He put me down and looked at Trent and stuck out his hand. "Hey," he said. "We met?"

"Trent Jessop," Trent said, and studied us. "We met last night."

Dirk pulled his hand back when Trent didn't take it. "Right. Dude, you were at Allie's apartment. It's okay. Allie and I are friends. Aren't we?" Dirk put his arm around me and gave it a squeeze.

"We are," I said, and turned to Trent. "Dirk is here to film the television pilot. The one that Paige won the right for filming background shots."

"Allie is helping me learn more about solving murders." He grinned. "We had a great dinner date last night." He pulled out a tabloid from his back pocket. "Got some great publicity from it." He opened the rag and there was a picture of him helping me into the open carriage. My skirt had slipped a tad too high. I was smiling from the warmth of one too many glasses of wine. The headline said, HOLLYWOOD HUNK FINDS NEW GIRL ON SMALL BACKWOODS ISLAND.

"What?" I grabbed the paper. "They make me sound like a good-time honey."

Trent pulled the paper out of my hands and scanned the photo. "Right. It doesn't look like you are just friends."

"It's Jenn's dress," I said. "I told her I shouldn't wear it."

"She looked amazing in it," Dirk said, and stuffed his hands in his pockets. "It's my fault. I told her to wear something great. They take pictures wherever I am." He glanced around and we noted that people were taking pictures of the three of us.

"I think we should go inside," I said, and put my

arms through each man's and walked them both back to the alley behind the McMurphy. We didn't say a thing until we were safely inside.

"Wow, that was crazy," Dirk said, and pulled away. "What's up, are you like Allie's boyfriend or something? If so, I'm so sorry, dude. I thought that Rex was the one."

"Rex Manning? How do you know Rex?" Trent asked, and crossed his arms over his chest.

"Dirk had been shadowing Rex to develop the police chief character in the pilot," I said.

"Yeah, he's let me watch him investigate the murder."

"Murder?"

"She found a body in the alleyway," Dirk said. "The killer seems to be leaving clues just for her."

"What? Allie? Are you okay?"

"There have been a few problems, but nothing I haven't handled," I said.

"Did you get the blood cleaned up?" Dirk asked.

"Blood?" Trent glared at me.

"Someone pranked my guests by hanging a headless chicken in their window. It was a bloody mess, but no one was hurt."

"What window? How did they get to it?"

"The police came and checked it out," I said. "I'm getting corner cameras."

"I'll have an alarm company come in tomorrow," Trent said.

"You will do no such thing." It was my turn to cross my arms over my chest. "The McMurphy is my business not yours. I will take care of it."

"I know a good business in Mackinaw City," Trent said. "I have friends in the area."

"I can use Yelp just like anyone else in the area," I said. "I don't need you to take over." I was so angry that I walked off. I swear if I stayed next to him I was going to lose my cool. How dare he think he could do better at caring for my business than me.

"Allie, stop," he said, grabbing my arm.

"No," I said. "Please just go."

"Dude, I'd back off if I was you," Dirk said.

"Yes, well, you aren't me," Trent said. "So stay out of it."

"I think you need to take your own advice," I said, and took Dirk's hand. "Come on, Dirk. Let me show you around the McMurphy." I pulled him up the stairs.

The front door to the McMurphy opened and the bells jangled.

"Hey, Trent," I heard Jenn say. "How long are you staying on the island?"

"Not for long," Trent said and he stormed out the door.

Dirk and I stopped on the landing. "Dude was upset," Dirk said. "Is he really your boyfriend?"

"He was my boyfriend," I said with a sigh. "We broke up. Well, he broke us up and then I broke us up."

"Sounds complicated."

"More than I could ever say," I said.

"Hi, Dirk," Jenn said. "What brings you to the McMurphy?"

"Dirk, this is my friend and assistant manager, Jenn. Remember?"

"Sure, how could I forget a woman as beautiful as you?" Dirk said.

Jenn blushed. "Thanks. Where are you two headed?"

"Allie was going to give me a tour of the McMurphy."

I winced. "I was angry at Trent and wanted to get away."

"I'll be happy to give you the tour," Jenn said, and hurried up the stairs to the landing. "I know Allie has some rooms to clean."

I laughed and shook my head. "Yes, I do have some rooms to clean. Do you mind, Dirk?"

"Not at all," he said, and pulled Jenn's arm through his. "Lead on, lovely lady."

"Great, how about we work our way from the top down?" Jenn said. I watched her take him up the stairs.

"No fair showing him the apartment," I said. "I haven't had time to tidy it up."

"I'll start with the office," Jenn shouted down the stairs.

"Right," I said to myself. Mella came up the stairs and wound her way around my legs. I bent and picked her up. "Well, my Mella," I said. "Are you still glad you picked the McMurphy as your forever home? Things are pretty crazy here."

I glanced over my shoulder to the front lobby. Trent may never speak to me again. I wasn't sure that was what I wanted. At this point I wasn't sure what I wanted, but I knew one thing: Dirk Benjamin was not on my boyfriend list. I thought back to the photo in the tabloid. He used me to get on the front page of the paper. I'd be mad at him if he hadn't been completely up front about it. If I was going to be mad at anyone about the picture, it would have to be myself. He'd told me what would happen. I'd gone to dinner anyway. Maybe I really did want to be noticed.

Chapter 15

The rest of Saturday passed quickly. Most of the rooms were empty. That meant that I did a deep cleaning on them, taking special note of necessary repairs. Sandy's cousin came in and did his magic to the stains in room 216. I don't know when Dirk left, but I figured Jenn took good care of him. She seemed taken by his movie star good looks.

I called a security company. The service would be pricey, but necessary. I talked to them about installing electronic door keys. The total dug into the money I had set aside for my roof improvements. But I wouldn't have any roof parties if I didn't have any guests. Right now, ensuring my guests were safe was number one on my list.

Mal got up from her cuddle bed in the office and jumped up on my lap. It was a sure sign she needed a good walk. I shut down my computer and went downstairs. She ran ahead of me and did circles on the landing. "You are so impatient. Let me get down the stairs." I hit the lobby and noted that it was empty. Jenn must have gone off to spend time with Shane. I grabbed my phone and texted that I was going to walk Mal. With a killer on the loose, I needed to ensure that someone knew where I was at all times. I grabbed my jacket, slipped on my shoes, and headed to the door. Just inside the back door was a set of hooks where I kept one of Mal's halters and leashes. There was a duplicate halter and leash upstairs in the apartment for late night walks.

I helped Mal step into her halter, grabbed a poo bag, and stepped out into the back alley. Mal ran across to her favorite patch of grass. I stared up into the dark night sky. It was cloudless and the stars twinkled. I had been right to be angry with Trent for thinking he could solve all my problems. But perhaps I hadn't handled it as well as I should have.

Truth be told I wasn't sure yet what I was doing. If I took him back, I would spend my life playing second fiddle to his work. Mal finished and I decided to take a walk down by the marina. It was one of my favorite walks with Mal. Especially when the island was quiet and the breeze blew softly off the straits.

We walked down to the end of the alley. I frowned. It had been a couple of days since I had seen Mr. Beecher. Usually I saw him at least once a day cutting through the alley on his walk. I certainly hoped he was okay. I turned to Main Street and waved at Mary Emry, who was cashiering at Doud's Market. Then Mal and I turned toward the fort. The lawn was filled with fireflies. The glowing bugs added a twinkly dimension to the expanse of grass. A horse and carriage passed us on the road. There was a group of four people inside, laughing and sharing a glass of wine. Mal tugged me across the street to the marina. She had a fascination with the water ever since we found the dead girl there. I think she liked to see what new things washed up against the docks.

There were a few boats. Mostly fishermen or people who summered on their yachts and were not ready to move south for the winter. A group of men sat around a small fire in a fire pit laughing. Children raced through the cool damp grass of late evening.

I pulled my jacket up around my chin as the breeze turned brisk. "Come on, Mal," I said. "Let's head home. It's been a long day."

She barked and tugged on her leash toward the pier. I laughed. "All right, one sniff, then we have to go home."

She dragged me a few yards from the group of men and sat down on the water's edge, barking.

"What is it?" I asked. Mal rarely barked. When she did there was usually a problem. I had gotten to where I was afraid to look. I peered over the edge and saw a dead duck floating on the water. I was at once sorry for the animal and glad it wasn't another person. "It's just a duck," I said. "I'm sorry but we can't take care of it. I'll call animal control when we get back to the hotel." I turned and came face to chest with Jeffery. "Oh!"

"Hey, watch what you are doing," he said, and put his hands on my forearms to steady me. "You'll end up in the drink."

"You startled me," I said with a hand to my heart. Mal jumped up on him as if to say hello.

"Hello, doggy," Jeffery said, and patted Mal's head.

"I didn't hear you walk up," I said with a frown. "What brings you out tonight? Isn't Mrs. O'Connor's place kind of far from here?"

"Not that far," he said with a quick frown and a

shake of his head. "I like to go out walking in the evenings. It clears my head and helps me work on the plotlines."

"I see," I said, and pulled Mal away from him.

"What brings you to the docks?"

"Mal likes the walk," I said with a slight shrug. "The weather is nice."

He shoved his hands into the pockets of his coat. "Getting cold, if you ask me," he said.

"How long are you going to be on the island?" I asked. "You've been here since May, right? Are you staying through the winter?"

"Don't know," he said with a frown. "Probably not. I've got to see how many changes they make to the script on the pilot." He narrowed his eyes at me. "Did Dirk say when they would start shooting?"

"I think he said Monday? But don't quote me on that," I said. "I thought you would know."

"Hmm." He shrugged into his coat. "I'm pretty sure the crew shows up tomorrow."

"How long does it usually take to film a pilot?"

"A couple of days," he said. "They get as many outdoor shots as possible. Then go back to LA to shoot in the studio."

"That's what I thought," I said. Mal barked and yanked her leash out of my hand. "Mal!" I shouted, and ran after her. She rushed toward the coffee shop. "Mal!" I grabbed at the leash she dragged. The second grab and I got it. Mal stopped short and sat. "What are you doing?" I asked her. She looked at me and then looked at the coffee shop. Someone sat against the building. The person was shadowed. "Hello?" I asked. "Are you okay?"

The person didn't move. I grabbed my cell phone

and hit the flashlight app on it. Light shown from my cell phone. I could see what appeared to be an old man. He wore dress slacks and a shirt with a vest. A fedora covered his face. My heart rate picked up.

"Mr. Beecher?" I asked, and stepped closer. "Is that you?" I knelt, swallowing hard, and touched the man's hand. It was frightfully cold. "Are you okay?" I shook his shoulder. He slumped down to the side-walk. Frightened, I stood and called 9-1-1.

"9-1-1, this is Charlene, what is your emergency?"

"Charlene—"

"Allie McMurphy," she cut me off. "Where are you?"

"I'm by the marina. The coffee shop, to be exact."

"I'm dispatching the police now."

I waited for her to make the call.

"What did you find?" she asked.

"There's a man here and he is cold to the touch. It's dark but he sort of looks like Mr. Beecher."

"Oh no," Charlene said. "I'll send the EMTs as well. I hope he didn't have a heart attack or anything. He's such a nice man."

"Yes," I said.

"You said you think it is him. Can't you tell for sure?"

"His face is covered by a hat," I said. "But he's wearing dress slacks and a vest."

"I don't know too many men who wear vests these days."

"I agree," I said, and glanced around. I didn't see Jeffery anywhere. "That's strange."

"What?"

"Jeffery Jenas was with me, but now he's gone."

"Who is Jeffery Jenas?"

"The writer from the television pilot."

"Oh," she said. "Yes, I heard a writer has been staying with Mrs. O'Connor this summer. Did you talk to him?"

"I did," I said, "but then Mal got away from me. She ran to the body and now Jeffery is gone."

"Sounds suspicious," Charlene said. "I'll let the crew on shift know to keep an eye out for him." She paused and I heard sirens in the distance.

"The ambulance is on its way," I said. In front of the ambulance were two police officers on bicycles. They pulled up and got off their bikes. I held Mal as they neared. "Rex and Officer Pulaski are here."

"Sounds like it's safe enough for you to hang up. Take care, honey," Charlene said, and the phone went dead.

"Are you all right?" Rex asked me as he approached.

"I'm fine," I said, and noticed that Dirk had appeared shortly behind the ambulance.

"What's going on?" Dirk asked in his perfect Rex imitation.

Rex shot him an angry glare over his shoulder. "We got a call about a dead body. Possibly Mr. Beecher?"

I swallowed hard. "He seems to be dressed like Mr. Beecher," I said, and pointed to where the body lay slumped on its side. "I didn't take off the hat to check. I didn't want to contaminate the crime scene."

"Smart girl," Dirk said as all three men headed toward the body.

"How did you know he was dead and not just sleeping?" Brent Pulaski asked.

"I touched his wrist. It was cold. I went to shake him when he tipped over and so I called Charlene."

Two EMTs came up with a stretcher and medical kits. One was George Marron, who had been the lead

EMT the first time I'd found a body on the island and was now a friend. Beside him was a young woman I'd never met. Her name tag said EMMERSON.

"The man's dead," Rex said. He had hunkered down and removed the hat. There was a bullet hole in the middle of the man's forehead. Thankfully, it wasn't Mr. Beecher.

"That's not Beecher," Brent said. He turned to me. "What made you think it was?"

"The clothes," I said. "He has on corduroy pants and a shirt and a vest. That along with the fedora is what Mr. Beecher wears every day."

"Beecher always wears a coat," Rex corrected me.

"That's true," I said. "I haven't seen him today and that's unusual. Do you know who the victim is?"

"He isn't familiar," Rex said. He glanced up at George. "Do you recognize him?"

"No," the EMT replied. He hunkered down and took the body's vitals. "He's definitely dead. Rigor is starting to set in."

"Did you see anyone near the body?" Rex asked as he stood.

"No," I said. "I was out walking Mal when we ran into Jeffery Jenas."

"Who?"

"The writer for the television show. He's staying with Mrs. O'Connor at the Sigmunds' cottage on Mission Point. I was standing near the marina when he came up behind me. Scared the devil out of me."

"Did he tell you what he was doing out here?" Rex asked, and made a note in his notepad.

"He said he was out for his nightly walk," I said. "You should talk to him. He might have seen something. The thing is I don't know whether he was coming from Mission Point or going back to Mission Point. But he was definitely in the area."

"I'll go talk to the men at the marina," Brent said.

I looked over to see that the men from the fire pit had all stood up and watched the action of the ambulance from a distance.

"They were all sitting there when I walked by."

"What brings you down this way?" Dirk asked, still channeling Rex.

Rex frowned at him. "Stop it, that's annoying."

"Just perfecting my part," he said with a shrug.

I looked at Rex. "Is there a note on the body?"

His eyes narrowed. "You think this is the same killer?"

"I did find a body near the water once," I said.

"I know," he said.

"There's a note in the vest pocket," George said. He pulled it out. George had on blue gloves so he could handle evidence. He held it out.

"I need gloves," Rex said. "Can you open it?"

The female EMT handed Rex a pair of gloves while George stood and shined a flashlight on the note. He looked from the note to me. "It's addressed to you."

I hugged Mal tight. "What does it say?"

"Knc3, bg7."

"More of the chess game," I said with a sigh. "I don't know chess."

"I thought you went to the senior center to practice with the chess club," Dirk said.

"I did," I said. "But a few random games does not a chess pro make."

"This guy has you really confused, doesn't he?" Dirk said.

"Does it say anything else?" I asked.

"Time is running out," George read.

I ran my hand through my hair. "What does that mean?"

"It sounds like a threat," Rex said. "He might be escalating things."

"That would not be good," I said.

"Are you going to try to figure him out?" Dirk asked.

"She needs to stay out of this and stay safe," Rex said as he bagged the letter.

"But this killer seems to think she should be able to figure out who he is," Dirk said. "Like one of those mystery shows. It might be someone she is close to. There has to be other clues."

"It's rare there are clues," Rex said. "This isn't a nice tidy thirty-minute television show. These are real human beings with blood and guts and gore."

"Clearly, it's someone who has followed all your cases," Dirk said.

"But why would anyone assume I know anything about chess?"

George stood. "There's not much we can do except store the body to go to the morgue in St. Ignace. Do you want to have Shane come out and document everything?"

"Yes," Rex said with a slight frown.

"I think Shane is on the island," I said. "Jenn wasn't at the McMurphy. I assumed she went to dinner with Shane. I can text her for you."

"I'll have dispatch call him," Rex said.

I pulled out my phone and texted Jenn. She

confirmed she was with Shane and they would be here as soon as they could. I glanced at the body. The man had a full head of black hair, but his mouth hung open and he had a couple of missing teeth. I frowned. "There's not a lot of blood."

"That's a good observation," George said. "There isn't any brain matter either."

"He was shot somewhere else and dumped here." Rex hunkered back down to study the body. "He has something on his fingertips."

"Is it a clue?" Dirk asked.

"Perhaps," Rex said. "We'll have to wait for lab results."

"You will get them tomorrow, right?" Dirk asked.

Rex made a dismissive noise. "Only in Hollywood. Our state-run lab is overworked and underappreciated. We'll be lucky to know next week. Definitely the end of the month."

"That's crazy, dude," Dirk said, falling back to his California accent.

My phone lit up with a text. "Shane's on his way."

"We'll stay until they release the body," George said to the female tech.

"Yes, sir," she answered, and stepped away from the body.

"Is this your first dead body?" I asked. I held out my right hand while I held Mal with my left. "Allie McMurphy."

"Joy Emmerson," she said, and shook my hand.

"I haven't seen you before."

"I usually work in Mackinaw City. I'm here to help out during vacations."

"Well, welcome to Mackinac Island." Mal reached out to kiss her cheek.

Joy laughed and rubbed my pup's ears. "It is definitely different here." She leaned toward me. "Is that really Dirk Benjamin?"

"It is," I said with a nod.

"He's even handsomer in person."

"Shush," I said. "Don't let him hear. It will go to his head."

Lavender Chocolate Fudge

2 ½ cups dark chocolate chips
1 (14 oz.) container sweetened condensed milk
2 tablespoons unsalted butter
2 teaspoons culinary lavender (divided)

In a double boiler, gently melt the chocolate chips and mix in the sweetened condensed milk until well combined. Remove from heat. Stir in butter and 1 teaspoon of lavender.

Butter and line an 8x8-inch pan. Pour chocolate in prepared pan. Top with 1 teaspoon lavender. Chill until firm. Store in a covered container. Enjoy!

Chapter 16

."What's going on?" Shane asked as he arrived on the scene.

"Allie, are you okay?" Jenn came straight to where I stood holding Mal.

"Yes, I'm fine. This gentleman, unfortunately, is not." I pointed toward the dead man. Shane borrowed gloves from the EMTs and hunkered down to study the man.

"Is that a gunshot wound?" Jenn's eyes were wide and round.

"Yes," I said, and turned my back on the poor man. "I was afraid it was Mr. Beecher."

"Why?"

"He was wearing clothes similar to Mr. Beecher's. I couldn't see his face. It was hidden by his hat."

Jenn put her arm around my shoulder and squeezed. "How terrible for you. I know how much you like Mr. Beecher." She patted me. "Do they know who he is?"

"Not yet," I said. "I hope he doesn't have family somewhere."

A crowd started to gather as the flashing lights of

the ambulance drew their attention. We turned to see Shane start his crime scene evidence collection.

"This could take a while," Office Pulaski said as he joined us on the outside of the crowd.

"Did anyone see anything?" I asked.

"The men near the bonfire say they saw you and Mal walk by. They said you were talking to a guy and then you ran off. The next thing they know the sirens were headed this way."

"Mal dragged me off," I said. "Did they see where Jeffery Jenas went?"

"Who?" Brent asked.

"Jeffery Jenas, the writer you were telling me about?" Jenn asked.

"Yes," I said. "He surprised me near the water. But after Mal found the body he was gone."

"Sounds suspicious," Jenn mused.

"I agree," I said.

"We'll send someone out to Mrs. O'Connor's to question him," Brent said. "I'll go talk to Rex."

"Do you want me to take Mal back to the Mc-Murphy?" Jenn asked.

"Would you?" I said, and passed the dog to her. "Please check on the guests. I would hate for something else to happen tonight."

"I'll see that everything is locked down. Did you have a chance to look into a security company?"

"It's going to cost me the roof budget," I said. "But we have to do it."

"Well, darn," Jenn said. "I was thinking up some great events for next season on your roof."

"Does that mean you plan to come back next summer?"

"Of course," Jenn said.

"Yay!" I hugged Jenn. "I feel so much better. We make a great team. Don't you think?"

"We do," she said. "Besides, I have a good beginning to my event planning business. I wouldn't want to abandon that."

"It's great to have some good news on such a horrid day."

"Allie." I looked over Jenn's shoulder to see Trent walking up. "What's going on?"

"She found another body," Jenn said. "Can you take care of my friend? I'm going back to the McMurphy to hold down the fort."

"Yes," Trent said. "I wanted to talk to you anyway, Allie."

"Dude," Dirk said as he walked up to us. I wanted desperately to tell Dirk to go away. I really did need to talk to Trent without any distractions. "Are you bothering Allie?"

"I asked him to stay," I said. "It's okay. Why don't you go see what Rex is doing?"

"Oh, man, he's just asking the same questions over and over. Dude's like a robot with that stuff."

"Is he getting any answers that are interesting?" Trent asked.

Dirk shrugged. "No clues to the killer anyway."

"I told you it doesn't work like on television," I said. "Murder is messy. Just like relationships." I eyed Trent. He wore a dress shirt with the cuffs rolled up on his forearms and dress slacks. The man looked like a walking cologne commercial.

"If you'll excuse us, I want to talk with Allie," Trent said, and put his hand on the small of my back to guide me a few feet away from Dirk. "Are you serious about that guy?"

"Dirk? No, I told you, we're friends. He's only interested in how I can make his series better and advance his career."

Trent seemed to relax. "Good, for a while there I'd thought you'd lost your mind."

"Because I might be into a handsome famous man who likes me for me?" I sent him a side-eye look.

Trent crossed his arms over his chest. "Because he's going back to Hollywood in a few weeks. I happen to know that you aren't dating guys who don't live on the island year-round."

I raised my chin. "Are we going to go over that old fight again?"

"No," he said with a shake of his head. "No, I can accept what you want and respect it. What would you say if I told you that I got my father to switch my duties and Paige's."

"You will be in charge of the island businesses?"

"I could be," he said. "But I don't want to make a pitch and upset my family if you aren't interested in seeing me anymore."

I put my hands up. "I don't want to be responsible for your decisions. That is not the point. If you switch with Paige, you need to do it because you love Mackinac Island and want to be here year-round." I swallowed. "I'm serious. If you do this you have to do it for you, not me. Rex can tell you what it's like to lose a spouse because island living isn't in their blood."

"I'm not one of Rex's wives."

"No," I said. "You aren't. But wait, isn't Paige happy with living on the island? The last time I saw her she was excited about her new assignment. That reminds me, I promised to meet with her regularly to mentor her on navigating the island."

Trent looked confused. "How can you help Paige? We grew up here."

I let that sink in for a moment. Counted to ten. "I summered here almost every year in elementary and junior high school. I'm not exactly a fudgie. That said, I did have a successful season. Paige wanted to have lunch and talk over any pointers."

He ran his right hand through his hair. "I'm making a hash out of this."

I crossed my arms. "Yes, you are."

"Look, I just wanted you to promise me that you won't make any decisions about dating until I talk to my father."

"Decisions?"

"You know what I mean."

"Do I?"

"Start dating Rex. I saw you kiss him at the reception."

And there it was. "That's why the sudden push to see me? I mean, the last month you've been pretty absent. Then you kissed Tori."

"Did you kiss Rex to get back at me for Tori?"

"No," I said. "I kissed Rex because you and I broke up and I felt like kissing Rex."

"Why? The man has failed at two marriages and who knows how many other relationships?"

"I don't have to explain myself to you, Trent."

"Right," he said. "Look. All I ask is that you give me a week or two before you move on. I want to show you that I can change. I will change."

"Only if you want to change," I said. "I don't want

to change you. You know that, right? I simply want what you aren't right now."

"But I can be," he said, and ran the back of his hand along my cheek. "Please, give me more time and in the meantime stay safe. I hate the idea of another killer messing with you. Did you get a security company?"

"I have one scheduled," I said. "Does Paige have security at her businesses? Because I know a guy."

Trent studied me for a long, silent moment. "I want to grab you and kiss you and keep you safe."

I blew out a shaky breath. "This island nearly killed my father. He couldn't breathe. When we moved to Detroit he blossomed. I don't want to see you in that situation. I know how much you love Chicago." I held up my hand in a stop motion. "I know I lived in Chicago, but it wasn't my love. My love and my dream is the McMurphy. I want to raise my children here. Can you see raising your children here?"

"I see my children attending the best private school in Chicago. I know that you would want the best for your children. Until you have them you won't know what you want for your children. What if you have a son or daughter who takes after your father? Would you restrict them to island living if they hate it?"

"Okay, this is ridiculous. We're debating where we would send our children and we aren't even dating anymore."

"I want to kiss you," he said with a grin.

"Allie," Rex called from near the body.

I turned toward Rex.

"I need you here a moment."

"I have to go," I said.

"I was very serious about everything I said. Allie," Trent said. "I'll be on Mackinac for the week."

"Tell Paige I'm free for lunch tomorrow if she wants to get together."

"I will."

I hurried to Rex. "What can I do for you?"

"Are you okay?" he asked. His gaze went from me to Trent and back to my face.

"I'm fine. Did Brent get ahold of Jeffery Jenas?"

"He took a statement," Rex said. "Jenas claims he was heading home from a walk around the island when he ran into you. That time line would exclude him from having anything to do with the body."

"I heard you say it was a body dump," I said. "Any idea where the poor man was killed?"

"No definite clues," Shane said as he came up. "I've got all the evidence I could collect at the scene. There isn't much. The body was moved. It's sitting on concrete. Not a lot of evidence. I've got George and Joy bagging up the body now. I'll take it back to St. Ignace with me. I can do more evidence-gathering right before the ME does the autopsy. We'll get back to you with anything significant."

"There was something on the man's fingertips," I remembered. "Any idea what it was?"

"Not sure," he said. "It was blue. Could be ink or paint. It's hard to tell. I've bagged his hands. We'll know more once I finish my exam in the lab."

"Okay," I said.

"This is the third note with your name on it," Shane said, and took off his glasses, wiping them with the bottom of his shirt. "I think you need to be vigilant. This killer wants to mess with your mind."

"Are you sure you don't recognize the handwriting?" Rex asked.

"No," I said. "I'm no expert but it sort of looks like a man's writing."

"I agree," Rex said. "The first sample was printed. So there's not much we can learn from it. The next one was carved. That's closer to handwriting. I'll send a copy of this note and a photo of the carving to a handwriting expert. Maybe we can figure out what the odds are that they all belong to the same person. The last thing I need is a copycat murderer."

Brent dispersed the crowd as George and Joy placed the body in the ambulance and drove off.

"Dude, I'm off to my room at the Grand," Dirk said, and clasped Rex on the back. "The production crew will be here first thing in the morning. They are doing setup for the first day of shooting." He looked at me. "I can walk you home."

"I'll see she gets back," Rex said dismissively.

"Dude," he said, and raised both hands in surrender. "Offering as a friend."

"Thanks, Dirk," I said. "I need to talk to Rex."

"Cool." He stuffed his hands in his back pockets and walked off. The darkness of the evening enveloped us. Stars twinkled in the cool air. I hugged myself.

"I saw you talking to Trent," Rex said as he wrote notes in his notepad. He glanced at me. "Are you okay?"

"I'm fine," I said. "It's an old argument."

"Still broken up?"

"Being single might be best," I said, and shrugged. "This killer seems to be messing with me."

"Any idea of who it might be?"

"No clue," I said. "The seniors don't seem to be in the know, either." I shrugged. "It could be anyone—anyone who has been here since May. They seem to be re-creating all the crime scenes."

"I noticed," he said. "Come on, let's get you home. You're shivering."

I noticed he was right. Shivers had begun to run down my spine and rattle my jaw. He put his hand on my back and guided me up to Main Street from the marina area. "I don't know either of the victims," I said. "I was so scared it was Mr. Beecher."

"I've sent an officer over to Beecher's house to check on him."

"Thank you," I said.

"How are you getting along with Dirk?" he asked in a soft, fierce tone.

I blew out a long breath. "He wants insights into solving cases. I think he imagines he could be an amateur sleuth. This television series was his idea. I think he may be footing some of the production costs."

"Ever since *CSI* started on television everyone thinks they are crime solvers," he grumbled.

"No, I think it goes back to *Perry Mason*, or maybe even further back. Grammy Alice used to love *Perry Mason*."

"You want to know how I got into law enforcement?" he asked.

"Sure," I said.

"I was a *Law & Order* fan," he said. "It seemed so cool."

I sent him a side eye. "Wow, I would have figured you for a *Friends* fan."

"Are you kidding me?" He looked affronted.

I laughed hard. "Yes, I'm kidding you. Although I

did wonder if you were going to say *CSI*. They made all the sleuthing look so cool and fast with their music montages and lab equipment right in the police headquarters."

"That was a real fantasy," he said with a smile. "You are right. I am still a fan."

"You watch it on cable?"

"I don't get cable in my cabin," he said. "I stream whatever I want when I get the chance. I rarely have time for TV."

"Me too," I said with a sigh. "Especially with Frances out. I've been working my job and hers and a bit of Mr. Devaney's as well."

"You should have hired a temp to cover for her," he said.

"Are you going to tell me how to run my business, too?"

He winced. "Jessop trying to tell you how to run things?"

"He seems to think he knows better," I said, and felt the back of my jaw clench. I worked to relax it as we passed Doud's. "I happen to be doing pretty well without anyone's help."

"You have been doing amazing," Rex said. "You should know that. Even with all the problems you've been having this season with the crimes."

"Thank you," I said, and stopped by the front door of the McMurphy.

"Listen, Allie," he said, pushing his hat up to expose more of his handsome face. "I want to cook dinner for you. You might like it. I have been told I make a heck of a steak salad."

"Do you want to talk about the case?" I asked, and drew my eyebrows together.

"Not particularly," he said. He studied me. "I want to have a relaxing evening talking to a beautiful woman over a glass of wine and my world-famous steak salad."

"Oh, it's world-famous now, is it?" I raised my right eyebrow.

His grin widened. "Yes."

"Then perhaps I need to try it."

"Great," he said. "How's Tuesday?"

"Tuesday works for me," she said.

"How about eight p.m.? I'll text you my address."

"I'd like that," I said.

"Good night, Allie," he said, and kissed my cheek. "I'll watch that you get inside safe. Lock the door behind you."

"Right," I said. I could still feel the heat and tingle of his kiss on my cheek. I went inside. The bells rang out as I entered and closed and locked the doors behind me. Rex tugged on the brim of his police cap and walked off into the darkness. My heart was racing and I felt warm and giddy with the hope of a new relationship. I turned off the lights as I walked toward the stairs, leaving only the night-lights. What would happen when I went to his cabin on Tuesday? I went up to my apartment knowing I couldn't wait to find out.

Chapter 17

The next morning, I finished the fudge and went upstairs to change out of my candymaking clothes. I couldn't clean rooms dressed in the same clothes I cooked fudge in. I headed down to the lobby wearing jeans and a white polo.

I stopped on the landing. There was a woman sitting in Frances's chair at the reception desk. "Can I help you?" I asked as I bounded down the stairs.

"No, thanks, I'm working," she said. She was an older woman with black hair pulled back in a braid. Her wide face had high cheekbones and coppery skin. Her black eyes seemed uninterested in me.

"Working?"

"Yes," she said. "My cousin Sandy said you needed a temporary reservation manager," she said. "It's clear you do."

"I see. Sandy Everheart?"

"Yes."

"Huh, and your name is?"

"Sharon Everheart," she said, and went back to reading her magazine.

"Right, is Sandy in yet?"

"She's setting a sculpture up at the yacht club. She'll be back in a half an hour. Oh, and you had a visit by a Jeffery Jenas."

"Sharon," I said, waiting for her to look up.

"Yeah?"

"What am I paying you?"

"Going rate," she said. "I already checked out the Goers in room 201."

That gave me pause. "How?"

"I've used the software before," she said. "I've substituted for Frances."

"Oh," I said. "Thanks."

"The room is ready to be cleaned," she said, and turned the page on her magazine. "You have two new guests coming in today."

"Right." I turned on my heel and went upstairs, pausing at the landing. "Could you tell Sandy I want to talk with her when she gets back?"

"Okay."

I watched Sharon for a moment, then went upstairs to clean the room. I pulled my phone out and texted Jenn. What is on your schedule today?

I've got a meeting with a young couple who are planning a wedding in May, Jenn texted back. Why?

Did you know that Sandy's cousin Sharon is working the reception desk?

Oh, yes, she texted back. I forgot to let you know. Sandy has seen how busy you are and suggested Sharon. So I hired her.

How are we paying her?

I used funds in petty cash. You have quite a bit left over.

Thanks.

I stopped short in the hallway. Room 201's door was open and Mella came strolling out. "Well, there you are," I said to the cat, and leaned down to stroke her back. "Find anything interesting in there?" I went over and opened the door wide. Why did the Goers leave the door open?

The interior of the room looked used but nothing scary. I stuck my nose in the bathroom. It was empty. There were towels on the floor. I shrugged and went to the utility closet for cleaning supplies. I turned on the light and was startled by something hanging from the ceiling. I might have said something profane. My heart rate was through the roof and I put my hand on my chest. I pulled out my phone and started taking pictures. Someone had been in my utility closet.

On closer inspection, it was a giant stuffed bear swinging from a noose. The noose was tied onto a hook where I hung mops. The bear was hung by the neck. It looked like it was bleeding. I stepped in for a closer look. A sniff test suggested ketchup. Frowning, I dialed Rex's number.

"Manning," he said.

"Hi, Rex," I said as I studied the bear's button eyes. "Do you have a minute to come over?"

"What's up?"

I texted him a picture. "I sent you a picture of what I found in my second-floor utility closet."

He muttered something dark. I could hear the scraping of his chair as he jumped up. "Are you alone?"

"Yes," I said. "No one else is inside here. Although I may have guests still on this floor."

"Don't touch anything."

"Okay."

"Are you inside the closet?"

"Yes." It was a large walk-in closet with shelves. It

held everything you needed for housekeeping in a hotel.

"Go out in the hall," he ordered. "Shut the door."

"Right." I did what he said. There were six rooms on the second floor and the utility closet was in the middle of the floor. There were two rooms filled with current guests. The other four were empty. Mella stalked over and rubbed against my legs. I reached down and picked her up to get a cuddle.

"Are you still on the phone?" he asked.

"Yes," I said. "I'm in the hall outside the closet. Mella is keeping me company."

"I'm nearly to the McMurphy," he said.

"You know, I don't think there was a note or anything," I said, frowning. "Do you think this is the killer? Or is this whoever pranked my guests before?"

"It could be either," he said. "I don't like that they are now inside the McMurphy."

"Me neither," I said with a sigh. "I may need to close this floor altogether."

"Are you working with a security company?"

"I can't lock people out of the McMurphy," I said in a low tone in case my guests were in their rooms. "It's a hotel, for goodness' sake."

"Is there anyone who might want you to close down?" he asked.

"No," I said, disturbed by the thought. "Do you think that's what this is about? Closing the McMurphy?"

"I'm not sure," he said. "If they really wanted to hurt you they would have done this during the season. Maybe they're simply trying to scare you off."

"Well, I'm not scared," I said stubbornly.

"I'm here," he said, and hung up.

I texted Jenn. **Are you out of your meeting?**

Be back at the McMurphy in fifteen, she texted.

Come to the second floor, I texted. We have another prank.

Oh, man, she texted back with an emoji of a scared face.

I heard Rex come up the stairs. "Allie?"

"Here," I said, and put Mella down.

"This has a familiar ring to it," he said.

"Yes, this is where we started, isn't it?" I said.

"I don't like it," he said. "Did you touch the doorknob?"

"Yes," I said. "I opened the door and then hit the light switch. That's all I touched. I was going in to get cleaning supplies to work on room 201. The couple who stayed there checked out and left the door open." I wrapped my hands around my waist as he opened the door and stepped inside.

"Is that odd?"

"What?"

"Leaving the room door open? Aren't they weighted to close on their own?"

"No, they aren't weighted," I said. "Usually people close them when they leave. It's sort of a habit. But when I came up to the second floor I caught Mella slipping out of the room. The door was open so I went in, but there wasn't anything out of the ordinary. I came over here to get the stuff to start cleaning the room. I have two guests coming in today."

"You may want to put them on the third floor," he said. "Do you have the rooms?"

"Yes," I said. "I can empty the floor if you think that's necessary."

He studied the hanging bear. "This is odd."

"Yes, it is," I said.

"Did you see anyone bring the bear into the Mc-Murphy? It's big enough to be noticed."

"I didn't," I said. "I'll ask Jenn and Sharon if they saw anything."

He glanced at me. "When did you hire Sharon Everheart?"

"I didn't, Sandy and Jenn did," I said. "It's fine. I can use the help and I understand she has covered for Frances before."

"Hmm," he said, and turned back to the bear. "I'll get Shane in here to dust for prints." He studied the red goo on the bear's neck. "Is that ketchup?"

"I thought maybe," I said. "But I didn't want to taste it."

"No, don't do that. You don't know what might be in it." He looked at the back of the bear. "No message?"

"It's weird, right? I mean, even the chicken came with the note on my door."

"When was the last time you were in your apartment?"

"I put Mal in there when I went and changed from my fudge making clothes to my housekeeper clothes."

"You put Mal in there?"

"Yes, she sleeps on the couch. It keeps her out of the way while I clean. If Frances was here, Mal would be allowed out. But when it's just me, I'd rather she was safe in the apartment."

"Why don't you go up and check your space," he suggested. "I'm going to call in some help. Don't forget to check your apartment door for any messages."

"Why would they put it outside my door if they were inside? It doesn't make sense."

"And hanging a bear in a utility closet makes sense?" he asked.

"I get your drift," I said.

"Hey, what's up, boss?" Shane asked.

"That was fast," I said as he walked to the closet. "You must have been on Mackinac?"

Jenn rounded the top of the stairs behind him. She looked flushed and her eyes sparkled. "What's going on?"

"That is a good question," I said with a teasing tone.

She straightened the silky blue top she wore. "I meant here. Why call Shane?"

"Come see for yourself," I said, and waved toward the closet.

"Oh boy, that's sick," Jenn said. "Was there a note?"

"I haven't found one. I'm on my way upstairs to check the apartment."

"I'll come with you," Jenn said, and put her arm through mine as we left the men in the hall.

"Why didn't you tell me you hired Sharon Everheart?" I asked. "It was weird to come downstairs to find her at Frances's station."

"I'm sorry," Jenn said as we climbed the stairs. "I meant to tell you but then you came home late last night and were making fudge when I left this morning."

"What else have you done without telling me?" I asked. I know I sounded a bit petulant but the McMurphy was my business. Jenn hadn't made any decisions without me before.

"Nothing," Jenn said. "I'm sorry if I overstepped. I was telling Sandy how busy you have been and she told me that your Papa Liam had used Sharon as temporary help in the past. I thought it would ease some of your burden."

"The thought is appreciated, but please don't hire anyone else without talking to me first. Okay?"

"Sure," she said. "No problem. I'm leaving soon anyway."

"Rex seems to think we should move all the guests to the third floor."

"Why?"

"Because this is the second prank on the second floor. He's worried about their safety."

"That makes sense," she said. "We have enough rooms free to do that."

I sighed as we approached the apartment. "I'll do it. I'll tell them that we are going to start renovations on the second floor and the third will be quieter."

"Good idea," Jenn said as I unlocked my apartment door. There wasn't any sign of a note on the front of my front door. "Where's Mal?"

"What?" I searched the apartment living area. "I left her in the apartment. Mal? Come here."

The apartment was silent.

"Oh no," Jenn said, and raced to the back bedrooms. "Mal?"

"Here, Marshmallow," I called. No answer.

"She's not here," Jenn said with panic in her voice.

The back door that led to the alley was locked. "It's locked," I said. "Both doors were locked. There isn't any way for her to get out."

"Mal? Here, girl," I called, and checked the living room and under the couch. "She's not here. I swear I brought her up when I changed my clothes."

"Did someone take her?"

"How? The room was locked."

"Maybe she squeezed out when I left and I missed it," I said. "She can be sneaky like that."

"True," Jenn said, but her expression told me that I was reaching. We both went out into the hall. "Mal!"

"Here, Mal, come on, girl. I have a cookie," I said as we checked the office, but the door was closed and I opened the room to find it empty and silent. By this time Jenn had run down to the second floor to ask the guys if they had seen my pup. I felt my stomach twist as I checked the third floor. Mal usually followed me or Jenn or Frances around all day. Once she met the guests at the front desk, she usually kept her distance, preferring to be with one of us. "Mal?" I called down the empty third-floor hallway. "Here, Mal."

A woman from 310 opened her door and stuck her head out into the hall. "Is everything all right?"

"Have you seen Mal?" I asked. "I thought she was in my apartment but I can't seem to find her.

"The little white dog?"

"Yes," I said.

"I'm sorry," the woman said. "I haven't seen her since I checked in. But then again, I haven't really been out. I'm a writer on deadline. I'm only here to get my work done."

"You're a writer?"

"Yes," she said.

"You wouldn't happen to be writing for the television show that is shooting this week, wouldn't you?"

"Oh no, I'm not a screenwriter. I write romances. Is there a television show filming on Mackinac?"

"Yes," I said. "It's a mystery series."

"Fun," she said. "Listen, I need a break. Can I help you find your dog?"

"Would you?" I asked. "Her name is Marshmallow, Mal for short. She's quite clever and loves people."

"Sure, let me lock up here." She came out of the room. She was about five foot four and older with dark blond hair that curled around her head. She wore jeans and a T-shirt that said WARNING, WRITER. WHATEVER YOU SAY MAY END UP IN MY NEXT BOOK.

"Mal," I called, and walked the entire hallway. She wasn't on the third floor. My heart raced and I wrung my hands.

"Would she go outside without you?" the woman asked.

"I doubt it," I said. "She never has before. I'm sorry, I didn't catch your name. I'm Allie McMurphy."

"Ah, the owner," she surmised. "I'm Terry Dubbs. Do you like science fiction?"

"Why?"

"Mal, it's the name of the captain of the *Serenity*. You know, *Firefly*? Nathan Fillion?"

"Oh, no, I don't know that. Sorry."

We headed down the stairs and ran into Jenn and Rex. "Have you found her?" I asked.

"No," Jenn said.

"And you are sure you locked her in the apartment?" Rex asked. "She could be in the lobby."

"I was sure," I said. "But now I don't know."

We hit the landing to the lobby. "Sharon," Jenn said, and the new woman looked up from her magazine.

"What is all the noise about?" she asked.

"Have you seen Mal?" I asked. "My dog. She's a white bichon mix."

"No, I haven't seen a dog," she said. "Cat's on the couch, though."

I hurried down the stairs and picked up Mella. "What are we going to do?" I asked.

"Let's try to stay calm," Rex said. "There wasn't a note or anything, was there?"

"No," I said in a half whisper. "I'm afraid after what they did to the chicken."

"Don't even go there," Rex said, a vein in his back jaw pulsing. He grabbed me and held me tight. Mella squirmed at the confinement and jumped from my arms. "That's not going to happen. More than likely she's sleeping somewhere."

"Have you checked the basement?" Sharon asked.

"I haven't been down there since Mr. Devaney left for the honeymoon," I said. "The door has been kept locked." I pulled away from Rex and grabbed the set of master keys from behind the desk.

"She's not in the kitchen or lobby," Jenn said.

"I'm checking the basement," I said. The door was locked, but I stuck the key in and opened the door. Turning on the light, I called Mal's name. In the distance I could hear a sound. "Mal?" I rushed down the stairs and turned on the main light. The basement was dark, filled with boxes and things. Mr. Devaney had a workbench down there with tools that had belonged to my grandfather. "Mal? Here, girl," I called, and then listened with my heart pounding in my ears. I heard the noise again. This time it was much closer. It sounded like Mal when she was scared. My heart raced as I moved toward the sound. "Mal, here, girl."

The whining was close. I moved a box to find a crate with metal slates for sides. On top of the crate was a big box. Mal stuck her nose out between the slates and cried.

"Mal!"

Rex was suddenly beside me. He pulled the heavy

box off the top of the crate. I shoved the lid aside and pulled my puppy out of the box.

"Mal, oh, Mal," I said, and held her close. She shivered in my arms, but seemed intact. No blood. No harm. She kissed my cheek and I held her against me. I stood and looked at Rex. "I did not put her down here."

"Someone has a key to your basement," he said, his voice gruff.

"That's not good," I said. "All I could see was that headless chicken."

"I'll have Shane come down here and see if he can't pull fingerprints or something." Rex guided me up the stairs. "I don't like this, not one bit."

I climbed up into the light of the lobby. "Oh, Mal!" Jenn said, and rushed over to me. She patted Mal's head. "Where was she?"

"She was in a crate in the back of the basement."

"A crate?" Jenn looked at me, her gaze concerned. "Did she fall into it?"

"Not unless she figured out how to put a heavy box on top of the crate and another box in front of the crate," Rex said.

"Someone put her in the basement? How?" Jenn asked.

"I don't know," I said. "The door was locked."

"But the keys are behind the reception desk," Rex said. "Is there a key to your apartment also on that ring?"

"It's a master key," I said. "So, yes."

"You need to keep those keys on you at all times," he said. "Leaving them down here is not safe. Especially with Frances and Mr. Devaney gone."

"Trust me, I'm not going to let them out of my

sight," I swore. I went over to the desk and took a treat out of the dish that Frances kept on the reception desk and gave one to Mal. "I'm so sorry you went through that, baby. When I find out who did that to you . . ."

"Don't say anything further," Rex said. "We all feel like you do, but no one's going to act like a vigilante. Shane will get some prints and we'll find out who did this."

"It might be a prank," Jenn said. "We didn't find any notes."

"This is nuts," I said. "It's broad daylight out. Who can come into the McMurphy, hang a threat in my utility closet, and then take my dog and put her in the basement like that?"

"It's the locked door part that bothers me," Jenn said.

"I'm calling the security company and doing whatever it takes to get them out here today," I said. "We're getting all the locks changed."

The doorbells rang and we all looked to see Sandy come inside. She froze at the front door. "What?"

"Someone played a prank on the dog," Sharon said without looking up from her magazine.

"Mal?" Sandy asked.

The pup brightened at the sound of her name. "They put her in a crate in the basement—the locked basement." I gave the dog a little squeeze.

"That's not good," Sandy said.

"Did you see anything unusual?" I asked. "I know you were in the kitchen after I went upstairs. Did you see anyone come in that didn't belong?"

"No," Sandy said. "Just the Goers, who checked

out. Oh, Mrs. Tunison's nephew Zack came in and bought a pound of fudge. But that's it."

"Did Zack go anywhere but the fudge shop?" Rex asked.

"No," Sandy said with a shake of her head. "He came in, bought some fudge, and left."

"It could have been a distraction," Rex said thoughtfully. "Who does Zack hang around with?"

"That Rick Sunjin is usually with Zack," Sandy said. "I didn't see him, though."

"What time did Zack come in?"

"It was just after Sharon came in," Sandy said. "So around nine a.m."

"I was upstairs showering then," I said. "I would have known if anyone came into the apartment and took Mal. At least I'd like to think that. I don't want to imagine that they came in while I was in the shower." I turned to Jenn. "I can't remember if I saw her after I got out of the shower."

"Let's try to stay calm," Rex said. "This sounds like a couple of kids playing pranks. I think we can rule out the killer."

"I'm not so sure," Sharon said. We all turned to look at her. She held up an envelope. "This was in the in-box on the reception desk."

Chapter 18

"Let me see it," Rex said, and held out his hand.

"It's my mail," I said, and handed Mal to Jenn. The pup squirmed and kissed her cheek. The envelope was addressed to me. The font used mimicked cutout letters for a ransom note. I took the envelope and opened it with the clean slice of the letter opener. Inside was a single sheet of paper. "Oh," I said as I read it. "You aren't as smart as you think you are."

"What?" Rex asked.

I showed him the letter. My hand trembling.

"There isn't a chess move," Jenn said. She handed Mal to me as Rex took the letter. "That means it's not the killer, right?"

"I'm afraid we can't rule it out," Rex said. "This is threatening." He looked at me. "I want to search the McMurphy from the basement up. If this guy is still in your house, I want to know."

I squeezed Mal. "I'm going upstairs to the office to call the security company."

"Jenn, could you go with her?" Rex asked. "I don't want anyone going anywhere alone in the McMurphy until we search every room." He got on his walkie.

"Charlene, get two more officers to the McMurphy. We're going to do a lockdown." He looked at me. "That means no one comes in or goes out until we search the place."

The bells to the front door rang out and we all turned to see Dirk entering the building. "Dude, I heard there was a problem. Is it part of the murders?"

"We don't know yet," Rex said.

"I thought you were filming this morning," I said.

"Oh, no, setup is today. Shooting was set for tomorrow, but who knows if it'll happen. Something happened to the equipment last night so they canceled today's setup," Dirk said, and put his hands in his back pockets with a shrug.

"What happened?" Rex asked.

"They were unpacking stuff and discovered some of the equipment had gotten crushed. Weird, though, as they really pack that stuff well. I mean it's make or break for a show, you know? Anyway, Jeffery was happy. It gave him more time to perfect his script."

"Was it vandalism?" Rex asked.

"Maybe," Dirk said. "I don't know. It's not my gig, you know?"

Officer Lasko and Williams came through the doors. "I heard you wanted a lockdown," Officer Lasko said. "What's up?"

"We've got a threat. I want the place gone over from top to bottom," Rex said. "Allie, I need to know who is in what rooms. I'll need you to come with me to search the rooms in use."

"Right," I said, and handed Mal to Jenn. "Find Mella, too, please. Keep my fur babies safe."

"I can do that," Jenn said. "Text me if you need anything."

I went to the receptionist desk, nudged Sharon out

of the way and pulled up the names of guests and their room numbers.

"I'll take my break now," Sharon said as she got off Frances's stool and went to the ladies' room in the lobby hallway.

"I've got the names," I said as I walked over to the printer and picked up the sheets. "Good thing we're not fully booked."

"You can check my room first," Terry Dubbs said.

I was surprised she was still there. "I'm so sorry," I said. "I didn't mean to keep you so long."

"No worries," she said with a smile and put her hands on Dirk's bicep. "This is great research. Hello, have you ever modeled for a romance cover?"

Dirk patted her hand. "No, ma'am, but I would consider it."

"I'm an author. I know a few people in the book business."

"Well, then we need to talk." Dirk pulled Terry to the settee and sat down. I shook my head. The man was always about advancing his image.

Shane came down the stairs with the bear under his arm. "Utility room has been processed."

"What are you going to do with that?" Jenn asked as she met him on the stairs.

"Evidence," he said, and pushed his glasses up on his nose.

"I need you to process the basement," Rex said.

"Someone took Mal and put her in a crate in the locked basement," I said.

"What? Who would do that?" Shane asked.

"A crazy person," Jenn said, and hugged Mal until the puppy squeaked. "I'm going to find Mella and take the fur babies up to the apartment."

"I saw the cat on the second floor," Shane said. "I'd put the dog upstairs first."

"She's not going up alone," I said. "Sandy, can you go with Jenn? I need to go with Rex to check out the guest rooms."

"Sure," Sandy said. "Come on, I'll get the cat."

"Thanks," Jenn said and they disappeared up the stairs.

"Was the basement door locked?" Shane asked as he put the life-size bear on the settee across from Dirk and Terry.

"Yes," I said. "I have no idea how they got her down there."

He studied the door. "It wasn't forced. They had to have a key."

"They could have gotten the master from the keys behind reception," Rex said.

"Hmm," Shane said. He pulled out his kit and dusted the door for fingerprints.

Rex looked at Officers Lasko and Williams. "Lock the front door and do a thorough search of the basement and first floor. Be careful in the basement. There's a tunnel but it was walled off earlier this summer."

"We'll check it, boss," Officer Lasko said.

"Come with me, Allie," Rex said. "Let's work our way up from the second floor."

We walked up to the second floor and passed Sandy and Jenn. Each woman had a fur baby in her arm and headed up to the apartment. The first two rooms were empty. The third room was the one that Mella had been inspecting when I'd discovered the utility prank.

"Is this the room with the door left open?" Rex asked as he carefully pushed the door farther open.

"Yes," I said. "I went in and didn't see anything unusual."

He carefully entered and checked the bathroom, closets, and under the bed. "Nothing."

"Do you think whoever did this is still in the hotel? I figure they might be long gone."

"It's better to be safe," he said and we walked by the utility closet. He poked his head inside. "Did you ever fix your attic problem?"

"Yes," I said. "No one has access to it but through my apartment."

"I'm going to have to check it."

"Sure," I said. "This room is occupied." I knocked on the door. "Hello? Management!" I waited to a count of five and tried the knock again. "Management. We're going to enter the room." I paused and still no answer, so I unlocked the door. Rex went inside. The curtains were closed, leaving the room in darkness. He turned on the light. "The Wrights are staying in this room."

They had left the bed unmade and their suitcases open on the suitcase bench. There were dirty towels on the floor, but no sign of anything untoward. The rest of the rooms on the floor were empty as well. Luckily, it was early enough that the people who were booked for the night were out sightseeing.

"Next floor," Rex said. We eased up to the third floor. This floor was more heavily occupied.

"Management," I said, and pounded on the door. A gentleman stuck his head out. "Yeah?"

"We've had a break-in," I said. "Have you seen anything unusual?"

"No," he said with a scowl and a shake of his head. "I've been watching sports."

"Do you mind if we search your room?" Rex asked. He had an intense expression that made most people do whatever he wanted.

"Search all you want," he said, and stepped aside. "I've got nothing to hide."

I glanced at my paper as Rex went inside. "Thank you, Mister Tiller."

"Grant," he said.

"The place is clear," Rex said. "Thank you for your cooperation."

"Sure," Grant said, and looked at me. "Certainly a lot going on lately. I booked the room after season thinking it would be quiet."

"I'm sorry for the inconvenience," I said, and walked to the next room. There were four people on the third floor. The rest of the rooms were empty. "Up to the apartment floor?" I asked Rex. "It seems futile. I mean, whoever did this is clearly gone by now."

"Let's not make any assumptions."

"Right," I said with a frown. "It's unnerving to think my guests might be in danger."

"And you are in danger," he said gently. "Most likely it's pranksters. I mean, they didn't harm Mal."

"No, but they wanted me to know that they could," I said and tears of frustration filled my eyes.

"Someone had to see something," he said. "It's a small island."

"Maybe I should get Liz involved," I said. "If the newspaper reports the incidents it will get people talking."

"Where has Liz been?" Rex asked as he waited for

me to open the office door and let him check it out. "She wasn't at the last murder scene."

"You're right," I said thoughtfully as I waved him inside the office. "I wonder if she's on vacation or something. Jenn would know."

"I thought you and Liz were friends," Rex said as he went through the office with a careful eye. My office was a large room. It held bookshelves and file cabinets with records that went back over one hundred years. Rex looked under the desks that sat in the center of the room.

"We are," I said. "I've been a bit distracted."

"When was the last time you heard from her?"

"I don't know. It was the first crime scene last week."

"I'll make a note to go check on her."

"Wait," I said, and put my hand on his arm. "Do you think something's happened?"

"I don't know," he said, and put his hand over mine and squeezed. "I think it's worth checking on."

"I'm the worst friend."

"Stop, we've all been busy."

"Hey, boss," Officer Lasko said, sticking her head into the office. "We're done with the basement. Shane picked up a few fingerprints, but that's all there was."

"We're almost done here," Rex said. "Why don't you check the attic?"

"This place has an attic?" she asked.

"Yes," I said. "Let me show you."

I unlocked the apartment and Jenn and Sandy sat on the couch talking. Mal jumped up to greet us.

"Find anything?" Jenn asked.

"No," I said with a frown. "Rex is going to check the apartment and Officer Lasko is going to double-check the attic. But it seems whoever did this is long gone."

"I don't like the fact that they got Mal out of the apartment," Jenn said. She stood and hugged her waist. "I've called a locksmith. He'll be over the minute the police allow us to open our doors again."

"I agree," I said. "I've got the master keys with me, but that doesn't mean the entire place isn't compromised. We know that it's pretty easy to make copies of keys."

"The attic?" Lasko asked.

"Through here," I said, and took her to Jenn's bedroom. It had an entrance to the attic. The McMurphy had had a secret passage that led to the attic and a dumbwaiter system from the early 1920s. But I had had that boarded off earlier this spring. Officer Lasko pulled down the stairs and went up into the attic.

"Check for squirrels while you're up there," I teased. She turned and sent me a narrow-eyed look. I raised my hands to say I didn't mean any harm by the comment. She pulled a flashlight out and went up into the attic. Rex came into the bedroom and checked the closets and under the beds.

"The apartment is clear," he said. "Lasko still in the attic?"

"She just went up," I said.

"I recommend that you get your security company in here to rework your locks."

"I'm on it," I said. "I'm adding cameras outside as well. If I didn't know better, I would say this prankster is trying to make me spend all my budgeted money on things I don't want to spend them on."

"That's what emergency funds are for, right?" he asked.

"I suppose."

He looked at his watch, then stuck his head under the attic opening. "Lasko, is it clear?"

There wasn't an answer. We looked at each other. It wasn't like her to not answer. He grabbed his gun and motioned for me to stay back. I took a step back and watched him disappear up the ladder steps. I held my breath and listened. There sounded like a scuffle, then silence.

"Rex?" I called.

"We're okay," he said back, his voice muffled.

I climbed the ladder and peered into the attic. Officer Lasko sat on the wooden floor holding her head. Blood trickled down her temple. Rex squatted beside her.

"What happened?" I asked.

"Your prankster was hiding in the attic," Rex said, his mouth a grim line. He stood and revealed a teenage boy handcuffed and sitting on the floor.

I studied the boy. "Ryan?" I asked. He turned and looked at me, his expression belligerent. Ryan was Mrs. Tunison's grandson. He sometimes portered for me, bringing suitcases up from the docks. "What are you doing?"

He turned his head away from me.

"Is she okay?" I asked Rex, and nodded toward Megan.

"I'm fine," she said, and touched the bloody spot on her forehead. "Just surprised me."

"Bitch got what she deserved," Ryan said.

"Ryan!" I exclaimed. "Your grandmother is going to be livid with you."

"I'm going to bring him down," Rex said. "Allie, call George and get him here to look after Lasko."

"On it," I said, stepped off the ladder and pulled out my phone.

"I don't need George," Megan said.

Rex pulled the teen down the ladder and into the bedroom. Officer Williams came into the bedroom. Rex handed the boy over. "Take him down to the station."

"Yes, sir," Williams said. He took the grumpy teen away.

Rex went back up the ladder and helped Officer Lasko down. I raced to the fridge, pulled out ice, and put it in a towel. "Here," I said. "Put this on the wound to help with the swelling."

"What happened?" Jenn and Sandy stood and flocked around the policewoman.

"He jumped me," she said. "I went up not expecting anything."

"How did he get up there?" Jenn asked. She turned to me. "I thought you had the entrances to the attic fixed."

"I did," I said. "He must have tucked up there when we entered the apartment."

"You mean he was up there when Sandy and I were in the living room?"

"I think so," I said.

Jenn frowned. "Creepy. What if he were a killer?"

I punched the number into my phone. "I'm calling the security company. I don't care what it costs. I'm going to get the McMurphy buttoned up and safe for everyone."

"I have a cousin who runs a security company," Sandy said.

"Thanks, but I think I'll stick to the guys I have."

"Suit yourself," Sandy said with a shrug.

I stopped Rex on his way out the door. "Do you think Ryan was responsible for the bear?"

"I'll let you know what I find out."

"But you're pretty sure the killer didn't have anything to do with the bear or Mal," I said.

"The probability that the pranks were pulled by Ryan is pretty high. I don't think he's a killer. Get your security in here and it will be fine."

"Thank you," I said. "Thank you, Officer Lasko, I appreciate your help in this matter."

"Just doing my job," she muttered as she headed out with Rex while holding my icepack gingerly against her head.

"You really should get that checked out," I said.

"I'm sure, I'll be fine." They walked out of the apartment.

I closed the door and turned to Sandy and Jenn. "Are you two comfortable with working here?"

"Sure," Jenn said. She held Mal in her arms. "But you'll get that security company out here, right?"

"Yes," I said. "I've got the number keyed up on my phone. What about you, Sandy?"

"I'm fine." She shoved her hands in her pockets.

"Thanks for recommending Sharon," I said. "I really needed the extra help."

She nodded at me. "Of course."

I hit the button to call the phone number. It was going to cost me a fortune, but it was worth it if I never had to go through another morning like this.

Gingerbread Fudge

½ cup packed brown sugar
½ cup molasses
⅓ cup evaporated milk
3 ¼ cups white chocolate chips
1 teaspoon cinnamon
1 teaspoon vanilla extract
¾ teaspoon ground ginger
½ teaspoon of allspice
½ teaspoon ground nutmeg
½ teaspoon ground cloves

Line an 8x8-inch pan with foil. Butter the foil.

Place the brown sugar, molasses, and
    evaporated milk in a medium saucepan. Stir
    to combine, then place over medium-low
    heat. Cook, stirring often, until the mixture
    barely begins to simmer.

Remove from heat and add in the chocolate
    chips, vanilla, and spices.

Pour into prepared pan. Place in the fridge to
    chill until the fudge has set, at least 1 hour.

Cut into small squares and serve. Store in a
    covered container. Enjoy!

Chapter 19

The next evening Sid, the supervisor of the security crew, walked me through everything they did. The security installation had taken up most of my Monday, but I think it was worth it. "Each of your guests' rooms has the new electronic key cards. I've trained you and your assistant manager and your desk crew on how that works."

"Yes," I said with a nod. "It seems pretty simple."

"We've got cameras on each corner of your building. They digitally record everything that happens outside your building. I've given you the password to the secure website that stores all the data. Here is a manual for best practices to keep it up-to-date. The apartment has fresh metal keys, along with the office. The place is locked down pretty tight. We put up the window clings explaining that they are under surveillance. We could still put cameras in the inside of the building. I'd recommend two in the lobby and one on each end for the hallways upstairs."

"I'm going to wait and see on that," I said. "I think my guests would prefer not to be on camera."

"I understand," he said. "You have thirty days to

change your mind and get the cameras installed under the installation fee you paid today."

"Okay," I said. "Thank you."

He tugged on his white cap. "Our pleasure. Remember, you have three free months of surveillance. Should you have any problems just call the number we've posted on the alarm systems at the front door and in the apartment. Here's a certificate you can give your insurance. It should lower your rates some."

"Good," I said. I handed him a check and he handed me all the paperwork that went with our new system.

In a flash he and his crew were gone. I'd left notes on all the guest rooms letting them know that we had new locks installed and the key cards were available at the front desk.

"This is kind of cool," Jenn said as she practiced using the software to code a room key.

"It should be, for the price," I said with a sigh. "So much for getting started on the roof project next year."

"Whatever happened to Dirk?" Jenn asked. "Wasn't he here yesterday talking to the romance writer?"

"He left with Rex yesterday afternoon," I said. "It seems the film crew got everything up and running this morning. He should be shooting for a few days now."

"Rex will be happy not to have his shadow."

I chuckled. "I'm sure he will be."

"What happened with Ryan?" Jenn asked.

"Rex is still questioning him," I said. "The kid hasn't admitted to much more than lifting a master key and bumming around the hotel."

"He's not admitting to taking Mal out of our apartment?"

"No," I said and my mouth went into a smooth, flat

line. "I want to give the kid a piece of my mind. He scared me and my poor puppy near to death."

"Do we know any more about the body you found the other night?" Jenn asked as she tried coding another key card.

"We were so busy securing the McMurphy that I didn't have time to ask Rex. I would love to know if they identified the man." I drew my eyebrows together. "Have you heard from Liz? Rex noticed that she hasn't been at any of the crime scenes lately. It's not like her."

"I think I heard that her grandfather was sick. I think he's in a hospital in Saginaw."

"Oh boy," I said. "I need to text her and see if she's okay. How long has he been sick?"

"I think it started with a cold or something," Jenn said. "I'm not sure."

"Who's writing for the paper?"

"They are rerunning old columns," Sharon said. She sat next to Jenn and thumbed through a magazine.

"Do you know Mr. McElroy?" I asked the older woman.

"Most of my life."

"Has he been sick before?"

"First time that I know of," Sharon said. She glanced up at the time. "Time to go. I've got a few errands to run."

"Do you want someone to walk you home?" I asked. I know it sounded silly but with the last couple of days I'd had, I wasn't sure anyone should be out on the streets alone.

"I'm good," she said, and tugged on a jacket. "Good night."

"Good night," I said. I picked up Mal and petted her ears. "Jenn, have you heard from Paige? She said something about having lunch a few days ago but I haven't heard anything."

"I saw her and Trent in the stables this morning," Jenn said. "They didn't look happy with each other."

"No?"

"They seemed to be fighting," Jenn said. "Any idea what that might be about?"

"Maybe," I said.

"Hold on," Jenn said to me, and then addressed the guests who were coming back to their room for the night. "Hello, we upgraded our room keys today."

"You did?" Mr. Angelus seemed surprised. "What prompted this?"

"It was planned," I said. "We had hoped to get it done before your arrival, but the workers couldn't come in until today."

"Here," Jenn said, and took their old key from them. "Here are the new key cards. This will be safer and more secure."

"Too bad," Mrs. Angelus said with a sniff. "There was charm in the actual key for the room."

"All of the island hotels will eventually go to key card," I explained. "It's for your safety."

"Come on, Irma," Mr. Angelus said. "You wouldn't have even thought twice about the key if we weren't upgrading. I'm tired. Let's go to bed."

We waited while Mr. and Mrs. Angelus walked up the stairs to go up to their rooms. Jenn came around the receptionist desk. "You know something about why Paige and Trent were fighting?"

"Their father is handing the business over to them."

"Cool, what's to fight over?"

"Paige got the island businesses and Trent got the Chicago businesses."

"Okay—"

"I told Trent I didn't want a long-distance relationship. So he's trying to get Paige to give over control of the island businesses."

"Hmm," Jenn said as she stroked Mella. The cat had jumped up on the receptionist desk to be part of the conversation. "Paige doesn't want to switch for Chicago?"

"I don't know," I said with a shrug. "But when I talked to her she seemed pretty happy with living on the island year-round."

"The real question," Jenn said with a wiggle of her eyebrows, "is will you take Trent back if he lives on the island full-time?"

"I'll cross that bridge when I come to it," I said, and turned off the computer and headed upstairs.

"Says the woman who has a date with Rex Manning tomorrow."

"He wants to cook me dinner," I said. "We'll talk about the murder case. Speaking of which, I haven't had any time to investigate. Did Shane tell you if they identified the man from last night?"

"Shane said that they are cross-referencing with any missing person's report. It could take a while. If the man lived alone, like the last victim, then it could be a while before anyone reports him missing."

"That's the saddest thing I've heard today," I said. "Come on, let's go upstairs. I have a nice bottle of wine to share."

We headed up the stairs with my fur babies in tow. "Do you think that Ryan was responsible for the chicken prank and everything that happened?"

"I don't know," I said with a shake of my head. "I don't understand why he would pull any kind of prank. I've been nothing but nice to him. I hired him to porter for me last month."

"It's probably how he got keys to get into the building and your apartment."

"It would also explain why Mal didn't bark or growl. She knew him."

"She just wants to cuddle with anyone," Jenn said. "She probably went right to him."

"Yes, it's why I need to keep an eye on her. She's a dear and very smart, but not the best guard dog."

"Good thing you got new cameras," Jenn said. We made it upstairs and I used the new key to open the double locks on the door.

"Feels a bit like a prison," I said with a sigh.

"Better to help keep people out of your attic. That's just creepy."

"I should check on Officer Lasko."

"Why? She clearly doesn't like you much," Jenn said.

"I know," I said, and locked the door behind me. "Any idea why?"

"I think she's sweet on a certain police officer who only has eyes for you."

"Seriously?"

"That's my best guess," Jenn said. "After all, you've had Rex's attention since you first came on the island. She's been working with him for what? Two years? Three? She might feel a bit possessive. You know how work romances can get."

"No," I said, and poured us both a glass of red wine. "I don't know anything about workplace romances."

"Well, let me tell you, they can be exciting," Jenn

said, and curled up on the couch with her glass of wine. "And frustrating."

"Especially if the one you're crushing on isn't interested in you back."

"Exactly," Jenn said.

I sipped my wine. "No wonder she doesn't like me much."

"You know what the answer is?"

"No," I said, and shook my head.

"Find her a handsome single man of her own."

I laughed. "I'm no good at romance. What makes you think I could help anyone else out?"

"Indeed," Jenn said.

"Did anyone hear from Mr. Beecher?" I asked, thinking of the older neighbor for the first time in hours. "The killer dressed the last body to look like Mr. Beecher. I haven't heard from him in days now."

"Maybe his granddaughter is visiting with her new baby," Jenn said.

"Oh, a baby?" I sighed. "I wouldn't have thought he was old enough to be a great-grandfather." I felt a moment of sadness. "Papa Liam would have loved to be a great-grandpa."

"I know," Jenn said, and patted my knee. "How are you doing with his loss?"

I ran my hand through my hair. "I've kept myself busy this season. Too busy to really grieve."

"You need to deal with it," Jenn said. "You lost an important member of your family."

"Yes," I said. "Funny how I'm fine and then I'll see something that was his and I get so sad."

"What would your grandfather think of your investigations?"

I leaned back into the couch and let Mal jump up

in my lap. "I think he would have gotten a kick out of trying to solve them."

"Speaking of solving, have there been any more chess moves?"

"No," I said with a shake of my head. "I think the killer has given up on my understanding his chess game."

"Aren't you going back to the senior center for this week's chess club?" Jenn asked.

"That's Thursday," I said. "Sandy already set it up. I think I'll go back up there tomorrow, though. I need to find out if anyone knows who the second dead man is. The rumor mill must be full. It's time I started looking into who this killer is before things get closer to home."

Chapter 20

The next morning, after I filled the fudge shop shelves with fudge, I made sure Sharon was good with the new key system. Then I left Sandy making chocolate in the kitchen and I put Mal's halter on her and went outside. I needed to check on Liz and Angus McElroy. The first thing I did was head to the little white house two houses down from the newspaper office. I knocked on the door while Mal sniffed around the tiny porch.

"Hello?" I called when I peered into the window. No one answered. Inside looked quiet and still.

"They are in Saginaw," Mrs. O'Malley said from the sidewalk. "Angus had a stroke last week."

"That's terrible. I hope he's all right," I said, and stepped off the porch to meet her on the sidewalk. "Jenn told me that something had happened. I thought I'd come by and see if they needed anything. But I see they aren't home yet."

"The ladies' auxiliary is taking up a collection to help Liz pay for the hotel she's been staying in since Angus went to Saginaw."

"How can I help?" I asked.

"We're having a bake sale as a fund-raiser. Would you be interested in donating some fudge and a couple hours of your time?"

"Yes, of course," I said. "When is it?"

"Saturday morning," Mrs. O'Malley said. "We have a space on the lawn in front of the fort reserved. We hope that with it being Saturday we'll get some traction from fudgies that come in for the day. The weather is supposed to be good."

"What time do you need me there?" I asked. Mal jumped up on her begging for a head scratch.

"Nine thirty," Mrs. O'Malley said, and patted Mal's head. "The ferries run the first group over at ten."

"I'll be there," I said.

"Say, I heard you found a second body."

"Yes, but I haven't heard if they have identified the poor man. Do you know?"

"Rumor is that it was Cyrus Johnson's nephew."

I drew my eyebrows together. "He looked older."

Mrs. O'Malley laughed. "Cyrus is ninety. So I'm sure his nephew would be older to you."

"Is his nephew missing?"

"The boy was always a bit of a hermit. Cyrus went out to his place this morning to see if he's alive."

"Wouldn't the people he worked with know if he was missing?"

"The boy hasn't worked since the 1990s. He was a postman. Did something to his back while working and they paid him a good sum for workman's comp. He moved into the family house and has basically retired ever since."

"Surely, he has some friends, someone to know if he is missing."

She shrugged. "He'd go in spurts. Sometimes he'd

be at the Nag's Head Bar for days on end. Then he'd disappear for a month or so. Suddenly he'd pop up full of stories." She leaned toward me. "The boy is a drunk," she said in a stage whisper. "Everyone knew it."

"Poor man," I said. "That's no way to live."

"It's the back injury. They say he got hooked on pain meds. Then when the doctors took those away he turned to drink."

"I certainly hope he's okay."

"Well, I'm not hoping he's dead, but it might be better than the way he's been living." She nodded and tightened her mouth into a straight line.

"If it is Mr. Johnson's nephew, why would someone want to kill him? I mean, he seems harmless."

"Probably a crime of opportunity," Mrs. O'Malley said. "Just like the last dead man. A single guy, loner, no one the wiser when he goes missing."

"Do you think the killer is looking for these kinds of marginalized men?"

"Marginalized?" she asked, tilting her head as she observed me.

"You know, living on the fringes of society."

"Humph, they live there because they choose to, you know," she said. "Not because anyone made them."

"Right, sorry," I said. "I didn't mean to imply . . ."

"Well, then you need to see that policeman boyfriend of yours and tell him to warn all the bachelors on the island. It could be that the killer doesn't like single men."

"Wait, my policeman boyfriend?"

"Honey, everyone knows you have a date with Rex Manning tonight."

"Sheesh, there are no secrets on this island, are there?"

She shrugged. "I don't know why anyone thinks they can get away with murder here. The truth always comes out in the end. Mark my words."

"Right, well, I need to go see Mr. Beecher," I said. "Thank you for your information."

"I'll see you Saturday morning bright and early, won't I?" Mrs. O'Malley asked.

"Yes," I said. "I'll be there." I tugged on Mal's leash and pulled her away from whatever smells she was interested in and down the street toward Mr. Beecher's house.

The good news was that Mr. Beecher was probably all right. Otherwise Mrs. O'Malley would have told me he wasn't.

Mr. Beecher lived two roads behind the McMurphy and two blocks down in a small bungalow that was painted a sunny yellow with blue trim around the windows. The maple tree in his front yard had begun to turn bright red in patches. I walked up to the door and knocked.

This time I heard shuffling as he made his way to the door and opened it. "Allie?" he asked as he opened the door. He was dressed in a smoking jacket and a pair of pajama pants. His face looked drawn.

"Hi, Mr. Beecher," I said. Mal pushed her way into the door and sniffed his leg. "I haven't seen you in a while and got worried. Are you okay?"

"Oh, yes," he said. "Come on in. Don't mind the mess. I've been under the weather lately. Can I get you some tea?"

"I don't want you to go to any trouble," I said.

"No, no, I'm making it for myself as well," he said, and waved me toward the living room. "Please, you and Mal have a seat. I'll be right out."

The home was small. You stepped into a small foyer that opened to a living area and dining area and then a small kitchen in the back. The place was decorated in dark wood and green and white paint with leather seating. There was a large fireplace off to the side and he had clearly been sitting near the fire reading a book.

Mal sniffed around. There was a pipe in a pipe tray. Next to a dark brown, leather-covered easy chair. I took a seat in the second chair. The chairs had tufted backs. The floor was covered in a plaid carpet. The wall opposite the fireplace was filled with bookshelves and books. The wall that was exposed was painted green. Mal enjoyed her sniff around. The room smelled of cherry pipe tobacco.

"Ah, I've made Earl Grey," he said, coming in with a tray filled with a teapot, cream and sugar, slices of lemon, and two teacups with saucers. He set them down on the small table between us. "How do you take your tea? Milk? Sugar? Lemon?"

"A little lemon, please," I said. He placed a slice of lemon on my saucer, poured the tea, and handed it to me. Then he made his with milk and sugar and settled back into his chair. His eyes shone with delight at the taste of his tea. "How have you been?"

"Ah, yes, just a little cold," he said. "That's what the doctor tells me. Plenty of tea and rest should do the trick." Mal jumped her front feet on his knee. He patted her head. "Hello, my little friend. I'm afraid I don't have any treats in my pocket today."

"It's okay," I said. "Mal missed you."

"What has been happening? Any news on the capture of the murderer?"

"No," I said. "I thought perhaps if I went to the senior center and tried to join the chess club I would learn something, but the trail had gone cold. That is until the other night."

"The other night?"

"Yes, I took Mal out for a walk along the marina and, well, we found another body."

"Oh dear," Mr. Beecher said.

"The worst part was that the body was dressed like you. Right down to the same waistcoat. He even wore a fedora like yours. The poor man's face was covered and I was so afraid something bad had happened to you."

"Oh dear," he said, and put down his cup. "Who was the poor victim?"

"We don't know," I said. "Rex hasn't given me an identity yet. I ran into Mrs. O'Malley on the street today. She said there is some speculation it was Mr. Johnson's nephew."

"Another loner," Mr. Beecher said.

"Yes," I said, nodding, and I sipped my tea.

"Was there a note?"

"Yes, another chess move. There seems to be a theory that the killer is replaying all of my solved murders. For each one he replays he is writing a move from—"

"An old Bobby Fischer game," he interrupted me.

"Yes," I said, and drew my eyebrows together. "How did you know?"

"I did some research on it. It's strange that he picked

that game. I wonder if there is any significance?" The old man sipped his tea thoughtfully. "That particular game was played in1956," Mr. Beecher said. "Perhaps the killer wants you to know something about that year."

"1956," I said. "I think that's the year my father was born. I need to check into that."

"Do you think the killer might have known your father?"

"I don't know. It seems though that they are busy killing men who live alone. It's why I came to check on you."

He laughed. "Oh, my dear, I am not even remotely a hermit like the first victim and the man we suspect was the second victim. My granddaughter comes to see me often. Plus, I have a housekeeper who comes in three times a week. I'm part of the library association and the Knights of Columbus on the island. People would miss me if I didn't get out in a day or two. Why, you even came looking for me and I've been sick only a few days."

"Oh," I said, and sat back happier. "That is good. I was afraid at first that you might be a victim. I mean, why else would they dress the latest victim to match your usual mode of dressing?" I frowned. "Who else knows you are sick and haven't been getting out?"

"I suppose anyone who is a regular on the island," he said. "Like I said, I'm not a hermit."

"Were you born in 1956?"

"I was ten in 1956," he said.

"So that year doesn't mean anything to you?"

"I was learning to play chess," he said. "The chess

club was quite the thing in those days. Nothing like it is today."

"Do you know if my Papa Liam played chess back then?"

"Oh dear, yes," he said, and drew his white bushy eyebrows together. "In fact Liam was very much involved in the chess club back then. I was a junior member of the team, but Liam was the one making all the waves. Your grandfather was a bit of a lothario in the day."

"Not to change the subject, but do you know Jeffery Jenas?"

"Hmm, no, why?"

"He's the writer for the television mystery show that is filming on the island right now. I guess he has been on Mackinac Island since I got here in May. He's spent the entire time writing half of a season's worth of scripts."

"What does this young man look like?"

I described Jeffery. "He's staying with Mrs. O'Connor."

"I have seen him on my walks," he said. "I understand he takes a lot of walks. Not much for speaking though. Nothing past a quiet tug on his hat and an acknowledgment of you walking opposite of him."

"I wonder if he has any ties to Mackinac," I said, and made a mental note to ask the ladies at the senior center if they might have known any Jenases who would have been on the island in or around 1956.

"Not that I'm aware of," Mr. Beecher said. "Unless he's related to the island Jenases. But I doubt that. When he first got here, he got a lot of guidance from the welcome center."

"How do you know that?"

"I know the ladies who volunteer there. They were always digging up old pamphlets and things to give him. The ladies were quite taken with him. Charming sort, I guess."

"He would have been here from the start of my adventures when I found Mr. Jessop in my utility closet."

"It could certainly be him," Mr. Beecher said. "You should look into his background. He is a writer, right?"

"Yes."

"Then he must have some sort of website or portfolio of work online. You should take a look. It could clear up a lot of things for you."

"Oh, true," I said. "I'll do that."

Mr. Beecher started coughing.

"Oh, let me get you some water."

"Kitchen," he gasped.

I went through the dining room and into the immaculate little kitchen. I opened the cabinets by the sink and found a glass, filled it with water, and brought it back to him.

He had a tissue in his hand and tears in his eyes and I handed him the glass. He took it and took a couple of swallows. "Thank you."

"You look tired," I said. "We'll go. Do you want me to get you anything? Do you have groceries? I can go to the store for you."

"I have chicken soup and crackers," he said with a half smile. "I'll be fine. The doctor says I need to give it time."

"Can I come back sometime? Say in a day or two?"

"That would be lovely," he said. "You can tell me what else you find out about this writer and if you find out for sure the name of the second dead man."

"I will," I said. "You get some rest and you really shouldn't smoke. Even a pipe isn't good for your lungs."

He chuckled. "I know. My doctor has been after me. I promise I haven't had a smoke since I got this darn cold."

"Good," I said, and leaned over and kissed his cheek. "Get well soon." I straightened. "Come on, Mal, let's go. Don't get up. I'll show myself out." Mal and I stepped out into the cool air. The breeze off the lake had the faint scent of fall. "Let's go see Rex, shall we?" I asked Mal. She jumped up. I knew she liked Rex. So did I.

The walk to the administration building was short and uneventful. We stepped inside the police station. Officer Pulaski sat at the front desk. "Hello, Brent," I said. "How are you today?"

"I'm good, Allie," he said. "Any problems at the McMurphy?"

"Not today. I was wondering if Rex was in?"

"I'll ring him," he said, and called Rex. "Allie McMurphy is here. Yes. I'll let her know." He hung up and looked at me. "He'll come out and get you in a minute. You can have a seat."

The hard plastic chairs in the foyer were familiar to me. I settled in and Mal begged for me to pick her up. So I held her in my lap. It didn't take long for Rex to come out and get me. "Allie, come on back to my office." He held the door open for me. I stepped inside and waited for him to walk me back to his office.

"What can I do for you today?" he asked as he showed me into his office and closed the door.

"I was wondering what you learned about Ryan. Did he admit to doing any of the pranks?"

"Yes," Rex said, and took a seat behind his desk.

"He admitted to the chicken and the bear and even locking Mal in the basement."

"Horrible," I said. "Did he tell you why?"

"He said that some guy paid him a couple hundred dollars to do it."

"Really?" I leaned forward. "Did he say who?"

"No," Rex said, and picked up a pen. He tapped the pen on the top of his desk. "He said he didn't know."

"How can he not know?"

"It was all done via e-mail. The request came through a social media direct message. Ryan told the guy that he needed to pay him before he did anything. The next day an envelope showed up at his door with fifty dollars in it."

"Can I press charges?" I asked.

"Do you want to?" Rex asked. "I mean, the disruption to the McMurphy is minor."

"The price of my security system is far from minor," I groused.

"Better to have it put in place over a prank than another murder," Rex pointed out. "You should talk to your insurance guy. I bet you get a better rate with the new system and cameras in place."

"Why would someone pay a kid to play pranks? Did he want me to have to get a security system?"

"I don't know," Rex said, and leaned back in his chair.

"Do you think it's the murderer trying to mess with me? If so, why wouldn't he do these things himself?"

"Maybe to throw us off the scent," Rex said.

"Did you identify the second body?" I asked. "Mrs.

O'Malley tells me they think it's Cyrus Johnson's nephew."

"Yes," Rex said. "Cyrus came to the morgue today and identified the body as that of his nephew, Tad. He also told us that those clothes didn't belong to Tad Johnson."

"I didn't think they did," I said. "I knew he was trying to make it look like Mr. Beecher was dead. I came here from checking on Mr. Beecher. The poor man has a cold and has been home sick this week. Whoever the killer is, he knows the island and he knows that I talk to Mr. Beecher nearly every day when he walks down my alley."

"That seems like a lot of work," Rex said. "Do you think the killer is stalking you?"

"I think he's familiar with the island," I said. "It's a small place. Whoever the killer is, they sure can scare me."

"Yes, I figured it was a local."

"Do you know what significance the year 1956 might have?"

"No, why?"

"It's the year that Bobby Fischer beat Donald Byrne in a chess match. The moves the killer is writing in the letters come straight out of that particular game."

"How do you know that?"

"I Googled it," I said. "And Sandy told me. Oh, and Mr. Beecher has studied the game."

"Interesting," Rex said.

"So any idea why that was an important year? Mr. Beecher said the chess club was big back then. He and my grandfather were members."

"Do you think Mr. Beecher is in trouble?"

"I'm not sure," I said, and shrugged. "But it might not hurt to keep an eye on him. He was with me when I found the first body."

"And the second body was dressed like him."

"Yes," I said. "I'm not into chess, but Mr. Beecher was."

"Interesting," Rex said, and sat back.

"Do you think it was the killer who paid Ryan?"

"We're looking into that."

"Does that mean that Ryan might be in danger?"

"I had a good talk with him. He promised not to ever do anything like that again. Officer Lasko is looking at pressing charges for assault."

"Oh," I said, and sat forward in my chair. "What will happen to Ryan?"

"I'm going to recommend community service," Rex said. "I know the judge."

"But won't it go on his record?" I asked. "The kid is young, it was a mistake."

"I can't tell Lasko not to press charges. He hit her hard."

"I understand," I said with a sigh, and sat back. "I wish he hadn't done it."

"I agree," Rex said. His look warmed me. "Are we still on for eight tonight?"

"Yes," I said, and felt the heat of a blush rush up my cheeks. I tugged Mal over to me and pulled her up into my lap. "What's the dress code?"

He raised his right eyebrow. "Wear something comfortable."

"Oh now, I don't slip into something comfortable on the first date," I teased.

His gaze warmed. "I didn't know you were a fifties kind of girl."

I smiled and stood. "I'll be there at eight."

"Maybe I should come and get you," he said. "It's probably not a good idea to go out alone."

"You don't live that far," I said. "I don't want you to burn dinner coming to get me."

"A carriage ride or a nice walk could be romantic."

"How much trouble can I get into in a mile walk?"

"Allie, this is you we're talking about."

I laughed. "I'll see you at eight."

Chapter 21

On the way back to the McMurphy I saw Jeffery walking ahead of me on Market Street. "Hello? Jeffery? Mr. Jenas?" I flagged him down.

He stopped and turned to see who called his name. "Yes? Allie, what can I do for you?"

"I thought you would be on set today. I heard they are shooting the pilot."

"I needed to take a walk," he said with a shrug. "Creative stuff." He wore a gray hoodie and blue jeans and shoved his hands in his front pockets. "I heard you had some trouble at the McMurphy. Makes me think I should have rented a room from you. I would have been in the middle of all the action." He tapped his temple. "Good fodder for further episodes."

"I was wondering if you knew a kid named Ryan?"

"Who?"

"He's a teenager. Mrs. Tunison's grandson. He sometimes will porter for me."

"I have no idea," he said. "Don't know that many people by name. I do see a lot of them on my walks.

Funny what you can learn about people simply by walking by their house or business every day."

"I was wondering, does the year 1956 mean anything to you?"

"What? No, why?"

"Just asking," I said. "How come you didn't stick around after Mal and I found the dead man?"

"I figured once you called the police there wasn't much for me to do. I'm on deadline. The last thing I have time for is sitting around while the police point fingers at people."

"Did you know Tad Johnson?"

"Who?"

"Cyrus Johnson's nephew," I said. Mal sniffed Jeffery's pant leg intently.

He stepped out of range of my dog. "No, I don't think I know Cyrus Johnson."

"Is this the first time you've spent any time on Mackinac Island?"

"What's with all the questions?"

It was my turn to shrug. "You said you spent the season here. I wondered if you'd ever spent time on the island before. I used to summer here every year growing up. So while this was my first season as the owner of the McMurphy, I'm pretty used to spending time on the island. Were you?"

"My parents brought me once when I was about eight or so," he said. "It's different as an adult."

"It certainly is," I said. "But I don't think it loses its charm. Do you?"

"Not one bit," he said. "I wrote some of that charm for the series."

"Good," I said. Then I drew my brows together.

"Wait, as the writer, shouldn't you be on set all the time?"

"Sometimes I need a creative break," he said. "The team knows it. As long as I'm not gone too long, it's okay. I'm still working out the last few episodes. I want to lead up to a killer season ending. You know we like to end the season on a cliff-hanger."

"Oh," I said. "Are you going to make it seem as if one of the principal characters is killed?"

He winced. "That's a cliché. I'm working on something even more interesting."

"Oh, what?"

"That's for me to know and you to watch the show," he said.

My phone rang. I answered it while he waved good-bye and kept going down the street. "This is Allie," I said.

"Allie, it's Paige."

"Hi, Paige, how have you been?"

"Busy," she said and I could hear the tiredness in her voice. "I'm sorry I haven't gotten together with you for that lunch. We need to do that. I was wondering if you had time today. I know it's sort of last-minute, but I would love to grab lunch."

I looked at my phone. It was 2 p.m.

"I've got Mal with me," I said. "When do you want to meet?"

"Why don't you come down to the marina? We can meet at the Island Café, say in half an hour?"

"Great," I said. "That'll give me time to take Mal home and check in on the McMurphy."

"Super," Paige said. "See you then."

Mal and I cut back down the street and through the alley to the back of the McMurphy. I unlocked the door and entered the building. It didn't take long to snap Mal out of her harness and leash and let her free inside. I placed the leash and harness on the hooks by the door and walked down the hall to the lobby.

Sharon was at the receptionist desk reading a book.

"Hello," I said. "Any trouble today?"

"Nothing," she said without looking up. "You've had three people check out as expected. Room 306 is running late for checkout. You might want to go up and check on them."

"Who is coming in today? Anyone new?"

"No, it's a slow day," she said. "End of season. Most people come in Friday and leave Sunday."

"Thanks," I said.

"Room 306," she said, and went back to her book.

Mal followed me up the stairs. I stopped on the third floor. It was quiet. The new door locks were a bit odd to see after seeing lock and key my entire life. I knocked on room 306. "Hello? Management." There was no answer. I knocked again, this time louder and longer. "Management."

I could hear banging around inside. Finally, the door opened to a bleary-eyed man in his twenties. "Checkout was at noon," I said.

"Right," he said, standing there in only a pair of jeans. His chest was bare, as were his feet. His thick dark hair stood on end. "Sorry. Overslept."

"We will charge you for the day if you're not out by three," I said.

"Got it," he said. "I'll be out."

"Thank you, Mr. . . . ?"

"Gold, Mike Gold." He grabbed a shirt off the back

of the chair and tugged it on. "Sorry, I got in late and the new key thing had me all confused."

"Sorry for the inconvenience," I said. "What about the new key system didn't work for you?"

"I didn't realize that you locked the front door after nine. I was out with my buddies until two and, well, it took me about an hour to figure out how to use the key card to get into the building."

"Oh," I said, and crossed my arms. "I didn't think it needed extra explanation. I'll be sure and note that for the future. Have a good day, Mr. Gold."

"Sure," he said. "I'll be out by three. Say, do you still have coffee in the coffee bar downstairs?"

"Yes," I said. "We have fresh coffee every hour except from eleven p.m. until three a.m."

"Cool." He closed the door and I went up to the apartment to get my purse.

"Hey, Allie," Jenn called as I walked into the apartment. Mal came in behind me and playfully chased Mella up onto the kitchen counter. She hissed at Mal, then settled down on the counter.

"Jenn," I said. "I just talked to Mr. Gold in room 306. He's a late checkout. Something about not understanding how to use his room key to get into the front door this morning. Do you think we need to put a doorbell on the front?"

"Oh gosh, no," Jenn said as she came out of her bedroom. She was dressed in a jean skirt and white peasant blouse. "Anyone could be buzzing you all night. No, we'll simply let them know when they check in. If they can't figure it out on their own after that, it's not our problem."

"Okay," I said, and drew my eyebrows together.

"What?" Jenn asked.

"You aren't usually so flippant when it comes to our guests."

She shrugged. "The only reason for anyone not to understand how to get into the building is that they are too drunk to figure it out. Drunks can sleep outside as far as I'm concerned."

"Wow, get up on the wrong side of the bed?"

"What? No," she said, and leaned against her doorjamb. "Just being realistic. Where are you off to?" she asked as I picked up my purse from the shelf in my bedroom.

"Paige called. She wants to meet for lunch."

"Oh right, so you can mentor her. Nothing like last-minute notice," Jenn said.

"Wow, what is up with you?"

Jenn sighed and ran her hand over her face. "I just heard from my boss in Chicago. She wants me there by the end of the week."

"So soon?"

"There's a big wedding and she wants to test my skills at last-minute problem solving," Jenn sighed. "It means my time on the island is over."

"Have you told Shane?"

"No, I just found out myself. I've been packing for the last hour." She frowned. "I'm not ready to go."

"So don't," I said. "You could stay and start planning for the winter and next spring."

"I have to. This is a great opportunity to get some name recognition. There are a lot of people in Chicago who summer on Mackinac."

I put my hand on her arm. "Do you want me to cancel with Paige? I can see her anytime."

"Would you?"

"Certainly," I said. I pulled out my phone and sent

Paige a text. Sorry, but something's come up. Can we try again next week?

She came back with a text. Certainly. Talk soon.

"There," I said, and put my phone and purse away. "Now let's talk about what you are going to be doing in Chicago."

I put on a pretty floral sundress for my date with Rex. There was no sense in going straight-up sexpot like I did for dinner with Dirk. It wasn't because I didn't want Rex to think I was sexy. But Rex had seen me at my worst more than once. So it seemed silly to try to impress him with one of Jenn's dresses. I chose to be myself—comfortable in a cute floral sundress. I had slipped my feet into a pair of sparkly sandals and grabbed a soft white sweater to cover my shoulders.

I stepped out of my bedroom and Jenn popped her head out into the hall from her bedroom. "You look cute."

"Thanks," I said shyly. Mal came out and jumped up on me as if to say she approved. I blew out a long breath. "I'm kind of nervous."

Jenn laughed. "That's a good thing."

"Okay," I said. "I'm off."

"By yourself?" she asked, drawing her brows together.

"Oh, not you, too?" I said. "It's only a mile. I'll be fine."

"It's just there's a killer out there," she said. "Mal and I can walk you."

"And who will walk you back?" I asked. "No, I'll be fine. I've got my phone."

"Hmm," Jenn said. "I guess. How about Mal and I walk you out and watch you catch a carriage ride?"

"I'm not sure there are any carriages out now. It's off-season."

Jenn gave me a narrow-eyed look. "You don't want to catch a carriage because you think Trent will find out."

"What?"

"The carriages left on the island are all out of the Jessops' stables."

"Now you're being ridiculous," I said. "I'm sure Trent already knows. It's a small island."

"Hmm. How about Mal and I walk you to the corner."

"Fine," I said. "Let's go."

"Bossy," she teased as we locked the apartment and went downstairs. We ran into a couple going up to their rooms. Otherwise the lobby was silent. "It's strange how quiet things get once the season is over," Jenn said. Tears welled in her eyes. "I'm going to miss this place."

I squeezed her hand. "You are always welcome here."

"I know," she said as I put Mal's halter on her and hooked up the leash. I handed Mal to her and we stepped outside. Rex lived up the hill behind the police station. Jenn walked me to the corner. "Looks like you were right. There aren't any carriages out."

The island was alive with the sounds of people in bars, laughing and drinking and playing music. The sky was dark and the stars had begun to pop out. The air was a cool sixty-five degrees and smelled of fall. I took a deep breath. "It smells wonderful, doesn't it?"

"It does," Jenn said. She gave me a quick hug. "Text me when you get there."

"Okay, bye." I watched her turn around to go back

to the McMurphy and walked up the hill. I felt safe until I got to the block behind the police station. I rarely came this way this time of day. It was clear that some of the homes were vacant during the week. I imagined they were still well used on weekends. The season might go until Labor Day, but more and more people were learning the joys of fall and winter on Mackinac Island. It meant that I would have guests as long as I wanted to stay open.

I hurried up the hill. At some point I thought I heard footsteps behind me. I turned but no one was there. I went back to walking and heard the footsteps again. "Hello?" I called. There was no answer. I gripped my phone and walked faster. The footfalls seemed to speed up with me. I stopped and turned toward the sidewalk behind me. "Who is it? It's not funny. Come out and face me."

No one answered. It's as if whoever followed me held their breath.

"Allie?" Rex's voice came from behind me.

I turned to see him walking toward me. "Hi," I said, and rushed toward him, putting my arm through his. "Am I late?"

"No," he said. "I got a text from Jenn saying you were walking up by yourself. I thought I'd come and meet you halfway."

"Thanks," I said, and glanced behind me.

"What is it?"

"I thought I heard someone following me," I said, and shrugged. "Whoever it was seems to be gone now."

Rex squeezed my hand. "Come on, let's get off the street. You look amazing, by the way."

"Thanks," I said, and nervously tugged my hair behind my ear. "You don't look too bad yourself."

He was out of his uniform. His wide action-hero shoulders were encased in a pale blue dress shirt. It was open at the collar. He wore dark wash jeans and cowboy boots.

"It's not every day I get to see you out of uniform," I said. I wasn't about to tell him he smelled nice. But he did. It was a combination of aftershave and warm male skin.

"I thought you'd be more relaxed if I wasn't on duty."

"Well," I said. "I certainly appreciate that."

"Good," he said, his gaze warm. "I wanted you to." He tugged me up on the porch of a bungalow that looked out on the straits. "I hope you like red wine. I've got a nice bottle breathing in the kitchen."

"I love red wine." I glanced behind me. Was that a shadow?

"Are you okay?" he asked.

"Yes," I said with a smile. "I'm just fine." I went inside determined to have a good time. After all, who would dare harm me while I was with Rex?

Chapter 22

"I've got a steak on the grill," he said as he handed me a glass of red wine. "I'm making steak salad."

"Your famous steak salad?" I asked, and smiled at him. "Not very action hero."

"Action hero?" He drew his eyebrows together.

"Yes," I said, and raised my glass in a toast. "You are my personal hero. Here's to good friends."

We touched glasses and took a sip of wine.

"Wow, that's great."

"It's from your cousin Tori's friend's winery in California."

"Tori always did have good taste," I said, and took another sip. "I like your home." I looked around. It was a classic 1940s bungalow. The front door opened into a living room, and a dining room that went straight back to a small kitchen. He'd opened the wall between the kitchen and the dining room, leaving a large island with a recycled glass countertop. The right side of the house was all bedrooms. Two of which were off the kitchen with a bathroom between. The third bedroom was off the living room. He'd turned it into a very masculine study. Complete with bookshelves and a large walnut desk. It was clear he sat in the easy chair often and read by the floor lamp. The books on the end table near the chair looked well read.

"What are your favorite books?" I asked, and went into the study to look at his collection of books. Most were private eye books. There was an entire collection of Louis L'Amour westerns and a few old Zane Greys.

"I like classics," he said. "Noir, police procedurals, and such." He leaned against the doorjamb and watched me as I trailed my fingers over the spine of his books.

"Agatha Christie," I said. "Nice choice."

"I thought you might like that one." He raised one corner of his mouth in a bit of a smile.

"How long have you lived here?" I turned and leaned against his easy chair.

"This was my grandparents' home," he said. "I moved in after my last divorce."

"So we're both living in our grandparents' homes. What a couple of weirdos."

He straightened. "Speak for yourself." He walked toward me and stopped dangerously close. "I happen to like the traditional nature of Mackinac Island."

"Yeah," I said, my tone breathy. "Me too."

There was loud knocking at the door. It startled me and I had to work not to slosh my wine. "Are you expecting someone?"

"No," he said, his eyebrows turning down in the center. "Hang on."

The pounding continued. "Boss!"

Rex opened the door to find Brent standing on his porch. "What's going on?"

"Sorry to disturb you," Brent said, and took off his police cap. His gaze went from Rex to me and back. "You weren't answering your phone."

"I turned off the ringer," Rex said.

"Well, we got ourselves a bit of a situation," Brent said. His gaze flickered back to me nervously.

"What's going on?" Rex asked, and put his drink down.

"It's Trent Jessop," Brent said. "He's missing."

"How long?" Rex asked, his face settling into the serious flatness of a cop on duty.

"Paige came into the station in a panic. She said he was supposed to be at the Jessops' office this morning but never showed. She spent the day trying to get ahold of him."

"Did he get called to Chicago?"

"Yeah, no one's seen him leave the island," Brent said. "There was a note. It was addressed to Allie McMurphy."

Rex said something dark and dangerous under his breath.

I put my glass of wine down on an end table and wrapped my hands around my waist. "What did it say?"

"We didn't open it," Brent said. He looked at Rex. "We tried to get ahold of you. Then we tried to get ahold of Allie and Jenn said she was here with you."

"Do you have the letter?" Rex asked.

"I thought it was best to keep it at the station," Brent said.

"Good call." Rex grabbed his keys from a small container near the door. "Shall we go?" He put his hand on my back and guided me out the door.

"How is Paige?" I asked.

"She's not good," Brent said. "She said they had a fight the night before. It seems the last thing she said to him wasn't very nice."

"What did they fight about?" Rex asked.

"Something to do with the business," Brent said. "I have Lasko taking her statement."

"You don't think Paige had anything to do with Trent being missing, do you?" I asked.

"No," Brent said, his mouth in a tight line. "No."

"Taking statements starts the file," Rex explained.

"You don't have to wait twenty-four hours, do you?" I asked, suddenly horrified over what could happen to Trent if the killer had him that long. Thoughts of the last two dead men rose in my mind.

"No," Rex said. "Paige is a reliable reporter. If she is worried, then we'll start the case." Rex looked at Brent. "That said, check the airport and the ferries. Make sure he didn't just leave the island. Also, call Chicago and see if anyone knows where he might be." He looked at me. "When did you see him last?"

"When we found the last dead body," I said. "He was there." I looked at Rex. "Do you think the killer saw me talking to Trent? Is this some way to get me to play?"

"We can't know that," Rex said.

We arrived at the police station. The activity at the front desk was busy. The officers were on the phone, trying to track down Trent. Rex opened the door to the offices and we walked into a bustling hive. Paige sat in Rex's office, her face puffy from tears. She had a wad of tissues in her hand.

"Oh, Allie," Paige said, and stood. She hugged me. "I'm so worried. Have you heard from him?"

"No," I said, and hugged her back. "Sit," I said. "Can I get you something? Tea? Water?"

"I'll get her a water," Office Lasko said. She stepped out and spoke to Rex in low tones.

Paige held my hands and I took the chair beside her across from Rex's big desk. "Tell me what happened," I said.

"I just . . . we fought . . . Please tell me you saw him today."

"No," I said, shaking my head. "I didn't. Things have been crazy. I found Mr. Johnson's nephew dead. That was the last time I saw Trent. He was still trying to convince me to date him." I squeezed her hands. "I . . . I'm sorry."

"He came to me the next morning," Paige said. "He wanted me to agree to give up the island businesses." She looked at me, her face an expression of guilt. "I told him no. I thought he was asking because he didn't think I could do a good job with the businesses. I was insulted. I told him Father wouldn't have given them to me if he didn't believe I could do a good job."

"It wasn't that Trent didn't think you could do it," I said. "He was trying to convince me to see him again. I told him that I didn't want to date a man who was gone all the time. I don't want to live in Chicago. It doesn't make any sense for us to see each other anymore. He has a wonderful opportunity with your father's businesses . . ."

"Oh," Paige said, and sat back. "Oh." She slumped in her chair. "The idiot."

"I'm sorry?"

"He must have thought if he had the island businesses you would see him as a viable candidate."

"I told him not to do anything for me. I don't want to be responsible for anyone choosing between opportunities. You and Trent have so many opportunities now."

"I'm afraid I said some very mean things to him," Paige said. "I told him to get out and not come back. He left. It was the last time I saw him."

"Are you sure he didn't stay at one of the hotels?"

"Yes," she said, and dabbed at her tear-filled eyes. "I contacted all my managers. No one has seen him. It's as if he vanished off the face of the earth."

"We'll find him," I said.

"Officer Pulaski said there was a note," Rex said as he walked in the room, all lethal muscle and action hero–looking.

"Yes," Paige said. She pointed to an envelope on the top of his desk. "I found it wedged between my storm door and the front door." She looked at me. "I was confused because it has your name on it, not mine."

"Who would put a letter in your door with my name on it?" I asked.

"That's what I want to know," Paige said. Her grip on my hands tightened. "I don't even know if it has anything to do with Trent's disappearance. It simply seemed so out of place."

"May I open it?" Rex asked.

"Yes," I said.

Rex slid on a pair of gloves, grabbed a letter opener, and sliced through the envelope. A careful examination of the inside showed only a single piece of stationery. The stationery matched the envelope. It was cream-colored and seemed expensive.

He pulled out the letter and opened it.

"What does it say?"

Rex frowned. *"Why aren't you trying? I'm upping the stakes. You have forty-eight hours to find him. Nxa4 Nxe4 and white faces considerable difficulties."* He looked at me. "Sounds like he's still playing the chess game."

"Yes, he seems to be playing both sides."

"Hmm, both sides," Rex said. "Anyone trying to help you with this case?"

"Mr. Beecher," I said. "Sandy and Jenn. Why?"

"You said that the notes reference a chess game and it appears the killer is playing both sides."

"So it's someone who is helping me," I said, and sat back.

"What do they mean by forty-eight hours?" Paige asked. "What will happen in forty-eight hours?"

"I don't know," I said, and gritted my teeth. "I don't want to find out."

"Are you white?" Paige asked. "It says 'white faces considerable difficulties.'"

"I don't know. I guess. Black opened the game. But why would the killer take Trent? It doesn't make any sense. We established that he's been killing loner men. Trent is high-profile."

"Why stick the note in my door?" Paige asked.

"The killer must believe that Allie and Trent are dating," Rex said.

"You think he's trying to scare me? Because it's working."

"Things are escalating," Rex said. "I don't like it.

Both of you ladies need to consider staying with friends. Better yet, leaving the island."

"No!" we said at the same time.

"This is my home," I said.

"I won't be run off," Paige agreed, and stuck her chin in the air.

"I've just installed a very expensive security system," I said. "Paige, why don't you come and stay at the McMurphy? We have empty rooms."

"I don't want to leave my home."

"Maybe you should go," Rex said. "It would be easier for us to send a patrol by one place every hour to make sure you are safe."

"I don't know," Paige said. "What if Trent comes home?"

"He will text you," I said. "Or call. Won't he?" I asked Rex.

"Most likely," Rex said.

"Fine," Paige said. "If you think it's best. I did call Mother. She's flying up tomorrow."

"I wish she wouldn't," Rex said.

"There's no keeping her from her baby," Paige said. She crossed her arms in front of her. "I don't blame her." Tears rolled down her cheeks. "Trent means the world to us."

"Us, too," I said, and gave her a hug. "I'm sure Rex will do everything in his power . . ."

"He better," Paige said. She eyed me. "And what about you?"

"She's going to go home and take care of you," Rex said. His gaze was serious.

"Come on, Paige," I said. "Let's go get an overnight bag and take you to the McMurphy."

"Brent, walk the ladies to Paige's place," Rex said.

"We don't need an escort," I said. "We'll stick together."

"I think it's a good idea for you both to be under police protection for a while," Rex said. "Please."

"Fine," I said, and stood. I took Paige's arm and looped it through mine. "Keep us posted on any updates. Okay?"

"Fine," Rex said. "Leave the investigation to us, okay?"

"Sure," I said. "Come on, Paige, let's let them get to work." We left the station with Brent in tow.

Paige lived in a large Victorian painted lady. It was two stories high with turrets and a pointed roof. It was a classic cottage. We went up on the wraparound porch and Paige unlocked the door.

"Let me check it out first, ladies," Brent said. He hit the lights in the foyer and left us to wait while he checked the house. After a few minutes he stepped outside. "It's clear."

"Thank you, Brent," I said. "We'll be fine now."

"Are you sure? Paige?"

"I'm sure," Paige said, and touched Brent's arm. "Allie and I won't stay. I'll pack and we'll go to the McMurphy."

"Okay," he said. "Text when you arrive at the McMurphy."

"We will," she said, and we went inside. Paige locked the door behind him. "You're going to do something, right?"

"I—"

"What are you going to do? I want to help." She wrung her hands. "I can't just sit and wait while Trent might be tortured or killed."

"When was the last time you saw him?" I asked.

"We fought and he stormed out," she said. "It was just after dinner that night. I thought he'd go down to the stables and work off the mad." She hugged herself. "He would have come around to my point of view sooner or later. He was open-minded."

"He is open-minded," I said gently. "He really loves you. He wouldn't want to jeopardize that."

"I didn't realize he was trying to get you back," Paige said. "He should have told me."

"I think it's because I told him not to do it for me," I said, and rubbed her forearm. "Come on, let's get you packed."

We walked up the stairs that reached up from the square foyer. She had the bedroom in the front of the house with a rounded turret. She grabbed a suitcase from the top shelf of her closet and threw in a few clothes. Her room was done in soft whites and blues. The four-poster bed was cherrywood and matched the dresser. The blue-and-white rug on the wood floor held a floral pattern that was mimicked in the thick curtains.

The overall effect was one of understated luxury. Unlike my mishmashed bedroom with wood-paneled walls, her room was light and bright and clearly well designed. "You think Trent went to the stables," I said. "Did you check with the stable manager?"

"Yes," she said. "He never got to the stables. The thing is that I can't imagine anyone overpowering him. Trent was pretty streetwise and in good shape."

I could attest to his great shape. "Whoever took him had to know him," I said. "Trent would be on his guard with strangers."

"Yes, that's what I was thinking," she said, and flipped the closures on her bag. "Or it was a woman in distress. He's a sucker for a woman in distress."

I smiled wryly. "What if whoever took him had a woman ask Trent for directions or help in some manner?"

"He could have been preoccupied when they over-powered him and dragged him off."

I frowned. "Someone should have seen it. It's difficult to move a man of Trent's size and stature. People know him."

"That's the thing that gets me," Paige said. "I can understand how it might be easy to prey on loners. People who live on the fringe of society are rarely noticed, but Trent. Trent was noticeable."

"Is noticeable," I corrected her again. "Whoever has him knows the island very well. That makes me think the killer is a local. But who? I am going to look into who was in the chess club in 1956. I think it will help point out who the killer is."

"I would have noticed Trent missing sooner if it weren't for that darn television pilot being shot. Because I won the outside shoot, I was busy this morning as they filmed outside the stables and all the other properties."

"Wait," I said. "They're filming?"

"Yes, I've been running around like a madwoman these last two days making sure they shoot my properties in a good light."

I frowned. "But Dirk was at the McMurphy Sunday. He said the setup day was canceled because the equipment was damaged. I thought that meant the shooting would be behind schedule."

"They were shooting Monday morning, right on schedule. Things must not have been too badly damaged. Do you think the damage might have something to do with Trent being missing?"

"I don't know. It's just random, you know? You said you were busy running all over. Do you think anyone on the film crew might have seen Trent?"

"We could check with the director, Troy Morrow," Paige said. "He knows most of what is going on. If anyone saw anything, he would know."

"Is it too late?" I asked.

"No," Paige said. "He told me to call him anytime. I think they were working on a night shoot at the stables."

"Let's go," I said. Paige picked up her overnight case and we left her house, locking it carefully behind us. The streets were quiet. Most people were either at a bar with friends or tucked in for the night.

Mackinac was like a small town. Once the sun went down the streets seemed to roll up. We walked from the Jessop cottage to the stables. It was a quiet and uneventful walk. I kept my eye out for anyplace that someone could have gotten Trent. The road was strewn with houses and tiny yards. There were a few gaslights along the street to illuminate it.

"He left after dinner. It was dark, right?" I asked her as we crossed the street.

"As best I can tell," she said.

"They had to have somehow gotten him in an alley or someplace where people weren't or the light is low."

"The stables open to an alley," Paige pointed out.

"Yes, but people come and go in that alley. Unlike this one between Market and Main Street."

"Should we go down that alley and look?" Paige asked.

"I think we should wait until morning," I said. "We need to be as safe as possible until we can figure out who has taken Trent."

Chapter 23

"Oh, there are some bright lights." We came upon a small crowd of people bustling about.

"Yes, they are shooting," Paige said. She tugged me over to the edge. "That's Troy there." She pointed to a tall, thin, young man in tight, colored jeans and a graphic T-shirt.

"Will you introduce me?"

"Sure, come on." Paige wound her way around people who were working, adjusting lights and ensuring the actors had good makeup.

"Hey, Paige," one guy who held a camera said.

"Hi, Bill," she said. "How's the shoot?"

"Going well," he said. "Lighting for a night shoot is always interesting."

"Hi, Troy," Paige said as we approached the director. "This is my friend Allie McMurphy."

"Hi, Allie," Troy said, and stopped long enough to shake my hand. "What brings you by? Hey! Don't put that in the shot," he called out over my shoulder. "Sorry about that. We need to keep going if we want to use the same light."

"Paige's brother, Trent, is missing. Do you know if anyone saw anything?"

"No," he said. "I'm sorry to hear that, Paige. How old is he? Is he a young kid?"

"No, he's a full grown man," Paige said. "That's a concern. What with the murders."

"Murders?" He said and looked concerned.

"Yes, two men have been murdered in the last week or so," I said. "Are you sure you didn't see anything unusual?"

"Nothing out of the ordinary," he said. "We keep pretty much on task or it drives the budget up."

"Speaking of driving up the budget, I heard that you had equipment problems the first day you were supposed to shoot," I said. "Are things back to normal now?"

"Yeah," he said. "It's weird, but a couple of my boxes of equipment showed up crushed."

"What happened?"

He shrugged. "There's no telling. I put in a call to the studio and they flew out a couple of extras. We only lost a few hours of prep time."

"Hey, Allie," Dirk said as he saw Paige and me standing by Troy. Dirk was dressed in a police uniform that mimicked Rex's.

"Hi, Dirk," I said. "You look official."

"He should," Troy said. "Costuming ordered it from the same place the police get their uniforms."

"Wow," I said. "Cool."

"So, did you figure out who stuck your doggy in the basement?" Dirk asked.

"Rex thinks it was Ryan Tunison. We found the kid hiding in my attic," I said.

"That's creepy," Troy said. "Can we use that in a story?"

"Sure, go ahead," I said. "How long have you been shooting here?"

"About ten hours," Troy said. He removed his glasses and cleaned the lenses with the tail of his shirt. He put his glasses on and peered at me. "You ladies didn't come out here just to meet me."

"Hey, Paige," Jeffery said as he came up behind her. "What's the suitcase for?"

"She's staying with me for a while," I said.

"Everything okay?" Jeffery asked.

"My brother's gone missing," Paige said. "Rex suspects foul play."

"Is Rex investigating?" Dirk asked. He looked at Troy. "Dude, I could totally go see how he handles a missing person case."

"We're shooting, Dirk," Troy said with a long drawn-out sigh. "You've had your week. I'm sure you have enough material to play a good cop."

"I'll go, boss," Jeffery said. "I'd like to see how it plays out. It might help me with my episode rewrites."

"Yes, go," Troy said. "At this point I'd do anything to help you write that story."

"Well, if you hadn't refused my chess story," Jeffery muttered.

I drew my eyebrows together. "You had a chess story?"

"Yeah," he said. "In it the killer was a disgruntled chess player from the 1970s."

"It was a horrible idea," Troy said. "Who knows anything about chess these days? You'd be better off writing about a spelling bee. At least that would have cute kids in it."

"Hey, Allie, isn't Paige's brother your boyfriend?" Dirk asked. "You must be beside yourself with worry."

"I am," I said, and glanced at my watch. "Come on Paige, let's go. It's late."

"Do you girls need an escort home?" Dirk asked.

"We're good, thanks," I said.

"Come on, people, let's get the next shot prepped," Troy shouted. "Nice to meet you, Allie. My parents used to come and stay at the McMurphy every Fourth of July. I have good memories of the old place."

"Thanks," I said. "You should come by and see what we've done with this year's renovations."

"Perhaps I will," he said.

I put my arm through Paige's and tugged her away.

"Catch you later, Allie," Dirk said with a quick wave and then he waded back into the small crowd, taking his spot in front of the cameras.

"Did you find out what you wanted to?" Paige asked me.

"I'm not sure," I said as we walked. "I learned that Troy has been on the island before. That makes him a potential suspect. I'm convinced that whoever is behind all this knows the island. I also discovered you know Jeffery the writer."

"Sure, he's been on set most of the two days I was a part of. Why?"

"Didn't he say he had an episode about a chess game?"

"Yes," she said unsure.

"And he's been here since I got here in May. He would know about all the murder cases I've helped to solve." I tapped my chin thoughtfully. "That makes him a suspect."

"I just don't see how either man could have taken Trent. Neither is that tall or that strong-looking."

"You'd be surprised how little effort it takes to subdue a man if you know about leverage."

Paige shivered. "I'm worried."

"Me too," I said. We arrived at the McMurphy and I opened the front door with my key card.

"That's different," Paige said.

"Yes, I spent quite a bit of money to upgrade it. But I think it's worth it. Sooner or later everyone will go to the key cards. Real keys are simply too easy to replicate."

Jenn popped up on the landing. "Hey, kids," she said with a smile. "Is this going to be a slumber party? Allie, I thought you had a da—" She paused and looked at Paige. "A dinner thingy."

"Trent is missing."

"Oh, no!" Jenn said.

"Paige is going to stay with us for a few days," I said. I turned to Paige. "You're more than welcome to sleep on the couch in my apartment. Or we can book you into one of the empty rooms."

"I really don't want to be alone," Paige said.

"Good, then it's a slumber party," I said and we headed upstairs. "Paige, is there any place that you can think of that Trent might be? I mean, we do need to rule out the fact that he would be off somewhere on his own."

"He had a conference call this morning that he missed," she said as I unlocked the apartment door. Mal came rushing out, jumping up on me and then Paige and Jenn.

"That is definitely unusual," I said. "I know how punctual he is with business meetings."

"Daddy always told us that meetings need to start on time. If you can't be at a meeting five minutes ahead of time, then you might as well reschedule."

"Does Trent have an assistant? Someone who keeps track of his calendar and buys his plane tickets, et cetera?" Jenn asked.

"There is Doris," Paige said. "She's been working in the main office for over thirty years. She knows more about where someone in the business is than I would."

"Does she schedule your day for the island businesses?" I asked.

"No," Paige said. "She schedules larger meetings and travel."

"Larger meetings?"

"When I have meetings with my father or the board of directors," Paige said.

"Did Trent have any larger meetings on his calendar?" I asked.

"I don't know," Paige said with a frown. She put her suitcase down beside my couch. "But the note proves he was taken, right?"

"The note?" Jenn asked.

"There was a note in my door addressed to Allie," Paige said. "It said we have forty-eight hours."

"To do what?"

"Figure out who he is, I imagine," Paige said with a sigh. "It's driving me nuts."

"It's got to be someone who is familiar with the island," I said. "They know about the other murders I solved."

"And they were able to take Trent without anyone else seeing," Paige said.

"That freaks me out a little," Jenn said. "I'm glad you have a new security system."

"That's why I'm staying," Paige said. "There's safety in numbers."

"I agree there," I said. "Come on, I'll show you where the linens are." We got out towels and sheets and an extra blanket and came into the living area. Mal was excited for the newest member of the apartment. Mella kept aloof, preferring to watch everything from the safety of the cupboards.

"What did you find out about Ryan?" Jenn asked as she poured glasses of wine.

"Ryan?" Paige asked.

"He's a neighboring teenager who has been playing nasty pranks," I said as I made up the couch for her bed and briefly described the pranks. "I talked to Rex. Ryan says someone paid him to do it."

"Who would do that?" Paige asked.

"I wish I knew," I said. "The fudge business is a bit cutthroat and I do have the exposure of the reality television show. Maybe someone was trying to slow our success down? Anyway, they certainly have upset my guests."

"That doesn't sound like anyone who lives on the island," Paige said.

I straightened from the couch. "I suspect it's all connected."

"What's all connected?" Jenn asked, and handed us our wineglasses.

"The murders, Trent's disappearance, and the pranks," I said, and leaned on the breakfast bar that separated the kitchen from the living room. "Whoever is doing this seems to have targeted me."

"That's obvious," Jenn said. "But why take Trent?"

"He is in love with Allie," Paige said. "Whoever is orchestrating this must think that they are still an item."

"I keep coming back to Jeffery Jenas," I said.

"The writer?"

"Yes," I said. "He's been on the island all summer so he would know about anything that has been in the press."

"Like the murders you have solved," Paige said.

"And your love life," Jenn said. "Let's face it, the Jessops are always in the *Town Crier* society pages."

"It's not something we think about," Paige said with a shrug. "It's basically been like that my whole life. We don't pay any attention to it."

"But others do," Jenn pointed out. "It's a good place to start."

"It's too bad that Liz isn't here," I said. "That reminds me, I need to send her an e-mail and see how she is doing."

"What's going on with Liz?" Paige asked.

"Her grandfather, Angus, had a stroke. They're in Saginaw while he goes through rehabilitation."

"Wow, that's terrible. I wonder if Mother knew what was going on with Angus? She keeps track of everyone in Mackinac society."

"Speaking of society, I need to see if the seniors have any information on the latest murder or even Trent's disappearance. The thing about seniors is that people often overlook them. They often see things that others don't notice."

"Oh," Paige said, climbing onto the bar stool. "Maybe they saw whoever took Trent. Someone had to have seen something."

"I'm sure that Rex is talking to everyone in the neighborhood," Jenn said.

"Yes, interviewing witnesses," I said. "Or in this case, looking for witnesses." I sipped wine. "The killer has to have a place where they take the men before they kill them."

"What makes you say that?"

"Because they re-dress and stage the bodies," I said. "The men haven't been killed on the spot."

"Oh," Jenn said, her eyes widening. "That means whoever is doing this is able to move bodies without anyone the wiser."

"Exactly," I said with a frown. "How can you move a body?"

"Carry it?" Paige asked.

"Someone would notice them if they were hauling around grown men," I pointed out.

"Well, we know it's not in a car or van," Jenn said. "They aren't allowed on the island."

"So, carriage or freight wagon," I said, and sipped wine. The flavor of the red washed over my tongue. I felt my body relax a bit. I hadn't realized I was so uptight.

"Not carriage," Paige said. "All the carriages left on the island are run through our stables. Our drivers would know."

"But others have their own carriages," I said.

"True," Paige said. "So no commercial carriages."

"Who owns the freight wagons?" I asked. Freight wagons hauled things from the warehouses on the docks to various homes and businesses. They also often worked from the airport, hauling freight from the warehouses by the airport to various businesses.

"We do," Paige said. "Oh, and the Jenases still have a few wagons. But the competition has basically left the bulk of the freight business to us."

"Jenases?" I pounced.

"As in Jeffery Jenas?" Jenn's eyes grew wide.

"Jenas is a pretty common name," Paige said. "If he were related to the Jenases from the island he wouldn't be staying at the boardinghouse."

"Do the Jenases have much property on the island?" I asked. "Jeffery might be staying at Mrs. O'Connor's to throw us off the track."

"He does go for a lot of long walks," Jenn said. "We've already established that."

"He could be taking the men and keeping them on some back property that the Jenases own."

"I'll call my mother," Paige said. "She'll know anything there is to know about the Jenases."

Chapter 24

After Paige talked to her mom, there wasn't a lot more we could do. Mrs. Jessop was taking the first flight onto the island in the morning and she would bring with her any information she could find on the Jenas family. In the meantime we all settled in for as much sleep as we could catch.

The next morning, I snuck downstairs at 5 a.m. to make fudge. I always made coffee for the coffee bar first, in case any of the guests came down for coffee before the office's 7 a.m. opening. Mal followed me down and I gave her breakfast and a treat. Next stop was to take her out for a short morning walk. I put on her halter and leash, grabbed a navy jacket, and stepped out the back door and into the alley.

She went to her favorite grassy spot to do her business. Behind the McMurphy was the alley, the small grassy patch, a fence and the backyard of the hotel behind us. I checked my cameras. They were originally pointed at my doorways, but now I had them on each corner covering the alley from edge to edge of the building. A quick glance up the steps told me that

Paige and Jenn were still fast asleep. The lights were out in the apartment.

Mal tugged on the leash, pulling my attention away from the building.

"What is it, Mal?"

She pulled me to the mouth of the alley. In the early morning light, the crews that cleaned the roads of animal debris were out, shoveling the horse manure from the day before. It was the least glamorous job on the island. I watched how they drove a wagon ahead of them, then jumped out to scoop up thick shovels full of debris before tossing it into the wagon as they traveled over every inch of Main Street. It was important to keep the roads clean and clear of debris. It wasn't something most people thought of, especially in places that had cars.

But on an island where the main mode of transportation included horse-drawn vehicles, it was a constant upkeep. I recognized one of the shovelers. "Ryan?"

"Miss McMurphy," he said, and skillfully shoveled up a cold thick pile. He tossed it into the wagon and then came over to me with his shovel in hand. "I wanted to tell you I'm sorry for having scared you so badly, I wasn't thinking clearly."

"I heard someone paid you to do those nasty pranks," I said. Mal didn't go see him. Instead she jumped up on me as if to say, *please pick me up.* "You really scared me and my pup."

"I want to apologize," he said. "I didn't mean any harm."

"Hey, kid, let's go," the driver called to him.

"Gotta go," he said, and headed back to the wagon

in a trot to catch up. He turned and tugged on the brim of his cap. "I will make it up to you. Please let me."

"Ryan!"

"Coming, sir," he said, and ran after the nonstop movement of the manure wagon.

"Allie?"

I turned on my heel, startled by the sound of my name. Rex was walking by the end of the alley.

"Oh, Rex, you scared the heck out of me," I said with my hand to my heart. Mal had raced to him, tugging on the edge of the leash.

He frowned at me. "What are you doing outside by yourself at this hour? The sun isn't up yet."

"Mal had to go out to do her business," I said. "I'm not waking anyone else up just to take the dog outside." I frowned at him. "What brings you by this early in the morning?"

"It was my turn to go by the McMurphy and check that everything was okay," he said, and ran a hand over his face. "I'm sorry you didn't get to eat any dinner last night."

"It wasn't your fault," I said with a shrug. "How's the investigation?"

"We can't find anyone who saw Trent after he left the cottage."

"We were talking last night," I said. "Whoever took Trent had to have a vehicle of some sort to put him inside. There was no way anyone could drag Trent off by foot. He's too big and people would notice."

"Certainly a vehicle would make the most sense," Rex said.

"Since there aren't any cars, it has to have been a wagon. Paige said that all the carriages left working the streets belong to the Jessops' stables. So, unless it was a private carriage it was most likely a freight wagon."

"That makes sense," Rex said.

"Except that Paige tells us that the Jessops own most of freight wagons as well."

"True," Rex said, and crossed his arms over his chest. He was dressed in a freshly pressed uniform.

"Except—get this—there is a competitive freight wagon company owned by the Jenases," I said.

"And?" He drew his eyebrows together, his hat lowering over his eyes.

"I think the killer may be Jeffery Jenas, the writer from the television pilot," I said.

"I don't know," he said, shaking his head. "What makes you think he's the killer?"

"He's been on the island since May when I got here. So he had access to the information about the other cases I've helped solve. Whoever is the killer has been following my escapades since May."

"That is everyone who lives on the island," Rex said.

"But not everyone is trying to write mysteries for a television show," I said.

"True."

"The killer is clearly trying to prove he is better than I am," I said. "Why else create the notes? Why put people in the spots where the other murders happened? Jeffery has been trying to get ideas off me since I met him."

"Hmmm," Rex said. "What's the motive? To prove he's a better killer than you are an investigator?"

"Yes, I think so," I said.

"I don't know," Rex said.

"Fine, but don't you think it's strange that there are Jenases with freight wagons? Just the kind of vehicle that could transport bodies without much questions."

"Jenas is a common name," Rex said.

I frowned. "Fine, I need more evidence."

"No, I need more evidence," he said gently. "You need to let me find it."

"I've got a chess club meeting at the senior center, tomorrow. I'm going this afternoon to take the seniors some fudge and see if anyone wants to practice with me."

"I'll send someone to escort you," he said.

"What about Trent? The forty-eight hours are almost half over."

"I'm doing what I can," he said.

"The killer has to have a place where he can keep, torture, and kill people without anyone knowing."

"Yes," Rex said.

"The Jenases own property just past the airport away from most of the town."

"There are a lot of families who own property back there," he said. "It doesn't mean I can just go in and search places. I have to have proof to get a search warrant."

"Trent could be dead by then."

"Allie, let me do my job. I know what's at stake."

"Do you?" I asked.

"I do," he said. "Trent is a friend of mine."

"Right."

"What time are you planning to go to the senior center tomorrow?"

"I don't know for sure. I guess around one p.m."

"I'll send someone over to walk you there. Please don't go unless you have someone to accompany you."

"I'm not helpless, you know."

"I know," he said. "But you are directly involved with a killer. A killer who has murdered two grown men and taken a third. There is safety in numbers."

"Paige thinks the killer took Trent because he's my boyfriend," I said. "That means you are in danger, too."

"Because I'm your boyfriend?" he asked softly. The heat in his gaze gave me a shiver.

"Just remember that this guy is targeting me. Even though you carry a gun, it doesn't mean you're any safer than Trent was."

"And you don't want to see me hurt."

"I don't want to see you hurt."

"Good," he said. "Then you know how I feel."

I blew out a long breath. "Come on, Mal. Let's go. I have fudge to make." I looked at Rex. "Please look into the Jenases. If they have empty property, Trent could be there."

"We're looking into all of the empty properties on the island," he said. "Please be patient."

"The clock is ticking," I said. "I don't want to find Trent dead." Saying it out loud hit me like a ton of bricks. My heart went into my mouth. I did love Trent. I didn't want to lose him like that.

"Neither do I," Rex said. "You're not alone in this."

"Good to know."

I turned and took Mal back to the McMurphy. My heart squeezed. I realized that Trent meant more to me than I ever imagined.

* * *

It was ten in the morning when Mrs. Jessop entered the McMurphy. The woman was a force of nature. She stormed into the building. A five-foot-two-inch tornado in four-inch designer heels. Her blond hair was bobbed to a fine edge. Her clothes had the finishes of wealth, but old wealth where you didn't need to talk about money for everyone to know you were born with it.

"Allie McMurphy," she called my name and I stepped out of the fudge shop. "Where are my children?"

"Welcome, Mrs. Jessop," I said. "Paige is upstairs with Jenn Christensen. I haven't heard any word this morning on Trent."

Her face momentarily reflected anguish. Then she schooled her features into a mask of efficiency. "Yes, well, I understand you took Paige in so that she would be safe last night. Thank you for that, but I want my daughter now."

"I'll take you upstairs," I said, and wiped my hands on a towel, removed my apron, and left the fudge shop. "Sharon, please let Sandy know I'm upstairs if she needs me. Also call me if we get anyone who wants to purchase fudge."

"Sure," Sharon said, never looking up from her magazine.

Mrs. Jessop's mouth moved into a tight line when she saw my interaction with Sharon. "You have to watch some people," she said. "They are not necessarily as hard workers as one would hope."

I walked up the stairs, letting Mrs. Jessop trail behind me in her heels. "Sharon has generously volunteered to take Frances's place while my manager is out on her honeymoon. I'm grateful for her."

Mrs. Jessop let out an inelegant snort, which I

chose to ignore. The two flights up did not wind her. I imagined she spent a good part of her days on a treadmill. She was whip thin.

"I suggested Paige stay with me because I just put in a new high-tech security system," I said. "We have new door locks and cameras."

"Yes, I saw the signs," she said behind me. "I have already tasked my property manager with putting similar systems in all the Jessop properties. If Paige is going to live on this godforsaken island year-round then I want to know she is safe."

The door to the apartment flew open. Paige came rushing out. "Mama! I thought I heard you in the hallway." She hugged her mother, who hugged her back just as fiercely.

"Please come inside," I said to them both. "I'll make us all tea."

"Have you heard any news about Trent?" Paige asked her mother.

"The police won't say anything other than they are taking his disappearance seriously," Mrs. Jessop said.

"I saw Rex this morning," I said. "He told me that they are looking into all abandoned buildings on the island. But there aren't that many policemen available. Paige said you might know where the Jenases own property. We can check that first."

"I do," Mrs. Jessop said. She took a seat next to Paige on the couch. I put a teakettle on to boil and pulled out four cups and saucers.

"I have a map of the island," Jenn said, and went into her bedroom. She came out with a paper map and unfolded it. She spread it out on the coffee table. Mella hopped up on the table and sat down next to the map as if to supervise the expedition.

I poured hot water into the cups and put a tea bag in each, then arranged them on a tray with milk and sugar. I brought the tray into the living room and handed the tea out, letting each fix them as they liked.

"Thank you," Mrs. Jessop said after she took a sip of her tea. "This hits the spot. I had Sophie fly me out here. She said she has not seen Trent since he flew in the other day. So we know he has not been back to the airport."

Sophie was the private pilot for the Grand Hotel and other bigwigs who needed to fly from Chicago or Green Bay or even Detroit. Sophie was a good pilot and knew everyone who came and went via the airport—even the freight pilots.

"Does Sophie have any ideas as to where Trent might be?" I asked, and sipped my tea. The heat from the water nearly scalded my mouth.

"No," Mrs. Jessop said. "She was distressed by his disappearance."

"We all are," I said, and sat back in my Papa Liam's old chair.

"Let's look at the map," Jenn said, and pulled a pen out and uncapped it. She put her cup down and pulled the map toward her. "We know that Trent left your cottage, here." She circled the Jessops' estate. "You said you thought he was going to the stables?"

"Yes," Paige said.

"What way would he have traveled?"

"This way," Paige said, and outlined the streets that would have taken him from the Jessop house past the police station and on to the stables.

I leaned forward and studied the area. "It looks like someone could have taken him here, and here,"

I said, pointing to two alleys between the cottage and the police station.

"Why before the police station?" Jenn asked.

"If he had gone by the police station, someone would have seen him," I reasoned.

"Hmmm," Mrs. Jessop said. "And the alleys are the perfect place to hide a wagon and then it's simply a matter of getting Trent into the alley, jump him, and tuck him up into a wagon."

"None of those things are easy," Paige pointed out. "My brother's pretty savvy."

"What if the killer has a woman working for him?" I asked. Mrs. Jessop looked at me as if I had lost my mind. "It's not far-fetched," I said, defending the premise. "He hired Ryan to prank the McMurphy. What if he hired a woman to call for help? We all know that Trent can't resist helping a damsel in distress. Paige said so herself last night."

"True," Paige said.

"So you think that the killer hired a woman to call for help?" Mrs. Jessop said.

"Yes," I said. "Or the killer might have taken a woman and let her scream for help when Trent walked by."

"But if he didn't pay her, then he had to either take her too or she would have gone to the police."

"True," I said, and sat back. "I think he must have paid her somehow. The killer pulled the wagon into the alley. Then they see Trent coming from the cottage. The woman screams and Trent goes running."

"Straight into a trap," Jenn said, and used her blue pen to highlight a possible route.

"The killer hits Trent over the head, tosses him in the back of the wagon, and takes off with him down the other end of the alley."

"But if a woman screamed, others would have heard it and come running as well," Jenn pointed out. "These alleys are behind the police station but there are businesses and homes in the area."

"Right," I said, a little defeated.

"Unless," Paige said with a frown.

"Unless what?" I asked.

"Unless they were filming in the area. If they were filming, people might have assumed the sound was from the television actors."

"Oh, yes," I said. "What was the filming schedule that day? Does anyone know?"

"I have a copy of the schedule in my purse," Paige said, and got up. She went over to her bag and pulled out a thick set of papers. "Because I won the rights to the outdoor shoots, I get a copy of their schedule."

"Brilliant!" I said as she came back to the couch and set the papers down on the table. I picked them up and thumbed through them. The pages held a film schedule of day shoots and night shoots. They were in order by day. I thumbed back to Monday. "It looks like they were filming on Main near the Island Bookstore," I said, and Jenn put an *X* by the area. "Then they were filming in an alley." I looked up. "This is the alley behind the police station."

"Close enough that a woman screaming could have been interpreted as coming from the filming."

"You know," Jenn said. "The killer could have hired a woman off the film crew. Like a stand-in or something?"

"They have stand-ins?" I asked. I knew so little about filmmaking. "What about the lead actress? Is she on the island yet?"

"Bella arrived on Friday," Jenn said. "She's staying

at the Grand with most of the more famous members of the crew."

"Where are the others staying?" I asked.

"They are near Mrs. O'Connor's in Mission Point."

"So the not-so-famous members of the crew get staff quarters with the workers on the island, while the two main actors get nice suites at the Grand."

"Yes," Paige said. "The camera crew is pretty rowdy. They tell me it's because they're working fourteen- to sixteen-hour days. Then get up and do it all again the next day. Especially the makeup artists and camera crews. They have to be around to block the cameras and run them."

"Makeup artists?" I said. "I haven't met any makeup artists."

"Oh, there's Candy and Phillip," Jenn said. We all looked at her. "What?" she asked. "I like makeup."

"Makeup artists could come and go unseen," I pointed out. "Whereas stand-ins might be missed."

"True," Paige said.

"So let's say Candy is paid to pull Trent into the alley. Trent hears a woman in distress and goes running. He sees Candy, who looks scared to death. He stops and the killer hits him from behind and tosses him in the wagon. Then the wagon takes off. It will have to go away from the police station," I said, drawing a line in the alley.

"So where does it go next?" Paige said as she leaned over the map.

"It can't go toward Main Street. Someone would see it," I mused. "Most likely it headed to the other side of the island."

"It would go by the airport," Mrs. Jessop pointed out. "The Jenases own property here." She pointed to a place in line with where the wagon might go. "No one would think twice about a freight wagon going that way."

"We have two buildings to check out," I said, and looked up at the women. "Who's willing to go with me to see what's out there?"

All three raised their hands. "Good," I said. "Mrs. Jessop, you need to change into some shoes that you can walk farther in. I think we should go out in twos. Jenn and I can go and pretend we are taking Mal for a walk. Paige, you and Mrs. Jessop can take your suitcase and walk as if you are going back to your cottage. Leave the bag at your house and keep going. We can meet you here at the first building."

"Do you think anyone will get suspicious?"

"I doubt it," I said. "After all, who pays attention to a couple of girls walking a dog?"

"Or a mom bringing her daughter back home."

"Exactly."

"Let's do it," Mrs. Jessop said.

Now all we had to do was hope that Rex didn't keep too close an eye on the McMurphy. If he even suspected that I might try to look into the Jenases, he would do everything he could to stop me. I wasn't going to let that happen.

Chapter 25

Mrs. Jessop and Paige left first. They went out the front door and toward Doud's Market. Jenn and I waited fifteen minutes and then put Mal's halter and leash on her and left the McMurphy in Sharon's and Sandy's capable hands.

I turned up my collar as we stepped out. The wind blowing off the lake was chilly. Jenn also had a jacket on. We headed down the alley toward the police station. "I went to see Mr. Beecher the other day," I said.

"I heard he's been sick. How did he look to you?" Jenn asked as we turned down the street toward the alley where we suspected that Trent was taken.

"He said he was recovering," I said. "But he looked pretty pale. I worry about him. He seems quite alone."

"I heard he's not that alone," Jenn said.

"You did? How so?"

"He has a girlfriend."

"What? Who? Do I know her?"

"It's Mrs. Cunningham. Do you know her? She has red hair with two white streaks down the sides."

"Oh, the pretty woman who is in her late sixties?"

"Yes," Jenn said. "She is at the beauty parlor most

Fridays. I see her when I get my hair done. I caught her looking at him once when he walked by. The next time I went to get my nails done, I saw her talking to him before she came in for her hair appointment. After that conversation, she came in looking all glowy and such."

"How sweet," I said. "I would have thought I would have seen her when I went to check on him. But there was no sign of a woman in his life."

"Perhaps they are taking it slow?" Jenn suggested.

"Hello, ladies." I looked up to see Brent and Rex walking toward us. I frowned. We were passed the police station. Why were they here?

"Rex, Brent," I said. "What brings you out this way?"

"I could ask you that," Rex said.

"We're walking Mal," I said. "We did a mileage check. It's exactly a mile and a half to the airport from the McMurphy. So we walk it for extra steps."

"What are you guys doing here?" Jenn asked.

"We went to check a few empty properties by the airport," Brent said.

"Did you find anything?" I asked.

"Nothing," Rex said. "You two stay together and go fast, okay?"

"We'll be fine," I said. "You checked out the buildings, right?"

"Yes."

"Then there's nothing to worry over," I said.

"Right."

"Look, I've got my phone," I said, and pulled the smartphone out of my jacket pocket. "I will text you if we get in trouble."

"I guess I can't ask for anything else," Rex said.

"I could go with you," Brent said. "Make sure you're okay."

"We'll be fine," I said. "Really. Besides, it would help me feel better if you spent more time trying to find Trent than following me around. Have you learned anything since last night?"

"We've been able to discount some things," Rex said. "But that's about it."

"Did you look at the Jenases? Maybe question Jeffery?"

"The writer?" Brent asked. "Why do you think he has anything to do with this? Isn't he slight? How could he have taken Trent? Jessop is a pretty substantial guy."

"The Jenases own some of the freight wagons," I said. "They would have access to a way to move bodies. Jeffery is a Jenas. He's most likely related."

"Jenas is a pretty common name," Brent warned.

"But he could be related," Jenn pointed out. "He has been here the entire season and would know about the murders Allie has helped solve."

"We're checking into his background," Rex said. "You two aren't sleuthing, are you?" He narrowed his eyes.

"No," I said, and lifted my chin. "We're walking Mal." I looked down to see my puppy sitting beside me, looking from me to Rex and back. "Well, we'd better get to it," I said. "Come on, Jenn."

"Bye, guys," Jenn said and we took off toward the building where we were to meet Mrs. Jessop and Paige. We walked a couple of blocks before Jenn glanced over her shoulder. "Do you think they bought it?"

"I'm not sure," I said, and looked over my shoulder. "They don't seem to be following us."

"Good" Jenn said.

"Why did you mention the Jenases to them again?" I asked. "Rex is pretty smart. He might figure it out and stop us."

"I thought they should know in case something happened to us."

"Nothing is going to happen," I said. "We're going to go look in an abandoned building and rule it out. That's all. No mess, no fuss, no danger."

"Got it," Jenn said. We power walked our way down the street. When we hit the place where we were to meet the Jessops, I stopped short.

"I'm surprised Paige and Mrs. Jessop didn't beat us here," Jenn said.

"Maybe they came across someone like we did," I suggested. "You never know who is going to want to stop and ask questions. The fact that Paige carried a suitcase might have opened some eyes and gotten tongues wagging."

"What if they don't show up?" Jenn asked.

"I'll give them fifteen minutes and then I say we go see Paige at the cottage. Does that work for you?"

"Sounds good to me."

We didn't have to wait long before Paige and her mother showed up. It was clear they had both changed clothes. They were wearing matching black slacks and black shirts. This time they both wore black flats and had their hair pulled back. They reminded me of an old Audrey Hepburn film.

"Wow, you two even have breaking and entering clothes," Jenn teased.

"We brought pepper spray," Mrs. Jessop said, and pulled a small can out of her pocket. "In the off chance we run into the killer."

"Let's hope that doesn't happen," I said. "Where are we going exactly?"

"They have an old storage barn about a block from here," Mrs. Jessop said. "I thought we would need to look there first."

"I have flashlights," Paige said. She held out two flashlights.

"Can I have one?" I asked.

"Sure," Paige said, handing me a flashlight.

"I'll use my phone," Jenn said.

We walked the two blocks through the wooded area. The old storage barn was run-down and the windows appeared to be covered in dust. There were tall weeds growing up around the building.

"It looks abandoned. There aren't any bikes near the building," I said.

"Good," Jenn said. "That's what we want, right? A building where the killer might be holding the men."

There was an abandoned wagon with weeds growing in the back of it in the area that might have once acted as a parking lot. We walked up to the front of the building and looked in the windows. The front doors were locked with a heavy chain and a padlock. Mal padded around the building with her nose to the ground.

I peered in the window next to the door, but it was coated in dirt and hard to see anything but my own reflection. "I'll go around to the left if you ladies want to take the right. If the killer is using the building, then there has to be some proof that they have been coming and going in and out of here."

"I'll go with Allie," Jenn said.

"We'll meet you around the back," Mrs. Jessop said.

We walked with Mal through the overgrown shrubs

and around the side of the building. It was a wood structure and clearly had once been a busy place where wagons had been stored. The windows on the sides were up pretty high. There wasn't any evidence of recent use.

We walked as quietly as possible to the back where we saw the Jessops. The back door looked as locked and undisturbed as the front.

"Did you see anything?" I asked.

"Nothing," Paige said. Mal jumped on her and she patted the dog.

"If they are using this building, then they are great at covering their tracks," Mrs. Jessop said.

"You said they had a couple of buildings," I said. "Where are the other buildings?"

"There's a small one right behind here through those trees," Mrs. Jessop said. "I didn't think of it first because it doesn't have a nice drive area. It's been abandoned longer."

We walked back through the strip of woods that separated the two buildings. The second building came into view. It was low slung and weathered. The roof looked as if it had seen better days. The drive was just a two-track trail.

"What was the building used for?" I asked.

"This was a small mill at one time," Mrs. Jessop said. "They would cut local pine and maple for wood to build furniture and such."

"It looks like it hasn't been used in decades," Jenn said.

We approached the building and I noticed a pair of wagon wheel tracks in the dry earth. "Look," I said, and pointed to the tracks. "Someone has been here in the last couple of days."

"We need to be especially careful," Jenn said. "They might still be around."

I clung to my phone. Mal pulled on her leash as we walked up to the building. This one had a wraparound porch. The doors were locked but not chained. I made a motion for us to split up and look at the back of the building. The sides were overgrown with weeds and shrubs. A mulberry tree was growing crooked from the side.

We got to the back of the building and a light was on over the door. Wide-eyed, I put my finger to my lips and we all crept toward one another and the back of the building. There were definitely signs of someone having been there. I didn't see a bicycle or even a wagon nearby, but that didn't mean no one was home.

I tried the door. It was locked. We peered in the window. It looked like a large room. There was a chair in the middle of the building and what looked like a rope. I tried the window and it creaked open. My heart rushed in my chest. Did anyone hear the sound of the window?

"What are you doing?" Paige whispered.

"We need to get inside," I said, and handed her Mal's leash.

"That's breaking and entering," Paige went on.

"I would argue that it's entering as the window is unlocked and hardly broken." I tugged the window all the way open and pushed my body through. I landed with a thud inside the building. I held my breath. I didn't hear anyone. That was probably good, except it would have been better to find Trent inside.

I went around to the back door, dodging a table full of old rusting tools. Opening the door, I let the others in. "It seems like no one's here," I said. "Be careful as you look around."

"Someone was definitely here," Jenn said, and pointed toward the chair in the center of the room with rope dangling from the bottom. There was also rope hanging down from the ceiling. The room, with its poor light and strange marks on the floor, had an eerie, sad quality.

"Is it blood?" Jenn asked.

I examined the small pool of red near the chair. "Could be," I said. I took a few pictures and put my foot near the spot to show size.

"It looks fresh," Paige said. She reached down as if to run her fingers over it.

"Don't touch it!" I warned. "It could be evidence and we don't want to contaminate it."

"Up close it doesn't look dry. That means it's not too old."

"I'm calling the police," Mrs. Jessop said. "This place looks like a crime scene."

"I agree," I said. I let Mrs. Jessop call Rex. Let him get mad at her, not me. Meanwhile I continued my investigation of the building. There were tools inside and a couple of old freight wagons. It could be the spot where the murders happened, but there didn't seem to be any sign of Trent.

Rex and Brent came up to the porch and inside. "Ladies, what are you doing here and how did you get inside?"

"The door was unlocked," I lied.

Rex gave me a slant-eyed look. I crossed my arms over my chest. "After I opened it," I specified. "I came in the window, which was also unlocked."

"Allie . . ."

"Look, it's clearly a crime scene," I pointed out. "It's why we called you."

"Then you ladies have been tramping on possible evidence," Brent said. "Respectfully, you should all step outside and let us take a look at things."

"I'll step outside," Mrs. Jessop said. "But I won't be lectured. My son is missing and I'm going to do everything in my power to find him. If you don't like it, you can lump it." She humphed, turned on her heel, and stalked out.

I followed behind. Paige paced outside the front door with Mal on her leash. "This is ridiculous. Trent is not here. What are we missing?"

"I don't know," I said with a frown. I left Jenn to comfort Paige and checked the outside of the building again. It was then that I noticed the door to the cellar. It was odd for an old building to have a cellar. Especially since it was a place of business and not a home. I jiggled the lock on the door. It was a heavy-duty padlock. I thought I heard a sound coming from the basement so I called for Rex. "Rex!"

Jenn came running. "What is it?"

"There's a basement," I said. "This lock looks new and I thought I heard something."

Jenn banged on the door and we both held our breath. There was a faint banging in response. She knocked five times with the old "Shave and a haircut" call. We both pressed our ears to the door and held our breaths. Finally, we heard the two-knock reply.

We jumped back and looked at each other. "Someone's down there," Jenn said.

"Rex!" I called again, and went hurrying to the front of the building. Rex came out with Brent and the Jessops in tow.

"What? Are you okay?"

"We found a cellar door," I said, and hurried toward the door. "There's a new lock on it and we think someone's down there." I stopped in front of the door and pointed.

Rex studied it and tried to open the door. "What makes you think someone's down there?"

"We did five knocks and there was a return of two knocks," Jenn said.

"Try it," I said.

Rex knocked in sequence. We all held our breath waiting for a reply. It came weakly. Two knocks.

"See!" Jenn and I said at the same time.

Rex glanced at Brent. "Do we have any bolt cutters?"

"In the ambulance," Brent said.

"Dispatch," Rex said into the walkie on his shoulder.

"This is Charlene," came the reply and I felt my heartbeat pick up.

"We need an ambulance sent to Forest Drive," Rex said. "Make sure they have bolt cutters."

"The ambulance is on its way," Charlene said. "Is everyone okay?"

"We may have a person in distress," Rex replied. "We'll know more once the bolt cutters are here."

I looked at Rex. "Please tell me we don't need a warrant."

"There's probable cause," Rex said. He went and

found a large rock and hammered away at the padlock, his muscles bulging and flexing while he worked. We could hear the sirens blaring in the distance as one of the few motorized vehicles on the island navigated the narrow streets. One more bang and the lock popped open. Rex and Brent opened the door and peered into the darkness. "Hello? Is anyone down here?"

A weak male voice called, "Help."

Chapter 26

Rex and Brent went down with flashlights leading and guns drawn. I picked up Mal and hugged her tight. Paige and her mom moved to the mouth of the basement. We all held our breath as it seemed to take forever for Rex and Brent to come up. The ambulance arrived as we saw Brent emerge from the darkness.

"Is it Trent?" I asked.

"Is he okay?" Paige asked. Mrs. Jessop covered her mouth.

Rex emerged out of the darkness with a grim expression. A man was leaning heavily against him, his face dirty. He looked up and I felt immediate disappointment. It was Dirk Benjamin.

"Dirk?" I asked.

"We got the call to bring bolt cutters," George Marron said as he strode up to us, cutters in hand.

"No need," Brent said. "Rex got the lock open."

"This man needs water and care," Rex said as he practically dragged Dirk up the steps. George helped Rex take Dirk to the back of the ambulance.

"What was he doing down there?" I asked.

"Was anyone else down there?" Paige asked.

"He was tied to a chair," Brent said. "It looked as if it was the place where the killer might have tortured the last two men."

"What about Trent?" Mrs. Jessop asked.

"There wasn't anyone else down there," Brent said. "I'm sorry."

Mrs. Jessop collapsed against Paige. I rushed over and helped her to the ground.

"Was it the killer?" I asked Brent. "Did Dirk say?"

"Rex is getting his statement now," Brent said. "I'm going to call Shane. We need a crime scene kit out here." He stepped away from us to make the call.

"Don't panic," I said. "Just because we didn't find him doesn't mean bad things have happened."

"But the killer has moved on to this Dirk fellow," Mrs. Jessop said with a tiny sob. "It can only mean one thing."

"Don't say it out loud," I said, and put my hands up in a *stop* motion. "I'm not going to even go there unless I see it with my own eyes."

I left Mal with the ladies and stormed toward Rex. He was talking to Dirk, who looked bewildered and in shock. "What about Trent?" I asked. "Dirk, did you see Trent at all?"

"Hold on," Rex said, and put a flat palm out against my shoulder. "I'm taking his statement and George is going to give him care."

"But Trent is still out there," I said, and waved my hand toward the trees.

"We need to deal with one thing at a time," Rex said. "Allie, go sit with Jenn."

George had Dirk on a stretcher and was administering IV fluids. "Dirk, did you see Trent?" I asked.

Rex put his hands on my shoulders and turned me around to face the building. "You've done a good thing here," he said. "Don't mess it up. Go sit with Jenn. See to Mrs. Jessop. I will debrief you when I can." He walked me toward Brent, who nodded and took my arm and guided me back toward the other women.

"It's not personal, Allie," Brent reassured me. "We have procedures for a reason. We need to see to Dirk's safety and the safety of you and the others."

Shane pulled up on a bicycle and parked it. He pulled his CSI kit off the back of the bike and walked toward Rex. I watched as they talked and then Shane put on gloves and headed down the basement staircase.

I turned to Jenn. "Shane must have been on the island to get here so fast."

"I don't know," Jenn said with a shrug. "He's been ignoring me this week."

"What? Why?"

"Because I leave Saturday."

"Oh," I said, and hugged Jenn. "I'm sorry."

"Thanks," she said, and hugged me back. "I didn't want to say anything because of what's going on with Trent and this killer and everything. I mean, it just seemed so trivial."

"Shane not talking to you is not trivial," I said. "Is he going to let you say good-bye?"

"I hope so," Jenn said. "I've tried to get him to come see me Friday night. One last time before I go. I want to plan when I will see him next. I need to prove to him that out of sight does not mean out of mind."

"That's really smart," I said. "It will show him you are serious about your relationship."

"I am serious," Jenn said.

"I'm done with waiting around," Mrs. Jessop said, and stood. "All of this is not helping us find Trent."

I stood with her. "I agree. Let's go see Rex." Everyone got up and we walked to Rex, who stopped us before we got to the ambulance.

"Ladies, what is going on?"

"We want to know if Dirk saw Trent," Mrs. Jessop said.

"He's not in any condition to tell us," Rex said.

"Is there any proof that Trent was in that basement?" Paige asked.

"We only have twenty-four more hours to find him," I pointed out.

"I will go through every empty building on Mackinac if that's what it takes," Mrs. Jessop said.

"Ladies, please," Rex said. "Calm down. We need to process this scene for clues. Right now we don't have any real information."

"Dirk knows something," I said. "I think we can presume he was a victim. Who did this to him? Let's find out and see if we can find Trent."

"This is a Jenas property," Mrs. Jessop said. "Go and arrest that writer, Jeffery Jenas. He has to know something."

"Hang on now," Rex said. "As much as I'd like to, I'm not arresting anyone just yet. To begin with we have no proof that Jeffery Jenas has anything to do with this. Next, it's not safe for you to go running around the island breaking and entering."

"Trent doesn't have much time," I said desperately. "We have to find him."

"You need to go home," he said.

"What about the other properties here?" I asked, waving my hands toward the other buildings. "They're locked, too. He could be in there."

"I will check the outsides of the buildings," he said. "But I don't have a warrant to go busting into every locked warehouse on the island." He stared straight at me. "Neither do you."

"Fine," I said.

"Good," he said.

"What?" Mrs. Jessop said in a strangled voice.

"We're going to go now," I said, and put my arms through hers and Paige's. "Come on, Mal." I pulled at her leash. "We'll be at the McMurphy."

"We will?" Paige asked.

"We will," Jenn said, and joined us.

"I'll be by later this evening," Rex said. "I need to take your statements."

"Will you tell us about your findings?" I asked.

"If I can," he said. "This is an ongoing investigation."

"Right," I said. "Come on, ladies, let's go home."

"But—" Paige started.

"We're going," Jenn said, and steered Paige down the drive. We walked to the street and turned out of sight of the police. "Okay, Allie, what's the plan?"

"We need to go see Jeffery Jenas," I said.

"Oh," Mrs. Jessop said, her eyes growing wide. "Of course."

I nodded. "Sometimes the best thing to do is to let Rex go about his investigations."

"But that doesn't mean we quit with ours," Jenn said.

"Where is Jeffery Jenas?" Paige asked. "Do we know?"

"Well, I don't think they are shooting today," I said. "It's pretty clear since Dirk was taken." I frowned. "Why didn't Troy say anything about losing his star for the day?"

"Maybe it was a break in the schedule," Paige suggested. "Sometimes it takes a while to move the sets. Especially with live backgrounds. I think they planned on filming on the docks tomorrow."

"So the film crew should be working setting up and tearing down," I said. "Maybe Jeffery Jenas is working with the crew or the director on the next shots."

"It could be," Paige said.

"If not, the crew should know where to find Jeffery," Mrs. Jessop said.

"Yes," I said. "Let's go down to the docks."

"Let's stop by the McMurphy and drop off Mal," I said. "I don't want to drag her to the docks."

We hurried down toward Main Street, passing the police station and the alleys where we thought Trent might have been taken. I took a moment to look down each alley that we passed in the off chance there was something we missed. Then we dropped Mal off at the McMurphy and headed toward the docks.

The area was bustling, but that was not new. Even on the slowest days the docks teamed with activity. It was one of two spots where freight and people were brought on and off the island. The crew was a third of the size that it was the last time I saw them. They seemed to be talking about staging and setting up and tearing down equipment.

"Troy," Paige called the director as we approached.

"Paige, how are you today?" he asked as he came flying over and gave her a kiss on the cheek.

"I've been better," Paige said.

"That's right, I heard about your brother," Troy said. "I'm sorry. Is there any news?"

"Not really," I said.

"Troy, you remember Allie," Paige said.

"Yes, of course, the girlfriend and muse for my starlet." He came over and gave me a short hug. "Who's this?" he asked as he addressed Mrs. Jessop.

"This is my mother," Paige said. "Mom, Troy is the director."

"Nice to meet you, young man," Mrs. Jessop said. "I hope you are giving us our money's worth in exposure."

"Yes, ma'am," he said with a nod. "We are doing all but the dock shots at a Jessop property."

"Good."

"Can I ask something?" I said. "Why isn't Dirk shooting today?"

"Oh, this is a tear down and set up day," Troy said. "Dirk will be coming in later tonight to do some night work and then we'll work here all day tomorrow."

"Have you talked to Dirk lately?" Jenn asked as she stepped forward.

"Hello," Troy said, and took her hand and kissed it. "And you are?"

"Jenn Christensen," she said with a blush. "Allie's and Paige's friend."

"She works with me at the McMurphy," I explained. "When was the last time you saw Dirk?"

"I saw him last night," Troy said. "I left him at the Nag's Head Bar. He was pretty much in his cups. I figured he'd spend today sleeping it off or doing more research with your police detective. Why?"

"We just discovered him tied to a chair in the basement of an abandoned building," Mrs. Jessop said.

"Excuse me?" Troy looked shocked and distressed. "What are you saying?"

"Someone tried to kidnap your star," I said. "We were looking for Trent when we found him."

Troy cursed under his breath. "Is Dirk okay?"

"Yes," I said. "We think so. They were taking him to the clinic to check for dehydration."

"Alice!" Troy called over a tall thin blonde.

"Yes, sir?"

"Who is in charge of Dirk today?"

"That would be Simon, sir," Alice said.

"Simon!"

"Yes, sir." A young man came barreling around the building.

"Are you in charge of Dirk today?"

"Yes, sir."

"When was the last time you saw him?"

"Last night, sir, why?"

"It seems our star was kidnapped." Troy pulled on his hair until it stood up on end. "When were we going to find out? When shooting started and you couldn't find him? What am I paying you for?"

"To take care of Mr. Benjamin," Simon said. He was pale as a ghost. "I thought he was sleeping it off, sir. Really."

"Where is Dirk now?" Troy asked us.

"They took him to the clinic," I said.

"Get down to the clinic and make sure our leading man is okay," Troy ordered.

"Yes, sir," Simon said.

"You are darn lucky nothing happened to him," Troy said. "You would never work in this business again."

"Yes, sir," Simon said, and took off running.

"Was there a note?" Jenn asked.

"A note?" Troy asked.

"Yes," Paige said. "When they took Trent, they left a note for Allie."

"Alice," Troy called.

"Yes, sir?"

"Did we get a note or message?"

"Mail just came, sir." Alice came over bringing a stack of letters. She handed them to him. "I'll get you some more coffee."

Troy went through the letters. "Junk, junk, junk . . . wait. This one is made out to Allie McMurphy." He held it out.

"That's me," I said. I took the envelope and opened it carefully. Inside was a single piece of paper.

"What does it say?" Paige asked.

I pulled the letter out and looked at it. It was typed neatly. *"How many more need to die? I thought you were better at this. F1 g3 Now Byrne is hopelessly entangled in Fischer's mating net."*

"What does it mean?" Jenn asked.

"I think it means the killer is closing in on me."

"Does it say anything about Trent?" Mrs. Jessop pulled the paper from my fingers.

"Not that I can tell," I said with a grim sigh.

"Have you seen Jeffery Jenas today?" Jenn asked Troy.

"Jeffery? He's back at his room putting the finishing touches on the last two episodes. Why? Was he kidnapped, too?"

"We suspect he might be involved in the murders," I said.

"Jeffery? Our Jeffery? No way. The dude is dark yes, but he's a writer. If they are going to mess with anyone's head they do it in writing. You know?"

"Thank you for the information," Jenn said. She put her arm through mine. "Come on, ladies, we have a meeting with a writer."

We left the crew to their shoot setup and walked down Main Street four across with our arms interlocked. We didn't have to talk; we all knew where we were headed—to Mrs. O'Connor's boardinghouse.

It didn't take long to walk the half mile or so to Mission Point and the white boardinghouse with black shutters. Mrs. Jessop charged ahead. She knocked on the door, tapping her foot. She knocked again and Mrs. O'Connor opened the door. "Yes? Oh, Mrs. Jessop. What can I do for you?"

"We need to speak to your boarder. The writer," Mrs. Jessop said in a clear, crisp tone.

"You mean Jeffery?" Mrs. O'Connor said. "I'm afraid he's out."

"How long has he been out?" I asked.

She frowned, drawing her eyebrows down and pursing her lips. "He left shortly after breakfast. For his daily walk, you know."

"When do you expect him back?" Mrs. Jessop asked. She glanced at her watch. "It is late afternoon."

"He is out longer than usual," Mrs. O'Connor said. "He usually comes back for lunch and works for a few hours before his night walk."

"Do you know where he goes when he goes for these walks?" I asked.

"Not really," Mrs. O'Connor said. "I never really thought about it. I figured he was going to a coffee shop or wandering the woods for ideas."

"Does he ever do anything suspicious?" Jenn asked.

"What do you mean 'suspicious'?" she asked. Then she studied us a moment. "Why don't you ladies come inside."

We all stepped into the wide living room of the boardinghouse. The living room had several chairs, a couch, and an assortment of small tables covered with doilies. There was a fire in the fireplace. The living area opened to a large dining room with a sideboard. Mrs. O'Connor disappeared into the kitchen. I stood and looked at the pictures on the walls. They were all original oil paintings.

"My sister painted those," Mrs. O'Connor said.

I turned to see her walk into the living room with a tray full of cups and saucers and a pot of tea. "She is quite talented."

"Was," Mrs. O'Connor said. She sat and poured the tea distributing cups to all of us. "Now tell me what all this worry about Mr. Jenas is all about."

"My son, Trent, is missing," Mrs. Jessop said. Her hands shook slightly as she lifted the cup of tea to her mouth.

"I heard about that," Mrs. O'Connor said. "Terrible thing that. Do you think that Mr. Jenas had anything to do with that?"

"We went out investigating," I said. "We discovered Dirk Benjamin in the basement of an abandoned building tied to a chair. The building was owned by the Jenases. We wondered if Jeffery was related to anyone on the island."

"You think Jeffery has something to do with all this?" Her eyes grew round with concern. "Surely not." She put her cup down in the saucer in her lap. "You think I might have a killer living under my roof?"

"Whoever is doing this has to have some connection to the island," I said. "They seem to know about every case I've helped solve this season."

"And you think it is Mr. Jenas because he's been here since May first?"

"It could be," I said. "It does seem to be more than a coincidence that his last name is Jenas and Dirk was found in the basement of a building owned by Jenases."

"Well," Mrs. O'Connor said back, and put her hand on her throat. "This is most distressing. I . . . I don't know what to think."

"Does Mr. Jenas ever talk about playing chess?" Jenn asked. "Or maybe he followed Bobby Fischer, the chess master?"

"Why, he wrote a biography of Mr. Fischer," Mrs. O'Connor said. "It did quite well from what I understand."

"We need to tell Rex," I said, and got out my phone.

"Why does his book about Mr. Fischer matter?"

"The killer has been leaving me clues about an old game of chess played by Bobby Fischer."

"Oh dear, that does sound suspicious. What can the police do?" Mrs. O'Connor asked.

"Keep an eye out for Mr. Jenas," I said.

"Am I safe if he comes back here?" she asked, her face suddenly pale.

"I think so," Jenn said, and patted Mrs. O'Connor's back. "The killer has been only harming men."

"Who would have thought. A killer in my home."
She hugged herself. "Terrible."

"We'll stay with you until the police come," Jenn
said.

I glanced at the clock on the wall. Time was running
out for Trent.

Chapter 27

"We've got everyone we can spare looking for Trent and Jeffery Jenas," Rex said later that evening. "I need you ladies to stay safely at the McMurphy."

"You don't have that many resources," Mrs. Jessop said as she sat on the settee in the lobby. "You need us out looking. I know you have a man at Mrs. O'Connor's. You have to have at least two on duty at the station. That only leaves two to search the island. My son only has a few hours left."

"That is if the killer is to be believed," Rex said.

"How can we not believe a man who has killed twice already? Why, if we hadn't gone looking earlier today Mr. Benjamin could have been the next victim," Paige said.

"I understand that you are feeling helpless at the moment," Rex said, his tone calm. "You have every right to worry, but if you leave here I can't guarantee your safety."

"I'll call my property manager," Mrs. Jessop said. "He can escort us."

"Please give us more time," Rex said.

"There isn't any time left," Paige said.

I pulled Rex away from the group. "What did Shane find at the Jenases' basement? Was there any proof that Trent had been down there?"

"No," Rex said. "There was blood at the scene but we won't have lab tests for a few weeks. We can't take a sample and confirm the blood belongs to Trent without any samples from Trent. It doesn't work that way."

"How did they take Dirk?"

Rex's mouth went into a flat line. "He says he stepped out of the Grand Hotel and heard a scream. He went to investigate and the next thing he knew he woke up in the basement tied to the chair."

"Does he know who took him?"

"He said he never got a look at the guy, but he has to be pretty big to haul Dirk down those basement stairs."

"Maybe there were two men," I suggested. "I mean, it has to be difficult for one man to haul these dead bodies around."

"It's a possibility," Rex said. "We've been looking into it."

"Someone is working with Jeffery Jenas," I stated. "Do you know who?"

"I don't know for sure it is Jenas," Rex said. He ran his hand over his head "I need proof, Allie."

"I understand," I said. "Let me talk to Dirk."

"He went back to his hotel. I think his director has people staying with him."

"There was a note for me in the mail on set," I said. I pulled out the letter. "Whoever is doing this expected me to go looking for Dirk. I think this is where he made a mistake."

"What do you mean?"

"I mean, so far the killer has been copying murders I solved and picking on the things I love—the McMurphy, Mal, and Trent."

"You love Trent?" he asked, his face strangely composed.

"You know what I mean."

"Do I?"

I yanked at my hair. "You know as much as I do."

"Let's go back to your point."

"My point is that I don't have any reason to care about Dirk."

"Maybe they read that story in the tabloids where you went on a date with Dirk."

"I think they are getting desperate. They want me to figure out who they are and they are reaching for straws. It might be a sign that they are cracking."

"What do you think talking to Dirk will do?"

"I don't know, but I'd like to find out."

"Allie, Trent could already be—"

I put my finger on his mouth to not hear the word that was about to come out. "Don't say it out loud."

"Allie . . ."

Tears filled my eyes. "It's Trent."

"You still care for him."

I swallowed my tears and dashed the wetness from my eyes.

"Come on, then. I'll walk you over to the Grand."

"I'll get my jacket." Mal followed me to the hooks and begged to go for a walk with me. "I'm sorry, baby, but you need to stay and keep Jenn and Paige company. Okay?" I patted her head and put on my jacket. "I'll be back soon," I said to the group.

"I've called my manager," Mrs. Jessop said. "I'm going out with him to look for Trent."

"I can't keep you safe," Rex said.

"We'll take our chances."

Rex escorted me out of the McMurphy. The sun had set and Main Street was cool and quiet. The island was usually quiet after the tourists left for the day. But the off-season made the place feel positively cozy. The walk to the Grand was about a half mile. We walked in comfortable silence.

"I'm sorry about Trent," he said.

"I've got to find him," I said, and crossed my arms over my chest. "I can't live with the idea that this might be my fault."

"Stop right there," Rex said, and stopped me in my tracks. "None of this is your fault. It's the fault of the man or men who are committing the crime."

"I just . . . What if it's too late?" I shivered and tears rolled down my cheeks. "It feels too late."

Rex grabbed me and hugged me hard against his chest. "We'll deal with that when it happens. Okay?"

"Okay," I said, and wiped my face. "Come on, time's ticking."

"Do you really think Dirk can help?"

"I certainly hope so."

The Grand Hotel was quiet. There was a receptionist at the desk and a bellhop at the door.

"Hello, Officer Manning," the receptionist said as she came out from behind the desk. "What can we do for you this evening?"

"We'd like to talk to Dirk Benjamin," Rex said. "I know his room number."

"Would you like me to call and let him know you are coming? I understand he has had quite the day and is recovering."

"Is Simon with him?" I asked.

Rex and the receptionist looked at me with surprise. "Simon?"

"Simon is Dirk's handler for today. I went to see the director, Troy, and let him know that Dirk was missing."

"I see," Rex said.

"Yes, I believe there is a Simon Green with Mr. Benjamin," the receptionist said.

Rex turned to her and raised an eyebrow.

The receptionist shrugged. "We keep a careful eye on our special guests."

"Did you see Mr. Benjamin leave this morning?"

"Yes," she said, and went back to her books. "He left at six a.m. this morning. We pay attention so that we can go in and straighten up the room right away."

"Do you know where he was going at six a.m.?"

"He went out wearing workout gear," she said. "I'd assume he went for a jog."

I looked at Rex. "Was Dirk wearing workout clothes when we found him?"

Rex frowned. "T-shirt and jeans," he said. He turned to the clerk. "Does he do that often? Go out jogging?"

"Most mornings, yes," she said. "Unless he has someone with him."

"Do you keep track of all of Mr. Benjamin's visitors?"

"Yes," she said. "We are discreet, but yes, we log all of his visitors so that we know who is supposed to see him and who we need to keep off of his floor."

"Interesting," Rex said.

"What are you thinking?" I asked.

"Somewhere along the way, Dirk Benjamin came into contact with our killer."

"Oh," I said, and felt my eyes go wide. "Perhaps the killer is in his visitor log."

"Can I see his records?" Rex asked.

"Only if I have Mr. Benjamin's permission," she said.

"Or I get a warrant," Rex said, and crossed his arms across his chest.

"I can ask the manager, but in general we keep that information among the staff."

"You seem to keep close tabs on who is in your building," I pointed out.

"We do," she said. "As part of our safety measures. Now, we do have a restaurant that is open to the public, but that is monitored with a camera."

"Has Trent Jessop come into the Grand in the last week?" I asked.

Rex glanced at me as if wondering what I was thinking.

"Let me see," the receptionist said, and went to her computer. I waited patiently while she dug through her computer records. "It seems he was here two days ago."

"Do you know why he was here?" Rex asked.

"No," she said. "There's a note that he met with Dirk in the lobby. The two men left. Mr. Benjamin came back alone some hours later."

I looked at Rex. "That means Dirk might have been the last person to have seen Trent alive."

"It could be why the killer abducted Dirk," Rex said. He turned to the receptionist. "Thank you. We're going to see Mr. Benjamin now."

"I'll make a note," she said.

We hurried down the hall to the elevators. Dirk was staying in a suite on the third floor.

"What do you think Trent wanted with Dirk?" I asked as we stepped out of the elevator.

"We're about to find out," Rex said. We walked by the security guard at the end of the hall. The guard acknowledged Rex with a nod of his head.

"Have you been here before?" I asked.

"What do you mean?"

"How does he know you?"

"The uniform," Rex said.

"Hmm."

Rex knocked on the door to a room.

"Yeah," Simon said, and opened the door. "Oh, Officer Manning."

"Can we come in?" Rex asked.

"Yes, sir," Simon said. "Dirk is out on the balcony recovering from his ordeal."

We walked through the room, which was decorated in bright red and green florals. There was a large four-poster bed on one side of the room and a couch with two chairs on the other. Rex wasted no time going straight to the balcony. We stepped out to the cool breeze blowing off the lake and a lovely lake view of the sunset. Dirk was lounging in a chair. He had a bandage on his forehead and a bruise on his jaw. Rather than marring his good looks, it simply made him look more masculine.

"Rex, my man," he said, and straightened. "Allie! What a surprise. Come, sit, sit. Simon, get these people something to drink. What would you like? Tea? Water? A beer? We have gin and tonic . . ."

"Water, please," I said, and took a seat on the patio chair he pointed toward. "How are you?"

"Better now," he said, and touched the bruise on

his chin. "I understand you were the one to find me, Allie. Thank you."

"You're welcome," I said.

"How did you know I was there?"

"We were chasing clues looking for Trent Jessop," I said. "I'm glad we found you. No one seems to even know that you were missing before we found you."

"Yeah, well, I don't blame anyone," he said with a shrug. "I'm a bit of a wild thing when it comes to being on set or not. That's why our illustrious leader has assigned poor Simon to babysit me."

"We understand you saw Trent Jessop two days ago. Is that correct?" Rex asked.

"Sure." Dirk sat up and put his elbows on his knees. "You said you were looking for Trent . . ."

"He's missing," I said. "We think the killer took him."

"Gee, that's one busy killer," Dirk said, and ran his hand through his thick, blond hair. "He jumped me and Trent?"

"We think he has Trent, yes," Rex said. "What did you meet with Jessop for?"

"Oh, dude, the guy wanted to make sure his sister was getting her money's worth on the shoots, you know? I guess she won the bid for the outside shots for the show." He shrugged. "I told him that I'm not the one that schedules those things. He needed to go see Troy."

"The director," Rex said.

"Yeah, dude, it's his job to plan these things. I'm just the talent. You know? I show up, say the lines, and I get paid."

"The reception desk says you left with Trent. Where did you go?"

"Dude, I walked him down to see Troy. You know, with the rest of the crew. I think they were working near the stables that day."

"Did you introduce Trent to Troy?"

"Dude, no, I got stopped to sign some autographs. When I finished the dude was gone. You know? So I figured he's a smart dude. He'll find Troy."

"What did you do next?"

"Went for a jog. Seriously, it takes a lot of work to keep this bod. You know?"

"I can imagine," Rex said.

Simon walked out onto the balcony with a bucket of ice and bottles of water and soda. He offered me the bucket. I took out a bottle of water and twisted the top off. I took a swallow of cold water and watched as Rex declined anything and Dirk grabbed a beer.

"What happened this morning?" I asked. "The front desk says you went out for a jog."

"Yeah, I go out pretty much the same time every day and run the island. It's like eight miles around, right?"

"The bike trail along the coast is, yes," I said.

"So I started jogging and I see this wagon stopped by the side of the road. It was early and there wasn't anyone else around. So I thought I should check it out. The last thing I remember is walking around to the back. Next thing I know I wake up in that basement. My hands were tied and I had a sock or something in my mouth. It was freaking cold and there was one lightbulb overhead."

"Was anyone with you?"

He shrugged. "I thought I heard someone walking around, but didn't see anyone."

"So you don't know if it was a male or female who took you?"

He laughed. "I doubt some girl is going to transport two hundred twenty pounds of muscle anywhere. It had to be a dude."

"Or two dudes," Rex said.

Dirk leaned forward. "You think there are two guys involved?"

"Trent isn't a small guy, either," I said. "Whoever is doing this is strong enough to haul around dead weight."

"Yeah, well, I don't know why they would want to take me," he said. "I'm glad you found me."

"Me too," I said. "But I really need to find Trent. The killer left a note that says we only had forty-eight hours and that was over twenty four hours ago."

"Ouch, I hope you find him."

"I have a question," I said.

He took a swig of his beer from the bottle. "Shoot."

"Do you jog in jeans? I mean, you were wearing jeans when we found you."

"Oh, yeah," he said, and touched the bottle to his head. "Caught that, did you? They told me you were clever."

"And?" Rex asked.

"It's no mystery really," he said. "I jog in jeans. I got this thing about pictures of me in shorts. Not the best calves, if you know what I mean." He shrugged. "It's a thing. Gotta protect my brand, you know?"

"Do you know where Jeffery Jenas is?" I asked.

"Jeffery? I don't know," he said, shrugging. "The dude's always walking about the island. I think he told me his uncle lives here."

"So he is related to the Jenases who own the building you were found in . . ."

"What?" Dirk sat up straight. "You think Jeffery has something to do with this? No way, no way, the dude is a writer. They don't actually do stuff. They just imagine what it'd be like to do stuff. You know?"

"When was the last time you saw Jeffery Jenas?"

"Yesterday," Dirk said. "The dude had some cool ending to the last show he wanted to tell me about, but I'm a busy guy, you know? I told him I'd look at it later. Look, I'm sure it's fine. You know?"

"Right," Rex said, and stood. "Thank you for your time."

"Cool," Dirk said, and relaxed back into his chair.

"Come on, Allie, let's get you home."

I stood. "There's just one thing I don't understand. Why would the killer let us find you but keep Trent?"

Chapter 28

"I told you I thought Jeffery was behind this," I said as we left the Grand.

"I've got my people out looking for him," he said. "No one's seen the man since last night."

"The thing I still can't get my mind around is how Jeffery could have dragged Dirk and Trent around. Jeffery's only about five foot ten and super thin."

"There has to be two," Rex said as we walked down the street.

"So Jeffery is the mastermind and someone else is the muscle," I said. "But who? And more importantly, where is Trent?"

"We've exhausted the clues, Allie," Rex said.

"I'm missing something," I said.

"That's what the killer wants, right? To outsmart you?"

We walked toward the stables. I glanced down the first alley on the right and stopped.

"What?" Rex asked.

"What if they didn't take Trent anywhere," I said.

"What do you mean?"

I walked over to the alley. "This is the way Trent went, right? He left Dirk at the Grand and the crew was shooting at the stables. What if, as I thought earlier, the killer paid a woman to scream? Trent would have run in and the killer would have knocked him out."

"And?" We stood in the mouth of the alley.

"What if instead of taking him out to an abandoned building, they simply moved him inside one of these businesses?"

"Hmmm," Rex said, and pulled out his flashlight. We walked door-to-door and accessed the back doors as if they would tell us something.

"I'm going to knock like I did when we found Dirk." I banged on each door and held my breath while I listened.

"We can't knock on every door," Rex said after the third door.

"Shush," I said, and put my ear to the door of the third building. I knocked again. I heard a faint noise. I pounded harder. The noise came back in response. I rattled the doorknob. "What is this building?"

Rex walked around the side, running his flashlight along the building, spotting a basement window. He knelt down and peered into the window. "Knock again."

I raced back to the door and pounded as hard as I could. No one answered. Frustrated, I knocked twice. The faint sound of two knocks came through the door. It sounded far away. "Did you hear that?" I called to Rex.

"Hey," said the neighbor who came out on his fire escape from the second-floor apartment. "What's going on?"

"Have you seen Trent Jessop?" I asked.

"No," the man said. "But I work nights and sleep days."

Rex came around and shined his flashlight up. "Kerry Mentor," he said.

"Hey, Rex, are you looking for Trent?"

"Have you seen anything unusual?"

"Like I was telling the lady, I work nights so no, I don't see anything."

A faint sound of banging came from deep inside the building. I turned to Rex. "We have to check it out."

"I can't enter without a warrant or cause," Rex said.

"Hang on," Kerry said. "That's the Billsleys' place. I have a key." He disappeared back into his apartment for a moment, then came loping down the stairs. "Bill Billsley is gone for the season. I stay year-round so I have a key to check for things like pipes breaking and such." He pulled a key out of his pocket and unlocked the door. He flipped on the light. "Hello?"

We all walked into the back room of the building.

"Hello?" I called. "Trent?"

Rex cleared the first and second rooms, then found a door in the short hall that led down to the basement. He flipped on the switch. I stood at the top of the stairs. The basement smelled musty. The temperature was noticeably cooler.

"Police," Rex said.

I heard muffled pounding and went racing down the stairs. "Trent?" I called.

Rex caught me. "Stop." I froze at the bottom of the stairs.

Rex cautiously turned the corner from the bottom of the steps. "Clear," he called after what seemed like an hour of my holding my breath, but was only a minute or so.

I raced around the corner to see a dirty mattress on the floor. Trent was tied up and lying on the mattress. His eyes were covered with a bandanna. Rex pulled something out of his mouth. "Trent!" I went over to him. He was warm to the touch. That meant he wasn't dead, at least not yet. Rex pulled Trent up to sit and pushed the covering off his eyes. Trent blinked and winced against the light from the single bare bulb hanging from the joists. "We found you. Are you okay?"

His lips were dry and cracked. There was an old cut on his temple and blood on the corners of his mouth. "Allie," he croaked out my name.

I grabbed him and hugged him hard while Rex untied his hands.

"What the hell happened?" Rex asked him.

"Water," Trent said.

I looked up at Rex. He called the ambulance to the spot. "We'll get you some water. First, are you hurt? Is anything broken? Can you walk?"

Trent tried to stand, but fell back. "Weak," he said. "I don't think anything is broken."

Rex and I helped Trent to his feet. I held my arm around his waist as he took his first wobbly steps. It took a while, but we managed to go up the stairs. By this time George was there along with Joy Emmerson. The ambulance filled the tight alleyway. They bundled him into the back of the ambulance and started an IV drip.

Brent and Officer Lasko showed up along with Shane and his evidence kit. I heard Rex tell them to interview the neighbor. I climbed up in the back of the ambulance with Trent and held his hand.

"Your mother and sister are pretty worried about you," I said, and squeezed his hand.

"Mom's here?"

"Yes, and she will probably meet us at the clinic. Who did this to you Trent?"

"I'm not quite sure," he said, and closed his eyes against the glare of the lights in the ambulance.

"Was it Jeffery Jenas?"

"Who?"

"The writer, Jeffery Jenas," I said. "Did he do this to you?"

"No," Trent said with a shake of his head.

"Then who?"

"Dirk Benjamin," he said.

"I'm putting something in to keep him calm until we can better assess the damage to his body," George said. "Are you coming to the clinic with us?"

I glanced out at the building. Brent stood by the door with his hands clasped behind him. "Yes," I said.

"Wait," Rex said, and climbed in the back. "I need his statement."

"He's in no shape," George said.

"I can talk," Trent croaked. "It was Dirk Benjamin who took me. Dirk is the killer."

"I think you're mistaken," I said. "You mean Jeffery Jenas, the writer."

"No," Trent croaked. "Dirk, Dirk Benjamin. He said he was coming back to administer poisoning." Trent winced as the IV needle punched through his skin.

"Lasko," Rex said, and stepped out of the ambulance.

"Escort the ambulance to the clinic and keep an eye on Trent and Allie."

"Yes, sir," she said, and climbed up into the ambulance with a sober face. She took a seat. The doors of the vehicle closed behind her and we moved slowly along. I held Trent's hand the entire time. George worked on him, checking vital signs and looking for bumps and bruises.

We got to the clinic in no time and the doors opened. Mrs. Jessop was there and so was Paige.

"Trent!" they called, tears running down their faces. I let go of his hand as George and Joy pulled the stretcher out of the ambulance and took Trent off inside the clinic. Mrs. Jessop and Paige went in with him. I stood outside and gave them room to assure themselves that Trent was going to be okay.

"I'm glad you found him," Officer Lasko said.

"Me too."

"He said Dirk Benjamin did this to him?"

"Yes," I said. "I want to go wrench that man from the Grand Hotel and give him a piece of my mind."

"Relax," Lasko said, and put her hand on my arm. "Rex has this."

I went inside the clinic to find Trent. Paige and Mrs. Jessop were fussing over him. He looked exhausted.

"I'm flying in Doctor Hendricks in the morning," Mrs. Jessop said.

"There's no need," Trent muttered.

"He seems to be dehydrated, but none the worse for wear," the nurse said as she checked his vitals. "We're going to want to keep him on an IV drip overnight and then he can go home. The doctor will want to observe him for a while."

I noticed that someone had bandaged Trent's wrists where the ties had dug in.

"I'd just like a shower and to go home," Trent said.

"I want him home," Mrs. Jessop said.

"Doctor's order to keep him here overnight," the nurse insisted.

"And I must insist that he goes home with me," Mrs. Jessop said. "I won't have him in this place overnight."

I stood in the corner and watched as Mrs. Jessop bullied the staff. Trent turned to me and held out his hand. "Allie."

Taking his hand, I smiled at him. "We thought you were dead."

"I'm glad I'm not," he said with a hint of his handsome smile.

"I don't understand how it could be Dirk," I said. "Earlier today, your mother, Paige, and Jenn and I found Dirk in the basement of the Jenas warehouse. He was tied to a chair. It was clear he was in the place where the other two men were killed."

"That man is not as stupid as he wants us all to think," Trent said.

I remembered suddenly how Dirk was able to mimic Rex so quickly and so easily. "He was playing the part of the dumb actor." I looked at Trent. "Did he tell you why he chose you?"

"It drove him nuts that you weren't really investigating. He said he had to up the pain point to get you to take notice."

I shook my head. "How did he get you?"

Trent swallowed. "He was taking me to see the director. When we walked by the alley, I thought I heard someone shout out my name. I turned and he was on me. Next thing I know I woke up tied up."

I ran my fingers lightly over his temple. "There's a pretty good lump on your head. You probably should stay for observation."

"I think Mother's had enough stress for a while," he said. "It's probably best if we all go home." He squeezed my hand. "I'm glad you came looking for me."

I smiled at him. "I can't have you dying on me."

"Then Dirk was right. You do love me."

"Of course, I love you."

There was the sound of a man clearing his throat. I looked up to see that Rex had just stepped into the curtained area. I knew from the look on his face that he had heard me. There wasn't anything I could do about it. The truth was I did love Trent, but love wasn't always enough to make things work.

"Officer Pulaski has offered to see that you get home safe and spend the night patrolling your property," Rex said. He looked at Mrs. Jessop. "If you feel the need to skip the doctor's advice, we can accommodate you."

"Finally," Mrs. Jessop said. "Someone who is listening. Come on, children, let's go home."

I turned to Rex and left the Jessops to gather Trent up and take him home. Taking Rex by the arm, I pulled him toward the door of the clinic. "Did you pick up Dirk?"

"Lasko and Anderson are picking him up now," Rex said.

"Do you think he's the killer?"

"I don't know," Rex said. "There is no evidence to suggest he did anything but take Trent. I need to question Dirk to learn more."

"He could have been working with Jeffery Jenas," I said. "Then Jeffery turned on him. How else do you explain finding Dirk tied to a chair?"

"I'll find out," Rex said. "You've had a trying time of it. I suggest you go home and get some sleep."

"What about the Jessops?" I asked. "Is Brent going to be enough protection to keep them safe?"

"It's the best we can do," Rex said.

"What about Jeffery? Have you found him yet?"

"We've got everyone looking," he said.

"And Mrs. O'Connor? Do you think she's still safe?"

"As best I can tell," Rex said. "Seriously, Allie, you need to go home and get some rest. You've done some good work today. There are two men who owe you their lives." He put his hand on my forearm. "Let me finish putting all the ends together."

"Okay," I said. "I guess I'll go home."

"Let me walk you home."

"I'm fine," I said. "Seriously, you need to see to Dirk and Jeffery."

"There is no way I'm letting you walk out of here alone," Rex said. "Do you need to say good-bye to Trent?"

"No, I'm sure he's busy with his family," I said. "Come on then, let's get me home." I pushed out the clinic door and strode down the dark, quiet street. Rex strode beside me.

We walked in silence for blocks before he finally cleared his throat. I glanced at him. "What?"

"I heard you tell Trent you were in love with him."

"I told him I loved him," I said. "It doesn't mean I'm in love with him. I wouldn't have accepted your dinner invitation if I were in love with Trent."

"I see," Rex said, and went silent again.

I refused to comment further. We got to the Mc-Murphy's front door, where Jenn stood by watching for me. She pushed the door open. "Oh, thank goodness you're all right." Jenn gave me a hug. "I heard you found Trent. Where was he?"

"He was in an empty house not too far from here," I said. Then I turned to Rex. "Thank you for walking me home."

"I know you have new security measures, but I'm sending a patrol by once an hour until we get this thing wrapped up."

"Thanks," I said.

"Take care," Rex said, and turned and walked down the street toward the police station.

Jenn pulled me inside and we locked the door behind us. "Was it really Dirk Benjamin?"

"Trent says Dirk was the one who kidnapped him," I said. "But it doesn't make any sense. Why did we find Dirk tied up, if he was the killer?"

"Maybe he wanted to throw off any suspicion," Jenn said. "I bet he didn't expect us to go out and snoop around."

"You think he tied himself to the chair? What about Jeffery Jenas?"

"They still haven't found Jeffery?" Jenn asked. Mal came running up to me and begged for me to pick her up. I did and rubbed her ears.

"He couldn't have gotten far," I said. "There are

a lot of people out looking for him. What about Mrs. O'Connor? Is she all right?"

"She's had the locks on the boardinghouse changed. If Jeffery comes back, he won't be able to get inside."

"That's good," I said. I put the puppy down and put my arm through Jenn's. "I saw Shane."

"We're having a good-bye dinner tomorrow night," Jenn said. "Come on, it's been a long day. Let's go to bed." We walked up the stairs to the apartment. I opened the door and Jenn had her suitcases sitting near the door.

"Oh," I said, and a sadness fell over me. I looked at her. "You started packing?"

"Yeah, I have a lot to pack."

"So, you're really leaving."

"I told you I was."

"I know, but . . ." I shrugged. "Thank you for helping me this summer." Mal looked from me to Jenn and back. She didn't look happy with the suitcases, either.

Jenn got tears in her eyes. She dashed them away with a smile. "It's been the best summer of my life. Don't think I won't take you up on the offer to return at any time."

I hugged her. "Good." Then I yawned. "It's been a long day. Good night." I took Mal and Mella into the bedroom and closed the door. What a day. I'd found Trent before he was killed. I'd rescued Dirk. The only one who hadn't been found was Jeffery Jenas. I went to my window and looked out on the street below. The street-cleaning wagon went by slowly. The two men working together. One driving the wagon and

the other jumping out and scooping up the remains
of a day of horse traffic.

It hit me then how easy it would be to simply not
see the people who clean the streets. I grabbed my
phone and went out the back door.

Chapter 29

By the time I'd gotten down the stairs and through the alley the cleanup wagon was nearly to the marina. I followed it from a distance. It made sense, really. No one wanted to look inside the wagon. The smell is ripe and would hide a dead body.

Hurrying behind it, I ensured I stayed in the shadows. Ryan was doing the scooping with a heavy shovel. Who was driving the horse? Where did they go with their load? The Carriage Company?

I hadn't given much thought to the street sweepers and cleaners and flushers who worked diligently to keep the streets of the island clean. It was clearly more than a two-man job in the height of the summer season. It was one of those jobs no one wanted to think about. What a perfect way to get by with murder.

The street cleaners finished their rounds and went back to the Carriage Company to empty their loads. The driver got down and I recognized him as Avery Banks. I frowned. I knew Avery from the occasional times he'd come into the McMurphy to ask if we needed any handyman work done. It had taken some doing, but I'd convinced him that Mr. Devaney had everything covered.

I sneaked around to the building to peer into the windows. The lights were on and I saw Jeffery Jenas sitting at a bench playing cards with two other men. Holding up my phone I snapped a couple of quick pictures and sent a text to Rex.

"Allie McMurphy."

I nearly dropped my phone at the sound of my name. I looked up to see Dirk Benjamin towering over me. "Dirk," I said as the spit dried up in my mouth. "I thought . . ."

"What?"

"That Rex had you down at the station," I said weakly.

"Clearly a mistake on your part." He grabbed my arm and dragged me around the side of the building and into the light. He plunked me down on an empty chair next to Jeffery Jenas. "We have a visitor."

"Well, crap," Jeffery said. "How the heck did you find us?"

I shrugged. "I saw the street cleaners and thought it would be a good way to move bodies."

"And you followed it."

"Yes."

"Out," Dirk said to the other men there and they picked up their cards and left.

"Do they know?" I asked.

"Know what?" Jeffery asked.

"That you have killed two men," I said.

"They don't know anything," Dirk said. "Because

Jeffery didn't kill anyone. Doesn't have the stomach for it. Do you?"

"I write mysteries," Jeffery said. "I don't commit crimes."

"But you left me the notes," I said. "You had to have. You wrote the book on Bobby Fischer."

"It wasn't the chess moves that were important," Dirk said. "I thought perhaps you were smart enough to figure that out. But you weren't, were you?" He tied my hands behind me.

"The chess moves weren't?" I paused. "No, they weren't the clue at all. It was the name . . . Donald Byrne. It was my clue that it was you all along, wasn't it, Dirk Benjamin?"

"Ah, now she gets it," Jeffery said. He leaned against the table. "D. B. I was afraid it would give it away at the start. But you didn't get it, did you?"

"I have to ask why? Why would you kill these men?"

"Research," Dirk said. "I wanted to know what it was like. But you see, I wanted to have a story. A real reason why I would kill someone, so I asked Jeffery for his help."

"That's crazy," I said. I looked at Jeffery. "Why would you go along?"

"Why does anyone do anything? Money," Jeffery said. "I was broke. Dirk brought me in to write the series. This was just an extension of that."

"But you won't have a series once you are caught," I said. "It doesn't make any sense."

"That's saying we'll get caught," Jeffery said.

"I found Trent today. He knows that Dirk is the one who kidnapped him. The police have figured out that you two are working together."

"And the publicity will make the series popular," Jeffery said.

"You are crazy," I said. "You can't write it in jail." I turned to Dirk. "You can't act in jail."

"What about that hot felon guy?" Dirk said. "He went to jail and his mug shot got out. One picture and now he's screwing some international hottie. No, jail is not a bad thing."

"Why me?" I asked. "Why draw me in? What did I do?"

"You've been all over the local news since May," Jeffery said. "I've been watching you. Dirk and I talked. We thought you would be the perfect foil."

"We were wrong," Dirk said. "You aren't as clever as we hoped." He sighed. "You made us kill twice. We had to hire pranksters when you stalled out on your investigation."

"You hired Ryan," I said.

"Again, you should have thought of that right off," Jeffery said. "The Jenases have run the street cleaners for years."

"Now that we have you, what are we going to do with you?" Dirk asked. He ran the back of his hand along my cheek.

"Rex is going to be here any minute," I said. I started to shiver terribly. It gave away the fact that I wasn't all that sure that Rex had seen my text.

"We shouldn't kill her here," Jeffery said. "The guys know she came here. Witnesses and all that."

"Killing me now will serve no purpose," I said. "You proved your point. I'm not clever. I'm just a fudge maker."

"You're the writer," Dirk said to Jeffery. "They have

an idea about Trent but no proof to track us to anything else. How do you want to play this?"

"Emma is about her size and weight, right?"

"Yes," Dirk said.

"Emma?"

"The stand-in," Dirk said. "Go on, Jeffery."

"The guys saw you bring Allie into the building. They need to see Allie leave."

"I'll call Emma," Dirk said, and got out his phone. "She can divert their attention." Dirk walked around behind me. "From the back they look the same."

"Police, hands in the air!" Rex's shout startled me. Jeffery scrambled out of his chair as Dirk backed up away from me. "I said hands where I can see them!"

Brent entered from the back door, his gun drawn. Officer Lasko came in behind him and encircled us.

"Dirk Benjamin, you are under arrest for kidnapping and suspicion of murder."

"Dude, all I did was play a joke on Trent."

"Anything you say can and will be used against you in court," Rex continued. Brent went around and slapped handcuffs on Dirk.

"Jeffery Jenas, you are under arrest for conspiracy to commit murder," Rex said, and waved Officer Lasko forward. She grabbed Jeffery's arms and cuffed him as well. "Read them their rights and get them to the station."

"Yes, sir," Officer Lasko said.

Rex came over and cut the ties that held my hands. "What did you think you were doing going out alone?"

"I had an idea and I wanted to see if it was true or not," I said as I stood on shaky legs and rubbed my raw wrists.

"And you couldn't just share your idea?"

"You were busy looking for Jeffery and protecting everyone. I didn't want to take you away from that focus if I was wrong." A giant shiver shook me, rattling my teeth.

Rex muttered something dark under his breath, took off his jacket, and wrapped it around my shoulders. I leaned into the warmth of his body heat.

"I'm taking you down to the station," he said none too gently. "We need to be debriefed."

"I know how they moved the bodies," I said.

"The street cleaners," he said.

"Yes, how did you know?"

"The building gave it away." He helped me outside. The air was cool and crisp and the stars filled the sky.

"For a brief moment I didn't think I'd ever see the stars again," I said.

"It's a good thing I've learned to watch for your texts," he said. "I wish they were a bit sexier."

"What? Solving murders isn't sexy?" I said through shaking teeth.

"No," he said. "Not in my wildest imagination."

Chapter 30

"So it was Dirk Benjamin all along," Jenn said as we sat at the Harbor Café for our farewell lunch.

"He hired Jeffery to write the notes," I said. "Jeffery thought it was funny to add the chess game because of the initials."

"You learned chess for no reason."

"Well, I did have fun playing and I learned that Sandy is a whiz at the game."

"I'm going to miss this island and all the cool people. Too bad I have to leave even earlier than planned," Jenn said, and sipped from her teacup.

"What time is your flight?"

She glanced at her phone. "It's about two hours away. I can't believe I was able to buy a ticket from Sophie. She was heading to Chicago anyway to pick up a client so she gave me a great deal on the price."

"I'll go to the airport with you," I said.

"No, thank you," she said, wiggling in her chair. "Shane is taking me."

"Did you ever work things out between the two of you?"

"I guess," Jenn said, shrugging. "He isn't happy but he understands the value in my going and gaining experience and such from the clients in Chicago." She leaned in close. "What about you?"

"What about me?"

"I heard that you told Trent you loved him."

"I might have," I said, and sipped my coffee. "So?"

"So you had a date with Rex the other night. Is that over?"

"How can it be over when it never really started?"

"Seriously, are you and Trent a thing again?"

"I don't think Trent wants to date a girl who gets his family in trouble. I mean, if he wasn't my boyfriend, he would have never gotten kidnapped."

"But you told him you love him," she said pointedly.

"Yes, well, love doesn't mean anything. We're two different people in two very different social structures." I sipped my tea. "Besides, I understand Mrs. Jessop is calling all of her children back to Chicago for the winter. It will just be me on the island."

"And Rex."

"Rex heard me tell Trent I loved him."

"Oh, that's complicated."

"Here's the thing, I think I love Rex, too."

"What?"

"I love them both, I just need to figure out if I'm in love with either of them."

"Ah," Jenn said. "I see what you mean. You know what you need?"

"What?"

"A third choice," Jenn said, grinning. "I know this guy . . ."

"Stop it!" I laughed.

The bells on the door rang and I looked over to see Frances and Mr. Devaney walking into the café.

"Frances!" I said, and called them both over. I got up and gave my manager a nice big hug. "Welcome back. How was the honeymoon?"

"We had a marvelous time," Frances said, and sat down. She took off her fall patchwork jacket, revealing a white shirt and embroidered Western skirt that touched the floor. She ran her hand through her short locks. "You really must go sometime."

"Go where?" Jenn asked.

"Why, to the Caribbean, of course," she said. "The cruise was amazing."

"Not nearly as amazing as my new wife," Mr. Devaney said, and lifted her hand to plant a kiss on the back.

"We just got off the ferry and saw you sitting here and thought we'd join you for lunch if that's all right," Frances said.

"Of course," I said. "Please take a seat. You were missed. Sandy called her cousin in to take your place for a while."

"We solved a mystery," Jenn said. "I'll let Allie tell you about it. I've got a plane to catch."

"Are you leaving?" Frances asked.

"Yes," Jenn said, and brushed a kiss on my cheek and then Frances's cheek. "I've got a new job in Chicago. But never fear, I will be back before you know it." She went to the door and I noticed Shane met her on the sidewalk with her suitcases.

"I sure hope she knows what she's doing," I said.

"She'll be fine," Frances said. "She's got a good head on her shoulders."

"So tell me, what has been going on while we were gone?" Mr. Devaney asked.

"Oh, Sandy's cousin Sharon stepped in and took over the front desk duties for you."

"Wonderful," Frances said. Her eyes twinkled. "Sharon always does a good job."

"There was a film crew on the island filming a murder mystery pilot."

"That's interesting," Mr. Devaney said as he brought Frances a cup of tea and set a number card down on the table. "I ordered your favorite salad," he said, and kissed her cheek and sat down beside her.

"Even more interesting is the fact that the star of the pilot and the writer were murdering single men who didn't interact much with society."

"What?" Frances blinked at me.

"Oh, and I had a new security system put into the McMurphy. We now have key cards and cameras and such." I sipped my tea.

"What kind of system?" Mr. Devaney asked, frowning. "Why didn't you wait for me to advise you?"

"You were on your honeymoon and there was a killer on the loose."

"Do you have things well in hand?" Frances asked.

I sat back with a smile. "Almost. There's a bit of an issue with Trent and Rex, but time will work it out."

"Ah, love can be difficult when you're young," Frances said, and put her hand in Mr. Devaney's.

I lifted my glass of tea. "A toast to the newlyweds. May your new life be filled with love and joy."

"Here, here," Mr. Devaney said and we all three touched cups. I looked out the window at the slow bustle of Main Street and knew, no matter what happened, Mackinac Island was my home.

Don't miss the next delightful
Candy-Coated mystery from Nancy Coco

Fudge Bites

Coming soon from Kensington Publishing Corp.
Keep reading to enjoy a sample excerpt . . .

Chapter 1

"You look amazing," Frances said to me. "Like the scariest of the walking dead."

I laughed. I could feel the makeup cracking and so I tried really hard to get it together. "Uh-oh, I've got skin flapping off my cheek." I pushed on the latex flap that concealed the gory makeup underneath. "I'm sure glad zombies aren't real."

"I love the idea of the zombie walk," Frances said. "The fact that the profits all go to the Red Dress Foundation is fantastic."

"I like the idea that all the bars and restaurants pitched in to supply food for the hungry masses," I said.

"Fudge isn't exactly food," Frances said. Frances, a stunning seventysomething, was my hotel manager. She had worked at the Historic McMurphy Hotel and Fudge Shop since before she retired from teaching. Thankfully, she had stayed as an employee after my Papa Liam had died and I had moved in to take over the family business.

My name is Allie McMurphy and at this very moment I was putting the finishing touches on my zombie pinup girl costume. I didn't usually participate in late-night events because I get up very early in the morning to make fudge. But October is off-season and most of the fudge is sold online during the off-season. It meant I didn't have to have fudge ready for when the tourists came in the morning. Yes, I got to sleep in until 8 a.m. if I wanted.

The zombie walk was for a charity close to my heart. Its purpose was to remind people that heart disease is the number one killer of women. The event was put together by the senior center. It was called the Night of the Walking Red. Mrs. Tunison—one of my favorite seniors—was the head of the committee. She had insisted I enter the walk. There was going to be a costume contest later.

I had made pumpkin chocolate chip fudge for the occasion. "You and Mr. Devaney should come out for the walk," I said to Frances. "You would make great zombies. I know you like to play with makeup."

"Well," she said as she adjusted the collar on my cardigan, "I did sell Mary Kay for twenty years."

"I have a lot of leftover makeup upstairs. You can use it. You and Mr. Devaney could be a married couple of zombies."

"I don't think Douglas is into that kind of silliness," she said.

"What kind of silliness?" I turned to see Mr. Devaney walking through the door from the basement. He had a first name—Douglas—but no one used it except for Frances. He paused when he saw me. "You been in a car accident?"

"There are no cars on Mackinac Island," I reminded him. Mackinac Island, Michigan, likes to call itself the fudge capital of the world. It's a small island in the straits between the Upper and Lower Peninsulas of Michigan. The entire island has been combustion engine–free for over a hundred years. The only way to get around is to walk, bike, or take a horse carriage. I love the traditions of the island. Things are slower and the sights and sounds of modern life are left behind.

Huge Victorian "cottages" with their turrets and gingerbread trim line the streets. For centuries the wealthy from Chicago and Detroit have escaped the hustle and bustle of the big city to spend the summer season on the island.

They usually came by ferries, although some came by private jet these days. My friend Sophie is a private pilot. She works for the Grand Hotel during the season, but also has her regulars who ask her to fly them on and off the island when the ferries quit running.

Sophie was meeting me for the Walking Red event. My best friend, Jenn Christensen, had left the island for an important job in Chicago. Sophie and Liz McElroy, the editor and lead reporter for the *Town Crier* newspaper, had stepped in to keep me from moping too much or feeling lonely. Jenn had come to Mackinac to help me through my first season. She was an excellent event planner and had connected with the islanders like a pro. Me, on the other hand, not so much. Even though my family had owned the McMurphy for over one hundred years, I had grown up in Detroit and gone to school in Chicago. I wasn't quite accepted as a true local, despite my efforts. I was slowly fitting in, but there had been a few bumps in the road.

Things had been going smoothly since Jenn left.

But it was the off-season and Jenn had left me with strict instructions. I had spent some time following them as closely as possible, but I didn't have the same knack with people that Jenn had. Truth was, I missed her.

I felt a bump on my leg and looked down to see my bichon poo puppy. Marshmallow—Mal for short—was nudging me with her nose. She jumped up and I scratched her behind the ears. "What do you think of my zombie look?" I asked the dog.

She seemed unfazed by the red-and-white makeup.

"I think I'll skip the zombie makeup," Mr. Devaney said as he poured himself a cup of coffee from the coffee bar at the far side of the lobby. "Go ahead and do it if you want to, Frances," he said with a warm look in his eye. "I'd love to see you have some fun."

"Oh, pooh," she said. "I've got to watch the front desk. We have a couple of families coming in for the weekend."

I glanced at my watch. It was getting dark at 5 p.m. "Did they say if they expected to arrive late?"

"Sophie is bringing them in in the next few minutes," Frances said. "I know it's close to Halloween, but I don't want to give them the impression that we aren't a warm and welcoming place."

"What's not warm and welcoming about zombies?" I asked with a laugh, and raised my hands like claws. "We only want to eat your brains."

The door to the McMurphy opened and Liz walked in. She was dressed like a ballerina with zombie makeup. Her curly dark hair was pulled up in a tight bun and she had makeup bite marks on her neck. Her leotard was dirty and torn and her tutu was ragged.

"Oh, my goodness, what happened to you?" Frances asked her.

"Nothing," Liz said with a smile. "I'm a zombie and a prima ballerina. Two things I always wanted to grow up to be. Thanks for sponsoring us."

"It was my pleasure," Frances said. "Douglas pitched in half."

"Thanks, Mr. Devaney," I said. Mr. Devaney was a retired schoolteacher who I had brought on to be the handyman for the McMurphy. It hadn't taken long before he and Frances had started secretly dating. In a whirlwind courtship, the two seventysomethings had gotten engaged and last month they had gotten married. You could see the joy on their faces every time they were in the room together. It made my heart fill with hope that someday I, too, might find the love of my life.

At the moment I was sort of single as my ex-boyfriend, Trent Jessop, was in Chicago for the next few months. My attraction to Officer Rex Manning was progressing slowly. The problem with having two handsome men competing for your attention was that sometimes they both backed off. I think they were giving me room to decide. Maybe I needed the room.

"Mal can go," Liz said, her eyes lighting up. "They have zombie dog costumes."

"That's creative," Frances said.

"*I* don't have any doggy costumes," I said with a frown. Feeling the latex on my face crinkle, I smoothed out my expression.

"We can give her a black T-shirt with white bones painted on it."

"A black T-shirt?" I said. "We'd need a very small one. Mal only weighs twelve pounds."

"Oh, a onesie will do," Liz said with glee. "I'm going to run over to Doud's and see if they have anything on the shelf."

"I'll go with you," I said. We headed out the door.

The McMurphy is on Main Street and only a block or so from Doud's, the oldest market on the island. It was dark outside already and the air smelled of falling leaves, horses, and the lingering scents of fudge and popcorn. People were beginning to gather. The costumes were equal parts terrifying and funny.

We pushed into Doud's, the doorbells ringing behind us. Mary Emry, the cashier, was dressed as a zombie Minnie Mouse. She was waiting on a burly trucker guy with a cleaver buried in his skull. It almost looked realistic.

"This way," Liz said, and drew me toward the back where they kept a few items of clothing.

"Maybe we should have checked out one of the T-shirt places," I said as I eyed the sparse selection.

"No, this is perfect." Liz pulled a tiny sundress out of the racks. "Now we need a little blood . . ."

"I have plenty of makeup." I followed Liz through the store.

"This will do," she said, grabbing some red decorator frosting. "Come on." We approached Mary Emry.

Mary wasn't much for talking, at least not to me. "What's this for?"

"We're going to dress up Allie's dog, Mal," Liz said, and rubbed her hands together. "With any luck the red frosting will stain the dress and the dog will lick it and get red on her face."

"Disgusting," Mary said.

"But effective," I said. "Are you going to be in the Walking Red zombie walk?"

"Sure," Mary said. "It's for a good cause."

I paid for the purchases and we walked out of Doud's into the now crowded street. "I didn't know there would be so many people here," I said.

"It's for a good cause," Liz said. "My mom died of a heart attack."

"I'm sorry, I didn't know that," I said.

"This crowd is crazy. Let's go around and through the alley." As we turned down the side street, I noticed that it too was filling up with zombies, as well as people not in costume who carried blankets and came out to watch all the craziness.

We were a half a block away from the McMurphy, just behind the Old Tyme Photo Shop, when I noticed that my kitty, Carmella, was also walking toward the hotel.

Carmella was a stray calico cat who adopted me and the McMurphy. She wasn't a fan of Mal, who was a bit rambunctious yet as she was only seven months old, but Mella escaped the shenanigans by jumping up on the countertops. My cat was an indoor/outdoor cat. She loved to wander the back alleyways for an hour or so and then return to the McMurphy to beg treats from Frances and attention from the guests.

"Mella," I called to her. "Here, kitty." She walked over to me and I leaned down to pick her up.

"Wow, looks like you already have a costume started for Mella," Liz said.

I looked at the cat. She had wet paws that were a distinct brownish-red color, and her face had remnants of the same hue. "What did you get into?" I asked her. She wiped her feet on my sweater. "Is that blood?"

"Eww," Liz said. "She is coated with it."

I glanced around. It was too dark to see anything in the half-lit alley. We got closer to the McMurphy and the sensor lights I had installed came on. "It certainly looks like blood," I said, feeling a pang of concern, and held her up to the light. "Are you okay, Mella?" I asked. "Did you get hurt?"

She meowed at me as if indignant that I would think she would not win in a fight.

Liz ran her hands through Mella's fur and examined her closely. "I don't see any puncture wounds," Liz said.

"That means someone else is hurt," I said, and glanced back down the alley. It was darker now that the lights were on behind the McMurphy. "Let's take her in. I'll ask Frances to give her a bath and make sure it really isn't her who is bleeding."

"And while she's doing that?" Liz asked.

"I'll get a flashlight and we can check the alley. Whatever Mella got into may mean that someone has lost a lot of blood. We need to see if we can help."

Just then there was a scream from the dark alley. I hugged Mella tight and turned toward the sound. "Oh, my gosh!" It was Sophie. "Thank goodness you're out here."

"Are you all right?" I asked.

"No," Sophie said with trembling hands. She was dressed as a motorcycle gang zombie. "I think I found a dead man."

"Where?" Liz asked, pulling out her phone.

"Just over there," Sophie said, and pointed toward

the dark corner of the building that backed up against the alley. We all hurried over to where she pointed. "I was coming around this way to avoid the crowd when I stumbled over something. I got out my flashlight and there was a crumpled body."

"Are you sure it's real?" Liz asked. "I mean, look at us, we're dressed like the walking dead." She waved her hand over her costumed self.

Sophie paused. "Do you think it might be a decoration? If so, it's gruesome."

We stopped in front of a dark lump. Liz and I pulled out our phones and opened the flashlight apps. In the twin beams the person looked like a man. His head appeared to be bashed in. He wore an old suitcoat with patched elbows and his arms were at odd angles. His legs were also at odd angles and one of his shoes was off. A large pool of dark liquid had seeped from his shirt and under his jacket.

"He looks real," I said, and hunkered down.

"Are you going to touch him?" Sophie asked.

"Should you touch him?" Liz asked.

"It's the only way to know if he's real," I said. "It's what they tell you to do with first aid." I touched his shoulder and gently shook it. "Sir, are you okay?"

His head rolled to the side, his jaw opened, and his tongue flopped out. I jerked back. Mella squirmed in my arms. I held her tight and put my fingers on his neck to feel for a pulse. He was stone cold and the blood was dark and had a surface on it.

"He's either dead or he's a very good Halloween effect." I stood and looked at my friend. "If he is a Halloween effect, why hide him in a back alley?"

"I'm calling 9-1-1," Liz said, and dialed.

I petted a squirming Mella, who seemed only to want one thing—to leave. Whatever she had gotten on her was getting all over me, but I didn't want to let her down. She might make things worse. Especially if this poor man was dead and she had already walked through the crime scene.

"Hi, Charlene, it's Liz McElroy," Liz said. "I'm in the alley behind Doud's and the McMurphy. I think we might have stumbled across a crime scene." She paused. "Yes, I know that the whole island is full of walking dead right now, but we think this one might actually be real."

Sophie shivered and hugged herself. I rubbed her arm to comfort her.

"Who is 'we'?" Liz said. "Sophie and Allie and I." She looked at us. "Yes, Allie McMurphy."

"I'll call Rex," I said.

"No, don't call him," Liz said. "Charlene is contacting him now. She started calling him the minute I said I was with you." Liz covered the phone with her hand. "She said you are the grim reaper."

"Oh, for goodness' sake," I said, and rolled my eyes. "I am not the grim reaper. Besides, Sophie found him."

"I think Mella found him first," Liz said, pointing to the dirty paws of my kitty. Mella had given up on her struggle and sort of hung in my arms, looking miffed.

I sighed. "My pets seem to have good noses for dead men."

Rex and Officer Charles Brown walked into the alley carrying flashlights. They were an imposing pair. Rex was about five foot ten with an action-hero physique and shaved head—although you couldn't tell because his hat covered it. I knew well that he had killer blue eyes ringed with black lashes and a kiss that could curl my toes. Officer Brown was tall and square with green eyes.

I let out a breath I didn't know I was holding. There was something reassuring about the pair.

"Charlene said you had a situation," Rex said.

Liz shone her flashlight on the dead man. "Sophie found him."

Rex squatted down to feel for a pulse.

"We thought maybe it was fake," I said. "But I followed first aid protocol and shook his shoulder and called out. Then I felt his neck and he was cold as ice."

"What's up with the cat?" Office Brown asked.

"I think she walked through the blood," I said, and waved her dirty paw. "I didn't see her do it."

"There are tracks through the blood pool," Rex said.

"Is he dead?" Sophie asked. "I'm hoping he's just a fake like our makeup. You know, for the zombie walk."

Rex frowned and stood. "I think some of this is makeup, but this man is clearly dead. I'll call Shane out here." He reached for the walkie-talkie on his shoulder.

"Let's step away from the scene," Officer Brown said as he motioned us across the alley.

The door on the building behind us opened and Margaret Vanderbilt stepped out. Maggs was Frances's best friend and worked at the drugstore beside Doud's. She had long, curly gray hair, incredible skin, and wide blue eyes. "What's going on?" she asked as she looked at us in our zombie makeup. "Are you going to the Walking Red Walk? It's starting in a few minutes."

"We were," Liz said, "but something more important has come up."

"What is more fun than raising money for heart disease awareness?" Maggs looked at Officer Brown and then over at Rex. "Oh! This doesn't look good." Her gaze went to the crumpled heap on the ground at Rex's feet. "Anthony?"

"Who?" Officer Brown asked.

Maggs pushed through us, but Charles held her. "Anthony? Anthony!"

"Who's Anthony?" I asked.

"My son," she said, and covered her mouth with her hands. "Please tell me, tell me it's not Anthony."

Rex stepped over and hid the body from her. "We don't know who it is, Maggs." He touched her trembling arm. "Why do you think it's Anthony?"

"He was supposed to meet me here. He was going to dress as a business zombie. I think that's his suitcoat. The one with the patches." She started trembling hard.

"You need to sit down," I said, and handed Mella to Liz. I took Maggs by the shoulder and helped her to sit on the edge of the brick flower bed beside the door. "Does anyone have a blanket?"

The ambulance rolled up to the mouth of the alley. EMT George Marron came out. "Charlene called," he said.

"We need a blanket, I said. "I think Maggs might be in shock."

"Got it," George said, and reached into the ambulance and grabbed a blanket. He came over and tucked it around Maggs's shoulders. "Are you hurt?" he asked her quietly and calmly.

"No," she said, gasping for air. "No, I'm okay."

"Are you sure?" He studied her with his dark eyes. His handsome face, high cheekbones, and copper skin gleamed in the light over the door to the drugstore.

"It can't be Anthony," she said, tears welling in her eyes. "Please tell me it's not Anthony."

George looked up at Rex. He shook his head subtly and my stomach tumbled. Rex knew everyone on the island. From the look on his face, he was sure it was Anthony. I sat down and put my arm around Maggs's shoulders. She rested her head on my shoulder. I turned to look at Sophie. "Call Frances."

Sophie turned her back to us and talked on her phone.

"We're going to find out what happened," I said.

Rex cleared his throat. "Margaret, Frances will be right here. Go with her, please. You shouldn't stay. We need to work this crime scene and find out what exactly happened."

I helped Maggs to her feet as Frances came over. "I've got her," Frances said, and put her arm around Maggs, carefully and quietly speaking to her as they walked the short distance to the McMurphy.

Shane walked into the alley with his crime scene investigator jacket on and his kit in hand. "What do we have?"

"A crime scene that is less than a block away from a crowd of zombies," Rex said grimly. "What's worse is the man's in costume, so it's hard to tell what is real and what is fake."

Shane glanced at Mella in Liz's arms. "Is that fake blood on the cat?"

"I'm afraid not," I said. "Do you need to bag her feet?"

"I need you to put her in a crate and take her to the vet clinic," Shane said in a serious tone. "I need to process the scene and I need evidence collected off of her before she cleans herself."

"Right," I said, and lifted Mella out of Liz's arms. I glanced at Rex. "Do you need me to stay?"

"No, go," he said. "I'll come around later for a debriefing interview. Whatever you do, don't change clothes. It looks like the cat smeared evidence on you as well."

"Right," I said, and looked down at the bloody paw prints on my pinup girl outfit. "What about chain of evidence? Do I need a policeman to go with me to ensure there isn't contamination?"

"Shane?" Rex asked.

"Probably a good idea," Shane said from his position beside the body.

"Fine," Rex said. "Officer Brown, escort Miss Mc-Murphy and her cat to the vet clinic and ensure the chain of custody isn't broken."

"Will do," Charles said. "Shall we?" He pointed toward the McMurphy.

"Okay." This was a fine kettle of fish. I was becoming an expert in crime scene investigation . . . and so were my pets.

Acknowledgments

Special thanks go out to my family for their love and support. The only way to get a book written is with a lot of help and patience.

Thank you to the team at Kensington. You all are awesome. Especially, my editor, Michaela.

And always, special thanks to my agent, Paige Wheeler.

Connect with U s

Visit us online at
KensingtonBooks.com
to read more from your favorite authors, see books
by series, view reading group guides, and more.

Join us on social media

for sneak peeks, chances to win books and prize packs,
and to share your thoughts with other readers.

facebook.com/kensingtonpublishing
twitter.com/kensingtonbooks

Tell us what you think!

To share your thoughts, submit a review,
or sign up for our eNewsletters, please visit:
KensingtonBooks.com/TellUs.